Set in 2008, *Site Fidelit* ...porary novel centering on the importance of "place" in a turbulent, changing world. The title refers to the ornithological term for birds' instinctive migration back to their place of origin.

Ann Norton Holbrook writes in her foreword:

> " . . . 'site fidelity' reflects a recurring theme [in the series] that becomes more forceful with each new story. As the beloved characters share the considerable challenges of aging within a community that has evolved with them, their ties to each other and to this beautiful, northern, lake-and-mountain-graced New Hampshire world grow stronger. These bonds give them the strength and joy to survive the increasing 'bombardment' of 'physical limitations . . . every moment of every day,' as well as the hope that endures despite political disappointment, tenacious regret, and inexorably imperfect human relationships."

THE SNOWY SERIES

THE CHEERLEADER

"*The Cheerleader* is a sensitive novel for grown-ups about what it was like to be a teenage girl in the 1950s: the discovery of boys and sex, and figuring out who you are and what you want to be."

—Nancy Pearl, author of *Book Lust*

"It's heartbreaking at times, hilarious at others."

—*Philadelphia Inquirer*

SNOWY
HENRIETTA SNOW
THE HUSBAND BENCH, or BEV'S BOOK
A BORN MANIAC, or PUDDLES'S PROGRESS
A GUNTHWAITE GIRL (a novelette)
SITE FIDELITY

By Ruth Doan MacDougall

THE LILTING HOUSE

THE COST OF LIVING

ONE MINUS ONE

WIFE AND MOTHER

AUNT PLEASANTINE

THE FLOWERS OF THE FOREST

A LOVELY TIME WAS HAD BY ALL

A WOMAN WHO LOVED LINDBERGH

MUTUAL AID

THE SNOWY SERIES

THE CHEERLEADER

SNOWY

HENRIETTA SNOW

THE HUSBAND BENCH, OR BEV'S BOOK

A BORN MANIAC, OR PUDDLES'S PROGRESS

A GUNTHWAITE GIRL (a novelette)

With Daniel Doan

50 HIKES IN THE WHITE MOUNTAINS

50 MORE HIKES IN NEW HAMPSHIRE

Editor

INDIAN STREAM REPUBLIC:
SETTLING A NEW ENGLAND FRONTIER,
     1785–1842, by Daniel Doan

Site Fidelity

by
Ruth Doan MacDougall

A sequel to:
The Cheerleader
Snowy
Henrietta Snow
The Husband Bench, or Bev's Book
A Born Maniac, or Puddles's Progress
A Gunthwaite Girl (a novelette)

FRIGATE BOOKS

At the author's Web site, **ruthdoanmacdougall.com**, items of general interest such as discussion guides, background information, and photographs are available.

SITE FIDELITY
Copyright © 2017 by Ruth Doan MacDougall

Foreword Copyright © 2017 by Ann Norton Holbrook

Cover art: Bill Tyers

Cover design: Richard Hannus

Publisher's Cataloging-in-Publication Data
MacDougall, Ruth Doan
    site fidelity / Ruth Doan MacDougall
                p. cm
              ISBN 13: 978-0-9981942-0-2 (paperback)
              ISBN 13: 978-0-9981942-1-9 (e-book)

1. Women—New Hampshire—Fiction
      I. Title   Series: Snowy
      PS3563.A292S58   2017
      813'.54

To

Penelope Doan

Thane Joyal

James P. Gibbs

Hamish Peter Doan Gibbs

Foreword

Site Fidelity is the sixth novel in Ruth Doan MacDougall's Snowy Series, but readers devoted to the Gunthwaite Gang have seen this phrase before. Technically it names a natural phenomenon: year after year, birds return to the same location to breed. It's also the title of one of passionate bird-watcher-and-feeder Snowy's poetry volumes. Most importantly, "site fidelity" reflects a recurring theme that becomes more forceful with each new story. As the beloved characters share the considerable challenges of aging within a community that has evolved with them, their ties to each other and to this beautiful, north-ern, lake-and-mountain-graced New Hampshire world grow stronger. These bonds give them the strength and joy to survive the increasing "bombardment" of "physical limitations . . . every moment of every day," as well as the hope that endures despite political disappointment, tena-cious regret, and inexorably imperfect human relationships.

Like *A Born Maniac, or Puddles Progress*, which takes place between September 2001 and January 2002, *Site Fidelity* portrays a recognizably specific moment in recent history, January through June of 2008. As the story begins, Barack Obama and Hillary Clinton fiercely contend for the Democratic presidential nomination; the worst recession to hit America and the world since the Great Depression has just begun, fueled by global financiers' outrageous greed and duplicity; gasoline costs more than $3 a gallon; and like some cosmic curse, winter storms repeatedly pummel the Northeast. Though they have never before been involved in New Hampshire's first-in-the-nation primary despite lifelong prox-imity, Snowy, Bev, and their friends campaign for Hillary, passionately hoping to see the first woman president even as they lament that "this is all so upsetting . . . The first time a woman could, the first time a black man could, and they have to be running against each other!" Readers may wince witnessing their hope and disappointment, knowing that Hillary will be defeated not once but a second time, in a high-stakes election threatening to worsen 2008's horrific problems—climate change, income inequality, lingering racism and sexism—and highlighting the backlash against personal and social progress women have made since Snowy and Puddles were Gunthwaite High cheerleaders.

Snowy lives, as does any person of a certain age, with a continuous sense of her own and the country's history running like a soundtrack in her mind as she nevertheless remains actively engrossed in the circumstances of her late sixties. A self-admitted "worrywart," she manages two and then three small grocery stores with her thirty-something daughter Ruhamah, maintains vigorous friendships with long-time friends, writes poetry that actually gets published and read (no small feat in a nearly poetry-free world), and loves the love of her life, Tom. Still, the past haunts, cruelly: despite her continuing affection and desire for Tom, she remembers another love, her husband, Alan, who committed suicide twenty years earlier and whom she still entreats to return: "You can come back now," she whispers frequently, fruitlessly. The small apartment she and Tom share above his coffin factory contains a hodgepodge of furniture and other memorabilia from both their marriages, as well as her late mother's collection of rooster knickknacks. Snowy the teenager hated these knickknacks as a symbol for what she saw, with the smugness of youth, as the conformity and triviality of her parents' lives; but now they seem precious, redolent of blood ties that matter, fundamentally, in a way her younger self did not appreciate.

Snowy, desperate for escape, fantasizes about Maine's tiny Quarry Island, where Puddles's ice-cream-empire husband's family has a castle—really—and a tiny population lives and works surrounded by ocean and little else. She adores New Hampshire—at one point, she refreshes herself with a country drive because she knows "she need[s] to show herself that New Hampshire scenery was lovely"—but just as she loved two men, she loves two states and longs for both. "Site fidelity" has therefore an ironic edge, as it does in the novelette *A Gunthwaite Girl*. Woodcombe nurtures Snowy and Tom; it can also become too familiar, too reminiscent of past tragedies and quotidian numbness, lacking the inspiration for fresh vision and energy they both need. Their trip to the Scottish Hebrides eight years ago gave them this briefly. Could Quarry Island's isolated, bare-bones environment be the answer now?

The theme of aging. We can never hear it enough, especially when we worry, like Snowy, that we are "old" and that we may have "used up all [our] courage, the daily courage necessary for daily existence and the courage for emergencies, for big stuff . . ." Previously casual, easy activities—shoveling snow and balancing on ice; sitting or driving on long rides; walking up mountains and even stairs—become annoying impediments to health and autonomy. We know, though, as Snowy and Tom know, that they are not really old, not yet; no drastic infirmities impair their work or movement, and they remain lovers, sex rarely mentioned in these later novels but lasting as an elemental, enduring bond.

MacDougall joins Alice Munro, Anita Brookner, and Doris Lessing, among other great women writers, in addressing life after sixty. All the Gang members face aging and adapt with individual "daily courage." Glamorous, beautiful Bev, once the ingénue and now a grandmother, will play old ladies in matronly hats rather than Emily in *Our Town*. She and Roger, like so many Americans, watch their considerable financial investments dwindle, threatening the comfortable affluence they pictured for their senior years; they weather timeworn quarrels and stand "together, for better or worse." True to form, the novel portrays someone who feels that "worse" got the better of her life: 88-year-old Mildred Cotter longed for romance and travel to exotic islands but, marooned in a nursing home, believes she had her heart and spirit "broken. Killed. Even in Portland, Maine."

Nonetheless, as in all the Snowy novels, optimism undergirds the quiet, layered realism of *Site Fidelity*. The Gang ages; beloved grandchildren are born. Couples marry, or don't, but commitment, "for better or worse," persists. Getting older entails loss, sorrow, remorse; but it also generates joyful memories and, frankly, gratitude for their young lives in a younger world, where, as Snowy and Bev marvel, entire stores sold only hats and tourists encountering New Hampshire's exquisite beauty looked at scenery rather than smartphones. Even—especially—in her happiest moments, Snowy still knocks on wood, knowing that life's "Left Field" will throw curve balls. Tom, Bev, Puddles, Dudley, Harriet, and even 100-year-old Gladys Stanton will, however, be on site with her, exasperating and predictable, loving and hopeful. May we accompany them into their next decade!

.

ANN NORTON HOLBROOK
Saint Anselm College

Acknowledgments

For their advice and help, my gratitude to:

Michele Chase

Jennifer Davis-Kay

George Geers

Sandra Gottwald

Dick Hannus

Don MacDougall

Glynis Miner

Molly Motherwell

Winifred Motherwell

Jane Rice

Jan Schor

Bill Tyers

Daniel Weene

Marney Wilde

1

SNOWY THOUGHT: THIS COULD be getting dangerous.

A ridiculous thought, because she was only in her snowbound backyard in the hazy dark before sunrise, shoveling a path through the latest foot of snow brought by yesterday's New Year's Day snowstorm. She was just aiming toward the pole from which hung two tube feeders for sunflower seeds and a suet feeder. A pole! She wasn't on the North Pole, the South Pole—or Mount Everest. The thermometer had told her it was twenty-six degrees this morning, a balmy twenty-six *above* zero. Central heat and safety were close by in the gray barn where she and Tom lived, where the outside light over the snow-clogged screen door of the back porch glared at the narrow slot she'd already shoveled from the porch steps. She was bundled up in her L.L.Bean gear, navy-blue parka, baby-blue fleece cap, and insulated boots. The fresh snow smelled like ozone, which should energize her.

Still, the snowfall had weighted down the trees and bushes, with a white pine's floppy lower boughs pushed so low they'd frozen into the snowbanks, and she felt smothered, fragile. The poor lilac bush was more bent over than she was as she chopped yet another square of snow, slid the shovel in to lift the top half, being prudent, not lifting up the whole twelve-inch chunk—

A banging on a barn window made her turn. Looking up at the lighted kitchen window of their upstairs apartment, she saw Tom, white hair once curly but now thinning, white beard neatly trimmed. Tom Forbes, whom she, Henrietta Snow, had started dating when she was a sophomore and he a junior at Gunthwaite High School. She waved a mittened hand, her fingers within cramped and cold.

3

Despite the storm window and the inside window, she heard him bellow, "For Christ's sake, come indoors!"

She bellowed back, "The birds!"

"Fuck the birds!"

"I'm almost to the feeders, I'll be in soon!"

"I've got the coffee made!"

She repeated, "I'll be in soon."

He gave up, left the window, and she continued shoveling. When men are scared or sad, they can't cry so they tend to get angry. Usually Tom cleared the paths with his snowblower, but his knees had given out during a similar session in the last snowstorm. His son David had volunteered to do the snowblowing, but right now David would be busy digging out his own house. Sunrise was about seven-fifteen today—the days *were* getting longer!—and with sunrise the birds would come zooming to the feeders, which they'd almost emptied yesterday during their frantic efforts to keep stoked throughout the storm. She couldn't let them find nothing this morning. What if a chickadee keeled over from starvation? So, after her shower, while Tom was taking his shower, she'd hurried downstairs into his workshop, the North Country Coffins factory on the ground floor, gone out to the porch, and started shoveling.

The problem was, they were getting old. Hell, they *were* old. Today was Wednesday, January 2, 2008. On his birthday in May, Tom would turn seventy. Sooner, in March, she'd be sixty-nine. And what jokes her dear friend Jean Pond Cram Hutchinson, aka Puddles, would make about that number!

Chop, lift, throw. She always did the tidying-up shoveling after Tom did the snowblowing. She could do this. Yet a sudden fear stabbed her. Had she used up all her courage, the daily courage necessary for daily existence and the courage for emergencies, for big stuff? Or was she maybe saving up any smidgen she had left of the quota of courage she'd been born with? Saving for the inevitable. She and Tom were old.

4

The black haze overhead had begun to lighten, pink. She heard a pickup truck set to work plowing. Ryan Hopkins, who had a home-services business, had arrived to plow out the parking lot of the little white clapboard post office next door. Beyond the post office was her store, the general store, whose parking lot Tom would be plowing out with *his* pickup after he did their driveway. The store opened at seven, and although people understood if she didn't open on the dot during or after snowstorms, she started shoveling faster. Chop, lift, throw. Her mother had died of a heart attack at age sixty-three, but while asleep, not while shoveling. (That strange milestone, reaching the age at which a parent had died, then living onward, older than they. A mixture of feelings: relieved, victorious, guilty, grief-stricken.)

Triumphantly she arrived at the pole. A chickadee zipped past to alight atop it and yell at her.

"Hold your horses," she admonished.

The suet feeder still held some scraps. She would do the messy job of refilling it later. She ran back along her path to the porch, into the workshop, where next to the back door stood a small garbage can with a metal scoop balanced on the lid. Instead of garbage, the can held sunflower seeds. After pausing to reach under her parka and into her jeans to adjust the waistband of her silk long underwear, she scooped up seeds. As she ran out toward the feeders trying not to spill, she felt as if she were in an egg-and-spoon race in a P. G. Wodehouse novel— and then she slid, slipped, and in a shocking split second landed flat on her back on the path.

Sprawled there, scared, she didn't move. Had she broken any bones? Had she broken her back? She knew what Puddles would say at this moment: "Now will you listen to me? I keep telling you to spend the winters in South Carolina!" Well, actually, since Puddles was a nurse, the first thing Puddles would do would be to minister to her wounds.

Chickadees darted down and grabbed the seeds scattered on the snow, then flew away. Slowly she tested her arms and legs. She was okay. She might have some bruises. The surprise of the fall was the worst part. And the most difficult part would be sitting up and getting to her feet. She flailed around, seeking purchase, hoping that Tom hadn't been looking out a window, hadn't seen her comeuppance. When she did her morning exercises on the living-room floor, she had to haul herself up with the help of a nearby chair. No help here. She rolled onto her knees, picked up the scoop, shoved it into a parka pocket, and crawled on her hands and knees to the porch, then grabbed the screen-door handle and pulled herself upright. In the workshop, she refilled the scoop. She walked carefully back to the feeders, taking baby steps, remembering that Dorothy Parker had named her canary Onan because he spilled his seed upon the ground.

The sunrise was becoming gorgeous, a deep rosy flood of color.

She heard Tom's Ford Ranger start up out front, and thus as she returned to the barn and stomped snow off her boots, she knew she would have the apartment to herself. She and Tom could still feel an exultant contentment about cohabiting these past twelve years after all the years apart, but some solitude was welcome too. She crossed the workshop, where two coffins were being built. Tom had mentioned that coffins were getting bigger because people were fatter as well as taller. She climbed the inside staircase and at the top removed her mittens, flexed her knobby arthritic knuckles, unzipped her parka. Into the kitchen she hurried, into the fragrance of coffee.

The apartment was small, built by Tom: this kitchen-and-living-room area, two bedrooms, a bathroom. Simple and practical, walls painted white, pine-board floors. She didn't have time for coffee, she would be making some at the store, but she was so cold! A compromise; she lifted the Gevalia coffeepot and poured coffee only halfway up a black Bennington Potters mug.

Tom had traveled light after his divorce and his move from Newburgh in northern New Hampshire here to Woodcombe in the Lakes Region. He'd bought some basic furniture and built the rest, including the kitchen trestle table. He'd built cupboards, shelves, bookcases. When Joanne, his ex-wife, remarried, she shipped him a bookcase and a record-player-radio cabinet he had made in high school shop and had given to his parents, who years later, retiring to Florida, had given them to him and Joanne. After his mother died four years ago after his father's death nearly twenty years before, he and his two brothers had chosen shares of her treasures, including his father's souvenirs from the Philippines during World War II; Tom had got a hand-made knife with a carved handle, a wooden plaque with a carving of the Philippine government seal, and a coolie hat (there *must* be some politically correct term for this nowadays).

But mostly the apartment seemed to Snowy packed to the ceiling with her own past. When in 1985 she and Alan, her husband, had bought Hurricane Farm and the Woodcombe General Store, the furniture they'd accumulated for their young-marrieds apartment in Eastbourne and their first house down in Pevensay, on New Hampshire's seacoast, had been transported here. But two years later, after Alan committed suicide when the general store was going bankrupt, she'd had to sell the house to save the store, and she'd also sold most of their furniture, only keeping enough for the apartment over the store into which she and her daughter, Ruhamah, had moved. Most of that had remained with Ruhamah in that apartment when Snowy moved into Tom's apartment, but after Ruhamah married and began furnishing her own home, Snowy and Ruhamah divvied things up. So Tom's living room now held the Martha Washington chair and glass-fronted bookcases that Snowy and

7

Alan had found in secondhand and antiques stores. Snowy had also taken her grandmother's braided rug, now on this floor. Ruhamah had hoseyed the wing chair that had been Alan's and the Oriental rug. On that rug, Snowy suddenly thought, baby Ruhamah had crawled, and this morning she herself had been crawling on a shoveled path.

Ruhamah would be thirty-seven in July. This seemed impossible. Well, a few of the houseplants throughout the apartment were nearly that old, such as the spider plant and Christmas cactus brought from Pevensay.

Snowy could see, across the living room on a wall in the bedroom, another of Tom's mother's treasures, the framed blue butterfly amid dried flowers and milkweed fluff that she had first seen in the living room of his parents' house in Gunthwaite the night of his junior prom. The night they'd begun going steady.

Going steady! Unmarried, they were going steady all over again.

The spare room had become her office when she moved in, and it was filled with equipment, including a computer desk on which elegantly reposed a new Mac laptop, a Christmas present from Tom to replace her big green iMac. Also filing cabinets, bookcases, the little fireproof safe in which she kept the poems she was working on, and her old mahogany veneer desk given to her by her parents in junior high. For reading, there was a sun-faded aqua butterfly chair she'd discovered in an antiques store, just like the one she'd had at Bennington except that one had been orange.

Everywhere, the past.

The two place mats arranged upon the table had been woven forty-seven years ago, a wedding present for her and Alan. Around the kitchen on shelves and countertops was her mother's collection of roosters, ceramic and otherwise, which in her teens she had despised, yet now she felt—well, the roosters were treasures. She had even started to add to it, most recently the rooster clock over the fridge.

The wall phone began ringing. Caller ID told her it was Bev Lambert (Beverly Colby Lambert), her best friend since elementary school, whose mother had woven those place mats. Bev wasn't using her cell phone or calling from her real-estate office; she was calling from her home, Waterlight, a big old winterized summer cottage on the lake in Gunthwaite, so Snowy pictured her in her kitchen, which held many more loons than her own held roosters—loon curtains, loon dish towels, loon pot holders. Bev, green-eyed, her naturally curly short white hair once auburn, would be looking beautiful even first thing in the morning at age sixty-eight, and she'd be having coffee in a loon mug. Her loon kitchen clock would soon herald the hour with a loon's primeval and maniacal yodel that could stop your heart. Snowy had made sure the rooster clock was a simple silent model before she gave in to the impulse purchase. But she knew she was on the lookout for rooster mugs. "Hi, Bev."

"I just had a call from Ruhamah." Lately Bev's voice over the phone jiggled with a hurried haste, as if she were constantly in a rush. The Christmas rush, Snowy had thought, but now that season was over. Bev asked, "You know I was going to show her the Oakhill General Store today?"

"I've been trying to repress it."

"Well," Bev said, "she says that something's come up, she's too busy, she had phoned Rita and got her to fill in for both of you at the Woodcombe store."

"Both of us?"

"Well, she asked me to call you and tell you this—and to show *you* the Oakhill store."

Snowy cried, "What? She knows I won't approve! She knows even the second store still makes me panic!" Three years ago Ruhamah had talked her into buying the general store in the neighboring town of Thetford. It was managed by a Thetford resident, Donna Welch. Now Ruhamah had taken a notion to buy a *third* store. The newscasts were reporting that last year had been the worst real-estate market in decades, but Ruhamah saw this as an opportunity. Did Ruhamah want to rule a general-store empire? "Besides," Snowy said, "I'm well-acquainted with the Oakhill store—and so is she—and it's a disaster. Moose Jackson got worn out and let it go to hell." Moose was a widower in his seventies, once hale and hearty, now wizened and cantankerous. He had closed his store with a slam last September on the day after Labor Day, put it up for sale, and moved to his daughter's place in Florida. The realtor with whom he'd listed the store had had no luck, so last week Moose had decided to give the listing to Beverly Lambert, Realtor. ("As," Bev had said when she phoned Snowy and Ruhamah to report this before e-mailing them the details, "he should have done at the outset.") He'd also lowered the price from $120,000 to $90,000, which grabbed Ruhamah's attention. Snowy asked, "Have you been in it yet?"

"Of course," Bev said. "And I know what you mean, but come have a look anyway. I think it really might have possibilities. And it's a bargain!"

"There's no apartment upstairs to live in or to bring in rent. No gas pumps. A general store needs both." In bewilderment Snowy added, "Has Ruhamah taken leave of her senses?"

"Humor her," Bev said. "This will be a chance to see each other."

Yes, for almost a month they'd only been catching up by phone and e-mail, not in person. The last time she and Bev had got together had been in early December to attend Hillary Clinton's visit to the Gunthwaite Conference and Convention Center, the first time they'd ever gone to any presidential candidate's rally during the New Hampshire primaries. Then the holiday frenzy hit, with Bev and her husband, Roger, readying Waterlight for their family. This was what Bev loved, and the grandchildren now numbered four. Down in Connecticut her older son, Dick, and his wife, Jessica, had five-year-old Abigail and two-year-old Felicity. In Massachusetts her younger daughter, Etta, had finally married Steve, her veterinarian boyfriend, and produced one-year-old Jeremy. In Gunthwaite, Leon, her younger son, kept his count to one, ten-year-old Clem. Although in nearby Leicester her older daughter, Mimi, with husband Lloyd, resolutely remained at zero, Waterlight had brimmed with grandchildren at Christmas. As for Snowy's Christmas, her roommate, Harriet, had come up from New York to spend the holiday with her Woodcombe boyfriend at the Gunthwaite house she'd bought for getaways, so of course there were visits to and fro fitted into the work schedules of Snowy and Tom and Ruhamah and her husband, D. J. (Dudley Washburn Jr.).

Seeing Bev would be good. Yet Snowy hesitated, fretting as usual. "But that'll leave Rita handling the store alone."

"The snowstorm's aftermath should keep things slow."

Not necessarily. Storms could make people head for the store, seeking company as well as groceries. However, Snowy suddenly, urgently, wanted to shove aside the daily routine, to escape, and she said, "Was it at nine that Ruhamah was going to meet you?"

"Yes. I assume the roads have been plowed. I've called Chip Bates, the man who plows and shovels out the store, and that'll be done by the time we get there. God, a New Year's Day storm—we'll be receiving another barrage of e-mails from Puddles ordering us to borrow her Hilton Head home."

During the six years of their marriage, Puddles and her second husband, Blivit Hutchinson, had driven from their home on the Maine coast down to South Carolina, to have Christmas with her twin daughters and her grandchildren, staying in the house in which Puddles had lived with her first husband, Guy Cram, and had kept after he died. Puddles and Blivit went back for occasional visits throughout the year, and Puddles repeatedly offered the house to Snowy and Bev, harping about it exasperatingly, maybe because of frugal Yankee guilt over an unused house. Snowy always told Bev almost everything, but she hadn't confided a desire that had been brewing within her in recent years, a vague and confused longing for a fresh start in a new place, a wish that Puddles would instead offer her a place to stay on Quarry Island. Year-round. This Maine island was home to Blivit's family, where the Hutchinsons' famous ice-cream company had begun.

Bev was saying, "I'll see you at the Oakhill store at nine."

"Okay," Snowy said and heard Bev's loon clock begin its yodel.

THE SUN ON fresh white snow could scald your eyes, but Snowy didn't don sunglasses when she got into her Subaru Outback, bought secondhand two years ago, blue like her previous Subaru Legacy (the Subaru before that had been white; in Woodcombe, you drove Subarus). Sunglasses of course changed scenery. Driving the woodsy road out of Woodcombe toward Oakhill thirty miles away, she knew she needed to show herself that New Hampshire scenery was lovely; she wanted to see everything true—particularly, as she neared the outskirts of Oakhill, the wide brook that this stretch of road ran alongside. The golden-brown water hadn't completely frozen, so between the snow-cushioned banks it flashed and foamed. Then the brook turned to slip away into the woods, always reminding her of the first grown-up Christmas cards she had bought, age fourteen, at the stationery store on Gunthwaite's Main Street. A box of ten cards, all with the same winter scene, a brook curving exactly as this one did, into secret woods in the snow.

Lovely. But she was also seeing Quarry Island. The Hutchinsons actually had a castle there as well as a farm and also a farm in the town of Long Harbor on the mainland near their ice-cream plant. She'd visited Puddles at the Long Harbor farmhouse several times, going there with Bev or Tom, most recently with Tom last October after the busy foliage season ended. On various occasions Blivit and Puddles had taken them on boat trips to the island, where they'd stayed at the castle. But what she was envisioning in her daydream was some snug little cottage for her and Tom to live in alone, retired. As snug as their barn apartment, but the scenery would be the ever-changing ocean, not the motionless mountains of Woodcombe. Stupid desire! She and Tom weren't retired; they would have to work on and on in the general store and in the coffin factory until they dropped in their tracks. Scenery. A change of scenery. Her 2005 collection of new poems, *Lazy Beds*, had been inspired by the trip she and Tom had made to Scotland in 2000 in pursuit of her MacLeod ancestors on the Isle of Lewis. Then at her editor's suggestion she had assembled *Selected Poems*. After it was published last year (and had won the Anne Bradstreet Poetry Award), she found herself writing mostly about Maine. Why? She'd already written about the ocean when she and Alan were living on New Hampshire's coast. When she was young. The different stages of her life. Different men in her life.

As usual Tom had read her poems if she thought they were finished enough, but she hadn't told him about the growing urge to live on Quarry Island.

He used to talk about an ornithologists' term for birds returning to the same place each year: site fidelity. Several years ago, Bev had been tempted to move to Santa Fe to join an old boyfriend but decided to stay, telling Snowy, "You and I grew up in a New Hampshire lakeside town, where I now have my dream home on the lake." Snowy had mentioned the term to Bev, who said, "It should be the title of your next collection of poems. I didn't understand how New Hampshire was in my bones until I read *Tapestry Granite*," one of Snowy's previous collections. The comment had inspired a poem that became the title for the collection published before *Lazy Beds*. And Snowy had dedicated *Site Fidelity* to Bev.

Who now would be driving to Oakhill to try to sell her a general store.

When Tom had returned from plowing, Snowy explained Ruhamah's change of plans and added, "D. J. was going back to Washington today." In addition to the worry of the stores, Ruhamah had her husband's re-election to worry about. After an earlier try at the U.S. House of Representatives, D. J. had at last won the seat in the Democratic landslide in 2006. Now he was running again. Snowy said, "Maybe the snowstorm screwed up the limousine service and she has to drive him to the airport. I hate how she's so busy, she's stretched too thin." On top of everything else, Snowy thought guiltily, Ruhamah maintained Snowy's Web site as well as the Woodcombe and Thetford General Stores' sites. Oh, the shame of only being able to do the basics in cyberspace!

Tom had replied, "She's young, she can manage." Yes, Snowy had thought, and Ruhamah had friends with whom she relaxed, especially a best friend from her teens, Kim Parker, who had returned to Woodcombe with a dentist husband after college and after working at an insurance company in Boston. Her husband joined a practice in Gunthwaite, and Kim became an instructor at the Gunthwaite Yoga Center and the mother of two daughters. Surely the yoga influence was good for Ruhamah.

The road climbed uphill to what was known locally as Cowshit Corner. Snowy braked. On one side of the long curve stood the Pikes' old farmhouse and barn, wood smoke pluming out of the farmhouse chimney, the driveway plowed, a path shoveled to the barn; across the road on the other side the pasture looked rocky even under deep snow. The last of Oakhill's old dairy farms was still in business, producing milk and manure. The Holsteins were in the barn now, but you always had to be wary. You were apt to come upon them being escorted from the barn to the pasture or discover the aftermath, the road so slippery that once last year Tom in his pickup had skidded sideways through the manure smack into the barbed-wire fence. As other drivers had done over the years. The road was clear today, but she rounded the curve circumspectly.

From the hilltop she drove down toward a mailbox set atop an iron chain welded upright to form a post. Behind it sat a double-wide with a big plastic Rudolph the Red-Nosed Reindeer on its roof. The older generation of Pikes had retired here from the farm, which had been taken over by a son and daughter-in-law. Beside a shed, two snowmobiles were resting after the holiday merrymaking.

She drove down the steep hill into the village, past a white Cape, a red Cape, a yellow Cape, a white Colonial. At one house, a bundled-up guy was using a long-handled roof rake to pull snow off the roof's edge, while at another house another guy was up on the roof shoveling. The square old white clapboard town hall suited the scene, but beside it the community church, built to replace the old church that had burned flat, looked like a 1960s A-frame.

The general store, a shabby shingled building with a small parking lot, was set between a brick fire station and Buddy's Auto Service, the grubby garage to which Tom brought his pickup or the Subaru for repairs, she following in whichever vehicle wasn't ailing. Sometimes after the garage negotiations they'd walk over to the store to buy a couple of bottles of Moxie, that gentian-root-flavored bittersweet soft drink either loved or hated; they loved it. Moose Jackson's establishment didn't have a welcoming appearance, not even a front porch for sitting on to watch the world (such as it was) go by. The paint on its overhead sign had peeled so much you could only guess that it was supposed to say Oakhill General Store. Compared with the Woodcombe General Store, this store always looked pinched and dark.

She saw Bev's car in the parking lot. Bev also had a Subaru, but her latest green Outback had been born more recently, a year ago. Snowy pulled in beside it and opened her door. The scoliosis that Puddles had diagnosed three years ago and a back X-ray had confirmed always hurt most when getting out of the car.

"A gathering place," Bev said, emerging too damn grace-fully from her car. She was wearing an everyday green parka, not one of her chic winter coats, and under it Snowy could see the turtleneck of a white sweater that Bev had had for years. Bev had chosen plain jeans, too, and her least fancy boots. Realtor Bev was dressing down, no frills and furbelows for Oakhill. But her green shoulder bag was beautiful, one of her collection of shoulder bags woven by daughter Mimi, who had inherited Bev's mother's weaving talent. Her hurried voice continued, "That's what Ruhamah kept talking to me about, how general stores serve as a gathering place for people, a third place besides home and work. The heart of the community."

"Well," Snowy said, "the way general stores are having heart attacks and closing, she should be considering the possibility that it's the end of an era. All I want is for ours in Woodcombe to hang on."

Bev repeated slowly, "The end of an era." She then added in a determinedly upbeat tone, "Ruhamah told me about how you're saving money consolidating orders and deliveries for the Gunthwaite and Thetford stores, how this would be part of all that."

"Um," Snowy said.

They walked over to Bev's realty sign sticking out of a snow-bank. In the store's front window there were still Moose's various signs, which he hadn't bothered to take down when departing. These included:

BAIT & TACKLE

Also:

DEER REGISTRATION STATION

This didn't mean that deer registered to vote here. It meant that during deer-hunting season you registered the deer you'd just killed.

One sign warned:

NO SHIRT
NO SHOES
NO SERVICE

Another said:

COLD BEER
HOT VIDEOS

Moose had updated this some years ago with a scribbled "& DVDs."

And then there was:

FRESH NATIVE ICE CUBES

Bev said, "Moose certainly is a riot," and reached into her shoulder bag. Taking out keys, she added, "He's keeping the store heated, that's one good thing."

Whenever Snowy had entered this store with Tom, she had felt the need for a password and imagined herself back in Prohibition days, entering a speakeasy. Moose and his cronies always turned from their huddled conversation at the counter and stared. Then they'd recognize her and Tom, and Moose would grin and holler, "Checking out the competition!" Much joshing, at which Tom was far better than she. Regular customers also got stares and banter and seemed to enjoy it as part of the shopping experience, while tourists looked nervous.

As Bev and Snowy stepped indoors, stamping snow off their boots, the furnace whooshed on, but the thermostat had obviously been set low. There were no accompanying noises from the empty freezer and coolers. The store was just barely alive. The cash register looked penniless. Empty shelves. A sign on a small refrigerator said Beware: Worms In Fridge, but the refrigerator was unplugged, no worms or other bait within.

Snowy remembered arriving in Woodcombe with Alan to meet a real-estate man and be shown the general store. Its owner was old and ill, yet unlike Moose he'd stuck with the place and it was still functioning, albeit just as a bread-and-beer store. Woodcombe folks had to go to Thetford or to Gunthwaite—the big city!—for groceries. Alan, a curator of the historic district of Old Eastbourne, had believed he could rescue and restore this ruin too. He would be his own boss at last. So they had bought it. Alan made the store welcoming again, from the deacon's bench on the porch to the wheel of Cheddar beside the pickle barrel. She, locked in the prison of agoraphobia, did what she could. The locals and the tourists returned. Alan was handling the finances and she thought they were succeeding; she didn't know about the near-bankruptcy until after his suicide. She was a widow at age forty-eight. It became her job to rescue Woodcombe General Store.

Bankruptcy.

She said, "Bev, I can't let Ruhamah buy this."

Bev snapped, "Ruhamah has a master's degree in business administration. As you've been known to point out, that's why you go along with her decisions. *You* were a literature major."

Stunned, Snowy gaped at her. It was okay to say this yourself, but to have Bev say it? In a cruelly waspish tone?

She saw tears well up in Bev's eyes and was even more stunned.

The front door opened and a woman paused on the threshold, fiftyish, short dark hair with some gray. She wore jeans and a flannel shirt under a parka she apparently had just tossed on, and she looked solid and practical except for her flirty cat-eye glasses. "Hi, Snowy. Okay if I come in?"

Snowy said, "Of course, Cindy." Cindy O'Donnell was married to Oakhill's road agent, Wayne. (This term for the person in charge of a town's highway crew always made Snowy think of Alfred Noyes's "Highwayman" poem, even though the agent was legal and the highwayman was not.) Cindy and Wayne and a twenty-something son lived a few houses down from the store; an older son and his wife had moved to Gunthwaite. Cindy, one of those women who cobbled together an income from many sources, did chair caning, sold her jams and jellies, babysat for young and old—and filled in for Moose when he took a day off. Sometimes she combined jobs. Snowy had once seen her changing a baby's diaper on the cash-register counter, to nobody's horror except Snowy's.

Snowy began introductions. "This is Bev—"

"Oh," Cindy interrupted, "I know who you are. Beverly Lambert! I've seen you on TV. You're great!"

Bev blushed and stammered, "Thank—thank you."

Snowy couldn't believe it. Bev was so used to getting compliments, she always handled them smoothly, even automatically.

The compliments in recent years were for her appearances on a Boston news program, giving tips about buying real estate in New Hampshire.

"But," Cindy said, "I haven't seen you on lately. I suppose second homes aren't selling much these days." She turned again to Snowy. "When I spotted your car going past the house, I just had to run over here. Does this mean you're interested in buying the store? It would be terrific—we're *stranded* without a store! Look, come see, I always thought Moose should do what you did with the Woodcombe store, add a back porch. There's a view of the brook, come see." She took both Snowy and Bev by the arm and propelled them down an aisle between empty shelves to the back door beside the empty meat case. "That damn Chip doesn't bother shoveling out the back—"

The store shook. Earthquake, Snowy thought. Earthquake! New Hampshire does get earthquakes! Rarely, so people think it's something else. On these rare occasions, she and Tom had thought it was a truck hitting the barn. She heard a roaring sound, an engine, and spun around and saw the front end of a big truck knocking over the bait fridge.

Bev screamed. Cindy flipped the back-door lock open, shoved her and Snowy out, and jumped after them into the snow.

"SPIKE JONES," SNOWY babbled to Ruhamah, standing with Bev in the kitchen of Ruhamah and D. J.'s farmhouse previously owned by generations of an old Woodcombe family, the Thornes. "That's all I could think of, the sound effects on the Spike Jones records, crash, bang, crash crash."

She and Bev had hung their parkas on the pegs near the back door while being greeted by Kaylie, Ruhamah's black-and-white border collie. Now Kaylie sat golden-eyed beside a bookcase full of cookbooks and seed catalogs, ready if these three keyed-up women needed herding.

Bev said to Ruhamah, "You're too young to remember Spike Jones, but Snowy is right, especially when the fire station next door let loose with sirens—"

"Spike Jones?" Ruhamah wore a blue Woodcombe General Store sweatshirt with her jeans, her dark-blonde hair in a pony-tail, a hairstyle that always reminded Snowy of photographs of herself in her teenage years. Snowy and Ruhamah did look alike, but Ruhamah was taller—especially, Snowy thought, now that I'm shrinking like Alice in Wonderland. Ruhamah explained to Bev, "I know Spike Jones. Alan would imitate the sound effects for me when I was little. He'd memorized Spike Jones records when he was a kid." She lifted the copper teakettle off the gas stove that had replaced Cleora Thorne's wood cook stove which, however, remained in the kitchen, cold, a houseplant stand, and she poured boiling water over the tea bags in mugs. Ruhamah didn't have loon mugs or rooster mugs. She had a mixture of Woodcombe General Store and Thetford General Store mugs, and she kept real chickens in the Thornes' hen house. "Sit down, you two. I think you're still in shock. The truck driver is really okay?"

"Not a scratch," said Bev, and remained standing.

Snowy dropped into a chair at the harvest table that she and Alan had bought decades ago; it had replaced Cleora's Formica table. After the town cop and the volunteer firemen and the garage guys had taken care of the Landry Lumber Company's logging truck, and after Bev with eerie efficiency had phoned Moose in Florida and then phoned a Gunthwaite contractor about repairs, Snowy had called Ruhamah's cell phone and been surprised to find Ruhamah at home, not driving D. J. to the Manchester airport or doing whatever else had made her too busy to meet Bev in Oakhill. Learning her whereabouts,

21

Snowy and Bev had decided to come give Ruhamah the details in person instead of over the phone. They needed distance from Oakhill. Distance might calm their pounding hearts. But before they left, Snowy tried to phone Tom and reassure him in case news of the truck accident had reached Woodcombe via phone or Internet. However, he hadn't answered the barn phones or his cell phone. Probably doing some Good Samaritan extra plowing, she assumed, or too busy on some workshop machine to answer. Then, in tandem, Bev leading, they had driven back to Woodcombe, turning off onto Thorne Road, known as the Roller Coaster Road. Through woods they jounced over its hillocks and bumps. Usually Snowy debated within herself about whether or not to slow down and study Hurricane Farm, which now belonged to Rita Beaupre Henderson Barlow. But today she only glanced at the plain white shutterless farmhouse and white clapboard barn hunkered below Mount Pascataquac. The first time she'd seen it she'd been reminded of the Gunthwaite farm she loved, the farm where Bev had grown up. It still reminded her. She kept driving on along the road two miles to the place that would always be known as the Thorne farm. Rundown and weathered to gray by the time Isaac Thorne and then Cleora died, the buildings had been resurrected during the eight years since Ruhamah and D. J. bought it, the Cape painted white again, the barn red. At the end of the road was the little neighborhood graveyard where the Thornes were buried.

Bev picked up two mugs and set one in front of Snowy. She said, "Ruhamah, you yourself should sit down. You don't look well."

"It's probably the flu," Ruhamah said.

Snowy said, "You had your flu shot last September."

Ruhamah shrugged and put a bag of gingersnaps on the table. "If you two and Cindy had still been at the front of the store when the truck came through it, could you have got out of the way in time?"

Bev suddenly collapsed into a chair. "There was no sound of screeching brakes. No emergency horn. No warning."

"Just Spike Jones." Snowy began to tremble. "Coming down the hill, the driver—he realized he didn't have any brakes. A runaway logging truck." What if, she'd been thinking over and over, what if Ruhamah had gone to the Oakhill store after all, to meet Bev? What if Ruhamah and Bev had been killed?

"Drink your tea," Ruhamah said to her. "Eat a gingersnap." Snowy obeyed.

Ruhamah sat down. "On the phone you said that Cindy wanted to show you her idea of copying our store's back porch, so you'd walked to the back. In honor of that, with gratitude for saving your lives—and her own—we'll build a porch and call it Cindy's Porch. And offer Cindy the job of managing the store."

Snowy stared at her.

Bev shrieked, "You're still interested in buying the store?"

Kaylie got up and crossed the kitchen, toenails clicking on the pine floor, and regarded Bev. Too well-behaved to beg at the table, Kaylie was concerned about Bev's unseemly racket.

"Sure," Ruhamah said. "Well, there's a lot to sort out first. Let's see, there's—"

Ruhamah with the MBA, Snowy thought. Ruhamah, calm and sensible. But like her lit-major mother, she had been hit with agoraphobia years ago. She was not tough, shatterproof, infallible.

"—the insurance," Ruhamah was saying. "And when Moose collects his wits, will he decide to return north and oversee the repairs, or will he want to stay in Florida and have us oversee them? And, of course, what with all these problems, will he drop the price some more?"

Snowy said, "Ruhamah—"

Bev jumped up. "I'll phone him from my office."

23

Exhaustion engulfed Snowy. What she needed, she realized, was the haven of Tom. She dragged herself to her feet, saying, "I'll get back to work."

Ruhamah stood up too. "Take the rest of the day off. You and Bev *have* had a shock."

Snowy didn't reply. She pulled her parka on, gave Ruhamah a tight hug, patted Kaylie, and followed Bev out the back door, across the porch, around the shoveled path to their cars parked in the plowed barnyard.

Bev said, "Don't worry. We'll go at this carefully."

Snowy couldn't help wailing, "How can I not worry? The store was bad enough before the truck ran into it!"

Bev opened her car door. "Here's something else to occupy your mind. Did you believe the flu story?"

"Story? Ruhamah forgot she had her flu shot."

"To my eyes," said Bev, "Ruhamah looks the way I felt during morning sickness." She stepped into the Outback and drove off.

Bev had been the star of the Gunthwaite High School's Dramatics Club plays. She still could make a dramatic exit.

IN A TRANCE, Snowy plopped into her car, switched on the ignition, almost backed into a snowbank, and drove onto the Roller Coaster Road. She was driving home to Tom, but she wanted to be telling Alan. This time she slowed at Hurricane Farm and looked at the fields, under snow, and the orchard, branches bare.

She had met Alan Sutherland in 1960 at the start of her senior year at Bennington, when she drove to Eastbourne on New Hampshire's coast to do research for her thesis on a nineteenth-century poet, Ruhamah Reed. Alan had graduated from UNH and was working for the organization that was restoring the historic waterfront area, where Ruhamah Reed had lived all her life.

Instant attraction! Alan Sutherland. Tall, brown hair cut collegiate (crew cuts were passé), his long-lidded brown eyes delighted at the sight of her. A habit of tilting his head. He had given her a tour of the Ruhamah Reed House and invited her to his apartment for lunch.

He had asked her, "Is it love at first sight?"

She had replied, "I think perhaps it is."

And off they'd rushed to his bedroom.

During their courtship, she had realized he had dark moods. But then and for years she hadn't recognized that they were more serious than simple depression. The blues. Down in the dumps. She hadn't even known the term "clinical depression."

When she and Tom were staying on the Isle of Lewis, she had been transfixed by the title of a poem she'd found in a book about the Hebrides. The poem was translated from the Gaelic, it was about lost love, and its title was "Farewell Forever to Last Night." The title threw her back into the last evening she had spent with Alan. After they had been to a 1950s party at Patsy and Nelson Fletcher's house, they returned to Hurricane Farm to unwind with some TV in the living room. Eventually she'd headed for bed, and Alan said, "I guess I'll stay up a bit. I'll be along."

The next morning she'd realized he'd never come to bed. She learned later from the chief of police, who had found his van and in it a half-empty half-gallon of gin and an empty bottle of Valium, that while she slept Alan drove to Woodcombe Lake and swam out and out and out.

Grandparents.

She started to count nine months ahead from—when? When D. J. had arrived home from Washington for Thanksgiving? A grandchild. A baby. Suddenly she thought of Phyllis, Alan's mother, who had died in Florida two years ago, lost to Alzheimer's for the last five of her ninety-three years. The mourners at the funeral in St. Petersburg, which Snowy and Ruhamah attended, had included Phyllis's grandchildren and great-grandchildren from Alan's sister, Margaret, and her husband, Howard. Phyllis had had great-grandchildren to love, even when she no longer knew who they were, but not Alan's grandchild. She would have *adored* that great-grandchild! A girl, Snowy wondered, or a boy? Pink or blue?

Then she got furious. What the hell was Ruhamah thinking? If Bev was right about pregnancy, it was crazier than ever to be buying another store, to be creating a veritable chain of general stores! And what about Ruhamah's work for D. J.'s campaign? Last time, Ruhamah must've helped organize a thousand potluck suppers and—

She remembered her fury during grief, fury and resentment. How could Alan have been so cowardly and selfish, to leave her and Ruhamah? Then the aching bewilderment would sweep over her again, as it did right now, despite all the reading about depression she had done since then. How *could* he have left them? Had he not loved them enough to stay?

She pressed down on the gas pedal and jounced and bounced out to the main road, which here ran briefly alongside Woodcombe Lake, where onto the snow-covered surface eager ice fishermen had hauled their bob houses as soon as the ice was thick enough. She sped toward the village. When she pulled into the North Country Coffins driveway, she saw Tom's pickup parked in front of the barn's big double doors. She parked beside it and entered through a smaller single door. He wasn't in the workshop. On his rolltop desk, the answering machine's red button kept blinking.

Then she saw snow plummeting past a back window. She heard scraping. The damn fool was shoveling off the porch roof! That was his son's job, and it hadn't yet had to be done this winter. She ran onto the porch, out to the path she'd shoveled this morning, turned, and yes, a ladder had been set against the roof and Tom was up there in jeans and gray parka wielding a snow shovel. By a trick of sunlight, at this distance and angle his rimless trifocals seemed to have disappeared. In high school, when he and she went parking he would take off his horn-rimmed glasses and hang them over the sun visor.

She yelled, "That's David's job!"

Tom paused and looked down at her. "David phoned, he's helping dig out at Lyman's."

Lyman Morrill, a neighbor of David's, had come home from the hospital last week after a heart attack. David's wife, Lavender, a certified nurse's aide, was keeping an eye on his recuperation. Snowy said, "Then wait until David can get here."

"And let the roof collapse?"

"Fuck the roof!"

Tom began laughing.

And so did she, weakly, then wildly.

"Almost done," he said. "Gardyloo!" This was a word he'd adopted after learning that in the olden days in Edinburgh it was what you yelled as a warning when you threw slops out a window. With the shovel he pushed and slid snow over the edge, tossed the shovel after it, and slowly clambered down the ladder. "How did things go at Moose's?"

"Come indoors. I tried phoning you from Moose's. I expect the answering machine has more messages than mine on it; the news probably has reached some Woodcombe folks."

"What news?" he asked, following her into the porch and workshop.

So, standing here amid the coffins and the machinery, she started telling him about the logging truck. He put his arms around her, and she completed the tale with her face against the chest of his parka.

27

"Christ almighty," he said.

She leaned away from him to see his face. "It's okay, I'm all right."

"Christ."

"I phoned Ruhamah, she was home, so Bev and I stopped there. Would you believe, Ruhamah still is interested in buying the place? A smashed-in front wall and wrecked counter and shelves! And on top of everything else—" Snowy stopped. Bev was just guessing. It wasn't a fact, not until Ruhamah made an announcement.

"What else?" he asked.

"Um, she wants to build a back porch there and name it after Cindy."

His arms tightened. "I want to give Cindy a medal and a parade."

She rested against him. Then she said, "It's lunchtime, I should get over to the store to help Rita," and the small barn door opened and in came David.

"Caught you!" he said, grinning. Tom's younger son had inherited Tom's reserved nature, which Tom himself hid under an easygoing manner, but as the years had gone by David seemed more outgoing—and definitely amused by his father's unconventional romance with Snowy. From Tom he'd also inherited a rugged build and a talent for woodworking. He had inherited Joanne's beauty, and it was aging as well on him as it had on her; he'd be forty-three this year. He unzipped his parka, obviously ready to tackle today's projects. He hadn't heard any news from Oakhill.

Snowy said, "I'm off," and left.

Walking past the little white post office, she pictured an even smaller one, the Quarry Island post office, which Puddles's husband called "postcard size," where more than two people would cause a crush. Every November, Cheryl, the postmistress (postperson?), sent out order forms to summer people back on the mainland, hoping they'd buy their Christmas-card stamps from

28

the Quarry Island post office to help keep it from being closed by the powers-that-be. Typically, Puddles had butted into this arrangement, giving Cheryl the names and addresses of friends and family, including Snowy's and Bev's. Bev ignored the inconvenience of ordering stamps. But Snowy had been buying her Christmas-card stamps from Quarry Island ever since, wishing herself inside that tiny post office in the island's village on the harbor, while feeling unfaithful to Woodcombe's post office.

She crossed the general store's parking lot. Kelsea and Cody Crowley, the young couple who rented the upstairs apartment where she and Ruhamah used to live, had shoveled the outside staircase before they drove off to work at, ironically, the big Shaw's supermarket in Gunthwaite. She hesitated. Would entering another general store bother her, would it cause some post-traumatic flashback? Nonsense. Onto the front porch she went, over the old worn threshold, into the store.

A gathering place after a snowstorm. Warmth. The noise of townsfolk talking. The familiar smell of coffee and lunch. Today's special was onion soup and roast-beef sandwiches. That's where most of the customers would be, sitting in the back of the store, on the stools at the lunch counter and in chairs at the tables. Safely in the back of the store. Snowy hurried there, past the old-fashioned cash register and the bulletin board on which people still posted handwritten notices such as "For Sale: 2001 Toyota Tacoma" and "Bobcat seen near Big Pine Corner" and "Wanted: Used Clothes Dryer," although Woodcombe now also had an online bulletin board. She continued past shelves of basic groceries, the meat counter. Old snowshoes and historical society reproductions of photographs of Woodcombe decorated the walls. On the wall behind the lunch counter was a little blackboard on which she'd written this week's specials she'd planned.

"Hi, Snowy." Rita was assembling a sandwich. In the Crock-Pot, the soup simmered.

"Hi." Snowy waved to the customers. They waved back, acting normal; they hadn't heard the news, and the guys were talking about the New England Patriots, who hadn't lost a game all season. She assumed that the women's subjects were, as usual, more varied. "Rita," she apologized, "I'm awfully sorry for Ruhamah's last-minute change of plans—"

"Glad to get out after being cooped up in the storm."

Rita had been a year ahead of Snowy at Gunthwaite High School, in Tom's class of 1956, and because she and Snowy were the same height they had been partners on the cheerleading squad. Very cute, very brunette, very stacked, Rita had caught Tom's attention long before he'd particularly noticed Snowy. He had dated Rita steadily for a happy-go-lucky while without being trapped into going steady. Well, Snowy thought, I have Tom now. And Rita had Hurricane Farm, having married Frank Barlow, who'd bought it when Snowy put it up for sale. Widowed, Rita lived there and filled in at the store not for the money but for the company and gossip; her granddaughter, Mallory, had lived with her since childhood and now attended the University of New Hampshire. Rita was still brunette and vivid. Although Snowy used the aids of hair coloring (blonde highlights) and makeup (splurging on Chanel), she nonetheless as usual felt invisible beside Rita as she moved to join her behind the counter.

Rita said, "I've got everything under control here. Joyce is ready to pay for her groceries, you go take care of that."

Snowy turned toward the front of the store and instantly in her head she was in Moose's store again and she heard Spike Jones.

"Hey, Snowy," said Greg, one of the town's selectmen, sitting down at the counter, his cell phone clamped to his ear, "what's this about you almost getting killed by a logging truck at the Oakhill General Store?"

2

THE DAMN FOOL HAD gone and done it, wrecked his knees shoveling off the porch roof. Thus, on the following Tuesday she and Tom went to Gunthwaite to see his orthopedist for a squeezed-in appointment at quarter of two. She was driving; Tom was the somewhat chastened but thoroughly pissed-off passenger.

South she drove on North Road. The weatherman's prediction of a "warming trend" had come true, cloudy and up in the forties today, so instead of parkas she and Tom were wearing fleece jackets, his blue, hers pink (boy blue, girl pink), and she felt light and unencumbered. Except for the worry about Tom. And about Ruhamah. The roadside was stabbed with campaign signs, as were front yards, mostly John Edwards here, some Hillary, some Barack Obama. Come summer, there'd be signs for New Hampshire's various candidates, including D. J.

She passed the old summer cottage named Bide-a-Wee that now contained Bev's real-estate office as well as an apartment for her grandson, Clem, and Clem's mother, Trulianne, who did small-engine repairs in the prefab building beside it. Bev had bought such an unlikely property because of this established small-engine repairs business, a way of luring auto-mechanic Trulianne from her Eastbourne home to Gunthwaite—and, most importantly, a way of bringing Clem into Bev's sphere. It had also kept him close to his father, Leon, a caretaker and handyman who lived across town in a mobile-home park with Miranda Flack, an Older Woman who cleaned houses, including Waterlight.

Grandchildren, Snowy thought. Bev and Puddles were doting grandmothers.

Bev in her realtor role was dealing with Moose and his insurance agent. She reported that Moose had declared he did not want to return north to see how his store, which had withstood blizzards and hurricanes, had "got stove up by one of Joe Landry's goddamn logging trucks." She was arranging the repairs with the contractor while pressuring Moose to lower the sale price. Ruhamah hadn't yet wanted to make an offer, choosing to wait Moose out. And nary a word about a grandchild.

Woods again. Republican signs in a row a la Burma-Shave. There were a few farmhouses remaining in fields, but ranch houses predominated and small pre-World War II summer cottages that weren't *on* the lake but on the way to it. At the stoplights near a strip mall, four young people were waving Obama signs. Then came Gunthwaite proper, once a mill town, a factory town, and now a small city supplying services.

On North Main, more sign-waving at stoplights. She turned onto State Avenue and drove past Trask's, where both her father and Tom's had worked, hers becoming the foreman of the lathe department, Tom's the head of tool and die. The old factory was now the conference center; last year she'd gone to her fiftieth high-school reunion there with Tom, and the year before she'd gone to his. And ahead was a self-service gas station, previously Varney's gas station where Tom had worked in high school.

At the sight of the gas-prices sign, he said, "Jesus H. Christ, how high is the price of gas going to go?" He had asked the same rhetorical question earlier this afternoon in front of the general store while he filled the Subaru's tank.

The price had got up to $3.10 today.

Next came the two brick buildings of the high school. Three years ago, Andrea (Andy) Edgecomb, executive director of the Association of New Hampshire Writers, had had a brainstorm: a series of minibus tours of the towns that had influenced New Hampshire writers. The first town to be toured would be Snowy's

Gunthwaite, on an August Saturday, starting and ending at the high school, with Snowy as guide. When Andy had told her this plan, Snowy had panicked, but Bev and Puddles had come to the rescue, doing a dry run with her, a dress rehearsal, Bev driving, Puddles supplying commentary from the backseat, and Snowy in the passenger seat making notes. It had steadied her. When the real event occurred, when the tour had unbelievably sold out and the minibus was filled with readers of her poems, she'd actually had fun. Then, after a (catered) sandwich lunch in the cafeteria, everyone moved to her old senior English classroom, where she presented a workshop on the subject of "The Importance of Place," using historical and general examples from *Beowulf* to Edna St. Vincent Millay, trying for perspective, but during the question-and-answer session the people began asking more elaborate questions about her connection to Gunthwaite than they had in the minibus. Her poems about Gunthwaite (and Woodcombe) made it clear that this was not Paradise, that she and the locale had their differences, but all at once she had to fight the urge to scream that this place had become a prison.

Tom pointed to a sign in the window of the restaurant on the corner of State Avenue and Elm Avenue and read aloud, "'Tripe Is Back!'" He added, "I take it that's not a political observation."

"Nope." Snowy flicked the directionals for Elm Avenue and drove past Ivythorpe Health Care Center and Retirement Community, a make-believe village of white condos and town houses where there would be old folks eager to partake of a nostalgic tripe dinner. Lots of John McCain signs around Ivythorpe.

The group of orthopedists had chosen to set up shop nearby, and they had also chosen to use the fancy spelling of their specialty, adding an "a," so the sign outside the newish blond building read: Gunthwaite Orthopaedics. Although the parking lot seemed full, she spotted an empty space down at the end. Before heading there, she pulled up to the front door and said to

Tom, "I'll meet you inside." She knew better than to suggest she help him out of the car.

Hanging onto the car door, Tom swung himself out, reached into the back for a walking stick that one of Bev's sons-in-law, Lloyd, had made from a sapling many years ago, and hobbled away. She parked. Off the backseat she took her shoulder bag and the Woodcombe General Store tote bag containing his library copy of Adam Nicolson's *Sea Room: An Island Life in the Hebrides* and her library copy of Sue Grafton's latest, *T is for Trespass*.

January 8. Today was the big day, New Hampshire Primary Day. The polls were saying that Barack Obama would win, as he had in Iowa. And everybody seemed to be talking about how yesterday, at a New Hampshire coffee-shop event, a woman had asked Hillary how she managed to keep going and Hillary had suddenly looked on the verge of tears as she replied that it wasn't easy, that she couldn't do it if she didn't passionately believe it was the right thing to do. Shocked, Snowy had stared at the TV screen—Hillary, losing control?—and felt tears sting her own eyes in response. Then Hillary said, "I just don't want to see us fall backwards as a nation. I mean, this is very personal for me, not just political. . . . It's about our country. It's about our kids' future. It's really about all of us together." Horrified, terrified, Snowy realized that Hillary *was* going to cry. Oh my God, no, Snowy thought, if she cries she'll never be president! And Hillary held back the tears. But the world had seen them ready to fall.

Hurrying to the entrance, her jacket billowing open, Snowy hoped that maybe this mild weather would help, would bring out lots of Hillary voters who either didn't give a damn about tears or actually applauded the glimpse of naked emotion. Maybe there'd be some indication in the microcosm of Woodcombe this afternoon. Last month Woodcombe's Democratic organizer had recruited townsfolk to hold signs at the town hall during voting, along with any out-of-state supporters who might be sent from Gunthwaite or other campaign headquarters. Snowy and Tom were scheduled for a Hillary shift from three to four o'clock. Now, because of his knees problem, Snowy had pointed out to Tom that it would be wise if he just went home after voting, leaving her to represent them in the sign-holding, but he of course was stubbornly determined to do it.

The waiting-room chairs were filled with people cuddling crutches and canes or rigid with braces or fenced in by walking frames. Those without equipment looked as if they needed some.

Tom was leaning on his walking stick in front of an aquarium, contemplating the little fishes flitting through the water. "Fish gotta swim," he said. "Humans gotta walk on their hind legs."

"Yes," she said, "and it's not one of Mother Nature's brightest ideas."

A nurse came into the waiting room and called, "John Marston?"

A gray-haired woman nudged the gray-haired man beside her, reminded him loudly, "That's you," and steadied his cane as he pushed himself to his feet. It hurt to watch him move after the nurse, his wife following, carrying jackets. Snowy appropriated the two empty chairs and took her glasses out of her shoulder bag, rimless Silhouette glasses like the trifocals Tom wore. Hers were only bifocals and she used them for reading, mostly, after she'd once happened to start descending stairs while wearing them. Eek! But Tom's *trifocals* didn't faze him!

She and Tom hid in their books. The men within earshot were talking about the Patriots.

Dr. Cochran's nurse came into the waiting room. "Tom Forbes? Oh, hi there, Tom."

Tom was a regular.

37

In the examining room, Snowy shut her eyes while Dr. Cochran injected Synvisc, an artificial collagen, into Tom's knees, as he had on other occasions. On those occasions he'd suggested that Tom think about knee replacements. Today he said firmly, "Tom. You're almost seventy. You've been postponing the inevitable long enough."

Snowy's eyes flew open. In Scotland she had learned a word that had made her collapse laughing because it supposedly summed up the Scottish character: thrawn. It meant that if told to do something, a Scot would do the opposite. Now, chilled, she waited for Tom to balk.

"Damn," Tom said. "Damnit. Goddamnit. Well, I can't face going through the ordeal twice. Can both knees be replaced at the same time?"

Snowy thought: At the *same time*?

"Yes," Dr. Cochran said and began discussing details.

Although she and Tom left the office with plenty of information, including reassurances that Medicare would cover everything, all she could think of was that she had to phone Puddles. Not only was Puddles a nurse, but she'd also been a hip-replacement patient.

Outside the building, Snowy said, "I'll fetch the car."

He didn't put up a fuss.

She drove back to the front door and looked at Tom waiting there leaning on that walking stick he'd used on hikes over the years, before trekking poles became popular. God, all the hiking he'd done, especially up and down Mount Pascataquac! Since 1987 he had worked summers atop this mountain, hiking up to the tower, keeping watch for forest fires, living in the fire warden's cabin on the two-thousand-foot summit, with a schedule of several days on, several days off, around which he fitted the North Country Coffins work. The trail was only a mile one-way, a distance he'd hardly noticed in his younger years. And in 1992, at age fifty-four, he'd hiked the entire Appalachian Trail, Georgia to Maine. But although he hadn't complained in recent years, she was well aware that the hike up to the tower was getting more arduous.

Their minds were apt to travel together, so she wasn't surprised when, after he stowed the walking stick in the back and lowered himself into the passenger seat, he said, "That's the end of the fire tower."

"Oh, Tom. Maybe not." She reached over and patted his thigh. "Your new knees will be better than your worn-out ones. It should be easier to hike than it is now."

"Yeah, sure," he said.

Physical limitations, she thought, driving away. She could sense how every moment of every day he hated the bombardment of limitations, every little daily example of aging—not being able to lift as much as he used to, taking longer to open a jar she still automatically handed him. She remarked, hoping to get a laugh, "Puddles has been singing the praises of her new hip in bed. Imagine what she'll say about your new knees."

After a silence, she got a strangled snort.

Then he said, "It's not cancer. It's mechanical."

And then he lapsed again into silence. She feared he was remembering how his left knee, banged up during high-school football, had buckled on the summit of Mount Daybreak when thunder and lightning had exploded out of the sunny blue of a June afternoon. He and she and his daughter, Libby, had been eating lunch there on the ledges, and though he'd yelled at them to get off the summit, to let him crawl off on his own, they had stayed with him, and Libby had been struck. Snowy knew that he was certain his knee had killed his daughter.

Driving home, she tried to soothe herself by thinking about food. And Maine. Tonight they'd have what she called a Maine supper, clams and blueberries; that is, canned Bar Harbor Clam Chowder and blueberry muffins made with the blueberries she

39

had picked and frozen last summer (in Woodcombe, not Maine). She pictured the blueberry barrens you drove through down to Puddles's town of Long Harbor. In winter there would be frost heaves on the peninsula road, and in the inlets the ice would be piled up like quarried slabs of rock. She pictured the harbor. At the wharf would be the mail boat, which was the ferry. She'd never ridden on the mail boat, she'd always gone out to the island on Blivit's boat or the castle's boat, but now she saw herself stepping aboard the mail boat, and in this daydream she no longer had any tendency toward seasickness, she didn't need Dramamine or ginger.

Years before their Scotland trip Tom had told her that, up in the fire tower pondering life, he had been thinking about how little traveling he had done outside of New Hampshire and how this limited his perspective. Limitations. But, he'd said, into his mind had drifted another thought: Americans tended to be rootless, moving, seeking some figment of home, so in a way didn't that make them the innocents and him the more deeply experienced?

Home. She snapped to attention and drove carefully down the hill into Woodcombe. Mountains cupped the village, Mount Pascataquac, Swiftwater Mountain, Mount Daybreak . . .

THE TOWN HALL, which dated back to 1893, stood on Main Street between the church and the library. Like them it was a plain white clapboard building, but today its solemnity was both heightened and lightened by campaign signs on sticks gripped by people out front in the wide shoveled dooryard. As Snowy maneuvered into the parking lot's nearest empty space, she thought how useful another type of sign would be, a driver's handicapped sign, so she could nip into one of those parking spaces. She tried to erase that thought. Tom, handicapped.

He roused himself and looked at his watch. "Almost three. Just enough time to vote before we replace a couple of Hillaryites." Reluctantly he added, "I guess I'll need that chair after all."

Over his objections, she had brought a folding lawn chair. She said, "I'll come back for it after we vote."

As they walked—slowly—to the front of the town hall, he said, his voice joking, even affectionate, "Democracy in action."

But she heard his serious undertone. Yes, the freedom to differ. She and Tom waved to friends holding Barack Obama signs high, other friends holding signs for John Edwards, John McCain, Mitt Romney, and Mike Huckabee. When she and Tom reached the Hillary contingent, she called to Jared, the true love of her roommate, Harriet, "We'll be right back to spell you."

He gave her a one-handed thumbs-up.

The town hall's dark varnished woodwork and wainscoting always reminded her of schools, the Gunthwaite elementary school she'd attended and dear old Gunthwaite High. From the foyer, where sample ballots were posted, she and Tom went into the busy meeting hall. Voting booths had been set up, with red-white-and-blue curtains for doors. The turnout seemed pretty good for a town whose population was now up to about twelve hundred. She and Tom, feeling foolish as usual, recited their names to the checklist people who of course knew them, had indeed been buying newspapers and groceries from her for years. The checklist people were amused too, but rules were rules. Forbes, Thomas, and Sutherland, Henrietta, were duly checked off and given paper ballots.

In a booth beside Tom's, Snowy put on her glasses, picked up a pencil, and voted for Hillary. Then she nearly burst into tears. A milestone. Would it actually happen, had she actually lived long enough to see a woman become president? She thought of how her grandmothers hadn't been allowed to vote until the nineteenth amendment passed. Tears spilled. She plucked off her glasses. Yanking a Kleenex out of her shoulder bag, she dabbed under her eyes, making a far messier job of tears than Hillary had.

Back outdoors, while Tom talked with some Obama-sign-holders, she returned to the car and got the lawn chair, metal, its plastic strips the green of a lawn fed too much fertilizer. As she began lugging it toward the Hillary group, a young man she didn't know, who was holding a Hillary sign, dashed over, saying, "Let me," and tucked the chair under his other arm. He was bundled up, apparently unaware of the warming trend. Knit cap pulled down tight, puffy parka.

"Thank you," she said. "I'm Henrietta Sutherland. You're one of Hillary's campaign workers?"

"Travis Fisher," he said. "Can't believe this town. I cannot, like, believe it."

She said, "It's been compared to Brigadoon. Where are you from?" Though she knew by his accent.

"New York. New York, New York. I can't believe all these small towns I've been seeing."

Could she resist playing local for this city kid? No. She said, "I expect you've been sent to the boondocks from Hillary's head-quarters in Gunthwaite." He nodded, so she continued, "That storefront that it's in on Main Street used to be an A&P grocery store. An old friend of mine used to work summers there as a cashier." (Puddles.) "You wouldn't by any chance be staying at the Washburns' house, that big Victorian house on the river? They've got a bunch staying with them. Dudley Washburn is another old friend of mine—and he's my daughter's father-in-law." Maybe this last, she feared, was overkill.

"No shit?" Travis halted near Jared and the other Woodcombe Hillary-sign-holders. "How many degrees of separation *are* there around here?"

"His wife and I were cheerleaders together."

Travis said wonderingly, "Mrs. Washburn's been feeding us amazing macaroni and cheese and stuff, bringing these humungous casseroles to headquarters. She and her sister. They're twins! Well, you know that, don't you."

Snowy laughed. Charl and Darl, the Fecteau twins. Charl had married Dudley; Darl had married Bill LeHoullier, another graduate of Gunthwaite High School and now the retired owner of Bill's Office Equipment. She said, "We've all been friends for a long time." Dudley the longest, since nursery school.

Tom had moved on to the Hillary group, to Woodcombe's oldest resident, one-hundred-year-old Gladys Stanton. He relieved Gladys of her sign and headed their way, looking ready to sit down.

Snowy said, "Tom, this is Travis Fisher, from New York, New York. Travis, Tom Forbes. The chair is for him. Knees."

Travis glanced up the street. "Somebody is supposed to be picking me up around now."

"New York?" Tom took the chair, opened it, and settled himself rather royally in it, holding the sign like a giant scepter.

As he and Travis began talking, Snowy went over to Jared. Her Californian roommate, after graduating from Bennington as an art major, had become a New Yorker, continuing with her painting, buying the art gallery owned by a family friend, and doing a lot of itchy-foot world travel. Harriet had met Jared in the Woodcombe General Store back in 1990 when she was visiting Snowy. Harriet had eyed with interest this handsome carpenter and the big tape measure he wore on his belt; he had admired the Jaguar she drove and offered her a ride in his pickup. That he was about twenty years younger than Harriet had daunted neither of them. Harriet had fallen in love with him and with New Hampshire. The New Hampshire place

43

she'd bought as a second home was the Gunthwaite farm where Bev had grown up, which Bev's mother and stepfather had sold when they retired to Florida. Ten years ago the owners decided to sell and gave the listing to Bev, who sold it to Harriet. Jared kept his cabin in the Woodcombe woods (a cabin with a hot tub), and if Harriet wasn't in Gunthwaite, he only went to the farm for caretaking chores. Snowy said to him, "My turn for that sign."

He looked down at her and asked, "It's not too heavy?"

"Wouldn't Harriet clout you with the sign if you asked her that?" Snowy held out her hands.

He lowered the sign's stick into them.

The sign wasn't exactly heavy, but it was heavier than it looked. Her back would be screaming when the hour was up. "Thanks," she said. "Is Harriet en route to the Galapagos as planned?"

"Yes. You really okay? Then I'll be off."

She watched him lope away to his pickup. She felt the weight of the sign.

Patsy Fletcher, holding another Hillary sign, walked over, a sociable slender woman a couple of years older than Snowy. She was also a brave woman, wearing just a yellow fleece vest over her turtleneck sweater and jeans. She said, "I've been thinking about my grandmothers. Not being allowed to vote until nineteen-twenty."

"Me too. My mother's mother would've been thirty-eight and my father's mother forty."

"They never talked about this. I hadn't known they couldn't vote until I learned about the nineteenth amendment in high school. I remember I was too flabbergasted to be furious."

Snowy saw an SUV pull up and Travis run and hop in, joining others inside. Then Fay Rollins, another Hillary-sign-holder friend, strolled over to her and Patsy. Fay was more cautiously

44

and warmly dressed in a long black down coat, and you'd expect her politics might be more conservative too, because she was in business, the owner of the Indulgences bakery in Gunthwaite, but no matter how she'd voted in the past in the privacy of the voting booth, it was Hillary publicly now. Fay asked, "Will the tears hurt or help?"

Patsy exclaimed, "They make her real!"

Fay said, "She must be exhausted. I wish she hadn't, but I'm glad she did."

"Oh," Patsy said, "this is all so upsetting! The timing of careers! The first time a woman could, the first time a black man could, and they have to be running against each other!"

Snowy watched the SUV drive away. The kid would be returning to Gunthwaite, then to New York, then maybe heading on to other primaries. Harriet was in the Galapagos painting portraits of tortoises. She herself was here in this small town and longing not for Manhattan Island or far-flung islands but for a little island off the coast of Maine. She had read that Maine had three thousand one hundred sixty-six islands if you counted islands now connected by bridges and every teensy blob of earth and rock on the sea. She hankered for Quarry Island.

Fay and Patsy's discussion had continued on to the advent of the Pill, and Patsy was telling about getting her first prescription in 1961.

Snowy thought that she could excuse herself, pull her cell phone out of her shoulder bag, and call Puddles from here. But she was too old, of the wrong generation or the wrong personality, to carry on a phone conversation in public, especially while holding a sign. So she waited. After she and Tom had finished their stint, she eased her poor old spine into the driver's seat of the car, he put the lawn chair in back and eased his poor old knees into the front, and she drove home along the street to North Country Coffins. While Tom stayed down in the workshop conferring with David, she hurried upstairs, took off her boots, peeled off her jacket, and rushed into her office to her desk chair and her real phone.

She had last seen Puddles in December, when Puddles and Blivit had stopped in Gunthwaite to visit Puddles's father and had spent the night at Bev's en route to Christmas in South Carolina. She stretched, rubbed her back, checked her watch. Four-twenty. Puddles's weekly schedule varied, but in general nowadays she worked at the Long Harbor clinic three mornings a week and coached her cheerleaders at practice several afternoons. Snowy called Puddles's cell phone, but she pictured the landline phone in the low-ceilinged kitchen of the Hutchinsons' big square white farmhouse. Puddles's cat, Pom-Pom, had died last year at age fifteen, so it would be Puddles's new cat dozing in the kitchen rocker. The humane-society young cat was a black-and-white cat like Kit, the cat Snowy had grown up with, but this one's color configuration consisted of a white front and black back and tail. Such cats were called tuxedo cats, yet to Puddles he looked like a puffin; puffins were called the clowns of the sea. In lieu of puffins' colorful beaks, he had a one-inch teardrop of reddish-brown fur behind his right ear. Of course Puddles had named him Puffin.

Instead of "hello," Puddles immediately said, "Son of a whore!" She had been born in Maine, and when she'd returned to her Maine roots upon her marriage to Blivit, she had enthusiastically adopted Maine sayings. "You voted yet? Hillary's botched it, hasn't she. Fucked it up wicked good and proper. Hell, now *I'm* going to cry. Again."

"I know. Where are you, at the school?" Snowy was now picturing the view from the hilltop school, down across small houses crouched together, to the waterfront and the ocean, the winter wind kicking up white spray. Beyond on the horizon was the silhouette of Quarry Island. Bali Ha'i, Maine-style.

Puddles sniffled. "I'm out on Route One, at the Home Depot, looking at toilets. The toilet in the bathroom off the back hallway started leaking."

"Oh, yuck!" Then Snowy remembered her purpose. "Puddles, Tom is finally going to have his knees replaced, we've been talking to his orthopedist about it, Tom wants both done at the same time and they'll actually do it, but it seems so drastic, both at once!"

"Yes," Puddles said, sounding suddenly nurse-alert. "Two surgeons, one for each leg."

"That's what Dr. Cochran told us. But it's so—*multiple*!"

"They do it all the time. Well, well, after Tom's been shilly-shallying for decades, he actually decided. Where's he going to have the surgery?"

"Dartmouth-Hitchcock." Snowy reminded herself that this would be the new medical center in Lebanon, New Hampshire, not the old Mary Hitchcock Memorial Hospital in Hanover where her father had been operated on for pancreatic cancer. Then she reminded herself of what Tom had said: It's not cancer. It's mechanical. She added, "The appointment hasn't been made yet, Tom will be getting a phone call about that."

"Knees are complicated," Puddles said, "more complicated than hips. But it'll be the same routine I went through afterward, with a visiting nurse and a visiting physical therapist and then PT at some place. When the PT is over, will you two finally give yourselves a vacation on Hilton Head? The house is yours!"

"Um, thank you, we'll see."

"Well, until then, after the surgery you'll just have to make sure Tom doesn't do anything stupid, being a male."

"Like try to climb a mountain? He's afraid he won't be able to work at the fire tower anymore."

"For God's sake, his first goal will be to walk to the bathroom. Speaking of which, I guess this smaller Kohler water-saving toilet

47

is the best bet, it's supposedly 'ideal for powder rooms.' I'll tell the plumber this is what we want. Why do they still call them powder rooms if we no longer powder our noses?" Puddles's voice turned mournful. "I'm feeling as low as a whale's belly. I couldn't help hoping we'd have a woman president before we die."

"Remember last month when Bev and I went to see Hillary in Gunthwaite and I told you how great Hillary was? She talked without a podium or notes for half an hour, and then she did another half hour of answering questions. Remember how I said even Bev envied that poise? Well, at the town hall just now, a woman friend said the tears made Hillary real. Behind the poise."

"You're saying women will vote for her because she almost bawled?"

"Maybe."

Puddles said, "Men will be afraid she'll have a hot flash and start a nuclear war. I'll call you tomorrow and we can cry some more."

"Okay."

But the next morning Snowy awoke to the news that Hillary had won the New Hampshire primary.

THE WARMING TREND continued, complete with rain that lowered snowbanks. Then on Monday there was a daylong snowstorm, then more snow on Thursday into Friday. Snowy shoveled, and Tom did his plowing but let David use the snowblower on paths and clear the porch roof with a roof rake and a shovel. As usual David cleared off the general store's roof. In the store, people talked about ice dams dripping into their living rooms and kitchens.

Hillary won the popular vote in Nevada's caucus.

Bev phoned Snowy the following Monday. Three years ago Ruhamah had insisted that Snowy start taking Mondays off as well as Sunday afternoons, so Snowy was working at home, in her office, on a poem about the junker vehicles decaying on an unnamed Maine island. Quarry Island, of course, but according to Blivit it happened on all islands. Old cars and trucks getting older, then abandoned.

Bev exclaimed, "Moose is whooping it up! The Patriots are going to the Super Bowl, and to celebrate he just called me to okay my suggestion of dropping the price by a nice round ten thousand. He wants the store off his hands *now*. I'm telling you before I tell Ruhamah."

So the price would be $80,000. Snowy said, "Ruhamah will say yes. I don't know, I don't know." She was picturing in her mind an ancient pickup lacy with rust, which on Quarry Island she'd seen abandoned headfirst in a clump of sumacs.

"A golden opportunity," Bev said.

Getting old. Rusting. But Ruhamah was young. Snowy said, "Yes." She heard Bev expel a lengthy breath of relief.

Then Bev said, "Good. I'll call Ruhamah and tell her. And about telling—still no news?"

"She hasn't announced anything. With those sweatshirts she wears, I can't *see* anything. If my guess is right that she got pregnant at Thanksgiving-time, she's about eight weeks along. I didn't show early. I did start napping." Fatigue, Snowy thought. Ruhamah might be young in other ways, but not in motherhood, having her first baby at age thirty-seven. Snowy herself had been thirty-two when she had Ruhamah and that was considered old in 1971. Ruhamah would be tired as well as nauseated and everything else, so how could she take on a third store at the same time as a baby?

Bev said, "Maybe the morning-sickness look was just my imagination, overwrought by a close call with a logging truck. How's Tom doing?"

The knee operation was scheduled for Monday, February 25. Snowy said, "He's still getting things organized with David. And with Jared, who'll be helping David. Tom's not thinking any further ahead than this except for predicting we'll have the storm of the century on the twenty-fifth."

"You can always drive over the day before and stay in a hotel. There's the Marriott we've stayed at." Roger was a Dartmouth graduate, and he and Bev went to reunions in Hanover.

"That's my Plan B. In any case, I'll make a reservation for the next night. I'll be in no shape to drive home after the operation."

"Snowy, are you really sure you don't want me at the hospital, waiting with you?"

"You're too busy, Bev. I'll bring a book, I'll be fine."

Bev murmured, as if she were talking to herself, "I'm not all *that* busy." Then she said briskly, "I'll call Ruhamah now. Then Moose."

The die is cast, thought Snowy.

Fifteen minutes later Bev phoned back to crow, "Moose accepted your offer, yours and Ruhamah's!"

Oh my God, Snowy thought.

Bev said, "The next step, an appointment for us at the bank."

The Gunthwaite bank where Bev's stepfather had worked. Snowy remembered the mortgages on the Woodcombe store and Hurricane Farm weighing down on Alan like the ton of snow outdoors.

This year Burns Night, January 25, fell on a Friday. A sunny Friday. Ever since she and Tom had gone to Scotland, Snowy had made a Burns Night supper of Cock-a-leekie Soup, from a recipe in a cookbook she'd bought in Stornaway on Lewis. She suspected that Tom liked this chicken soup mainly because the name conjured up so many jokes in his mind. Last evening she'd simmered a chicken in a pot, cooled it, cut the meat off the bones, and stored the pieces along with broth in the fridge. This evening she added barley to the broth, and while it simmered she washed and washed and washed the leeks, thinking of how this cookbook also had two haggis recipes, a traditional recipe and a modern recipe. The former began: "1 sheep's stomach bag, 1 sheep's lungs." She'd eaten haggis on the trip with Tom as well as on an earlier trip to Scotland with Ruhamah (that trip paid for by Harriet so Ruhamah could visit her Sutherland roots). Snowy had liked it—"You would!" Bev had said when told—but she wasn't about to make it even the modern way, not that you could easily get the ingredients for the traditional nowadays. Well, a couple of folks in Woodcombe did raise sheep. But! She chopped the leeks and added them. As she stirred the soup, she wondered if she were going stir-crazy. No; in winter you just thought more about food.

The soup was a success, as usual. And while they ate, as usual they reminisced about that trip to Lewis. Maybe because of the wild wind outdoors, they talked about how the wind had nearly blown them off their feet the first time they walked through the standing stones of Callanish.

"Remember," she said, "you took off your glasses for fear the wind would snatch them off your face and I thought it would rip my hoop earrings out of my lobes."

The contrast between the photographs they'd seen of Callanish and the reality was the same as with most photography, which cleaned everything up too bright and clear, and whereas in pictures the aisles of standing stones leading to the center circle were dramatic, in actuality the scene had struck her as simple, a green hilltop with some upright stones, sheep and houses nearby. Its very ordinariness caused goose bumps. Could the few other people walking along, bent and gasping in the wind, feel the presence of the prehistoric builders trying to make sense of the universe, feel an eerie yet intimate camaraderie, a sharing of intelligence and curiosity? She and Tom stopped and stood braced, looking at the low hills along the horizon that the moon skimmed every eighteen-and-a-half years, and she was sure her great-great-great-grandfather, Murdo MacLeod, had stood here and said farewell to the scene before he left for America.

Sometimes she made a Burns Night dessert of cranachan, a trifle with oats and whisky (natch), which they'd first had at their Lewis guesthouse, but tonight, her back aching, she simply opened a packet of shortbread.

"Remember," Tom said, "the dinner at the guesthouse when the dessert was cheesecake?"

"A berry cheesecake," she said. "We weren't sure what the berries were."

"And our host held out a cream pitcher and asked if we'd like cream on our cheesecake."

"And we were too stunned to be polite and say yes. We declined. But our dining companions, Scottish, accepted. Cream on cheesecake! Gilding the lily! Something we Americans had never heard of. We New Englanders."

They laughed. After Tom did the dishes, they settled down to watch their DVD of *Scotland Explored*. She tried to think that they were winter-snug, not imprisoned.

ON SUNDAY SHE awoke to the news that Barack Obama had won the South Carolina primary.

When the store closed at noon, the light snow of the morning had ended, and she walked home from work in pale sun, needing a longer walk outdoors. Snowshoes. Tom insisted on coming with her despite his knees, so together they went snowshoeing out behind the barn on the fresh white surface, across the brushy field, through woods, to the town's athletic field, where kids were doing some cross-country skiing. Winter *could* be fun! Snowy and Tom snowshoed up a low hill, stopped, and looked back. From here you could see all of Main Street, this little strip of striving civilization chopped out of the forest, circled by frigid mountains. But in her mind's eye she was seeing the breadth of ocean off Quarry Island, and into her mind sailed Byron's words:

> Roll on, thou deep and dark blue ocean—roll!
> Ten thousand fleets sweep over thee in vain;
> Man marks the earth with ruin—his control
> Stops with the shore.

Alas, she told Byron, that's no longer true, and man is ruining the ocean.

All the more reason, she told herself, to spend what's left of your life there, while you still can.

Monday, after the session with Bev and Ruhamah at the bank, Snowy e-mailed Cindy O'Donnell with the news of the store's purchase and the offer of the managing job. Cindy's e-mail reply was a thicket of happy exclamation points. Snowy forwarded it to Ruhamah, adding craftily, "Remember the diaper-changing I mentioned, Cindy changing a baby's diaper at the cash register? We'll have to make sure she doesn't bring her babysitting job to her managing job." Wouldn't that be a good opening for Ruhamah to announce a baby?

But Ruhamah only e-mailed back, "Stop worrying."

Had Ruhamah told *anyone*? Kim Parker or maybe her other friends? She had of course told D. J., hadn't she? Or maybe the pregnancy actually was a figment of Bev's imagination.

At the end of January, Snowy thumbtacked on the store's bulletin board the local snow amount: 73.3 inches. So far. Customers were talking about their mailboxes being dented or demolished by snowplows. They talked about the collapse of a Gunthwaite supermarket roof and the folly of building flat roofs in New Hampshire. They talked about the prices of gasoline, propane, and fuel oil.

And customers also talked about the local human snowbirds who had beat a retreat to Florida winter homes.

"Wimps!" they said. "Wusses!" Their tone, however, was envious.

But sometimes they talked about ice fishing on Woodcombe Lake and about the kids' ice-hockey games there. Winter, Snowy reminded herself again, *could* be fun.

On the first of February a sleet storm worsened during the night, the electricity went off but only for an hour, and on the next morning, Groundhog Day, she and Tom awoke to an inch of white ice everywhere. In New Hampshire, groundhogs were woodchucks and were still hibernating. During the afternoon the sun did peep out—and if an insomniac woodchuck had ventured out, he'd've seen his shadow. Snowy tried to imagine springtime and summer, when the vegetable garden would be planted and woodchucks were enemies to be dispatched by Tom with his rifle.

That afternoon Janice and Max Sewall, who lived on steep High Knoll Road, came into the store for mugs of cocoa and regaled everyone with the tale of how, last evening when they'd driven back from visiting friends here in the village, they'd found the road unplowed and too icy to drive up so they'd left the car at the foot—"and we *crawled*, on our hands and knees, up the road on the ice to our house!"

At sunset, the iced branches of trees turned pink. The next day, the perfect-season Patriots lost to the New York Giants.

Two days later came the Super Tuesday primaries, in which Hillary and Barack Obama were almost tied. Wet snow and sleet clogged David's snowblower. Tom, after plowing the barn's and store's driveways, had to ask for David's help up the stairs to the apartment, where David lowered him into a kitchen chair and Snowy grabbed his knee-wraps out of the fridge freezer and applied them fast, over his jeans and long underwear.

David said, "That's it, I'm doing your plowing for the rest of the winter."

"Hell," Tom said. "Goddamnit all to fucking hell."

Ruhamah now was spending most of her days at the Oakhill store with Cindy, seeing to repairs and restocking. One afternoon she returned to the Woodcombe store and announced to Snowy and all the customers, "The latest winter victim is Oakhill's salt-and-sand shed—its roof collapsed on top of the salt and sand as well as on a bucket loader, with a narrow escape by Cindy's husband, the road agent!" The response from the customers was commiseration and some nervous laughter.

The next day, more snow. After a town plow cleared Main Street, the town grader came though, pushing back the snowbanks to make room for the next storm. At the store, organizing newspapers, Snowy saw on the front page of the *Gunthwaite Herald* that the roof of a marina had collapsed, smashing expensive toys. Walking home after work, she thought of the driving that real commuters were coping with. Then she saw that somebody had made a snowman in the front yard of the Ramseys' Colonial across the street, a house closed for the winter while the Ramseys basked in Naples, Florida. The snowman wore a baseball cap, sunglasses, and a big bright Hawaiian shirt. Eek, were some year-round locals turning against the wimpy locals, would they next start burning down winter-empty houses? She told herself: Get a grip.

The next day's snow was the very beautiful type, wet snowflake-snow that clung to trees, but Snowy couldn't ooh and aah about this filigreed world. Over the phone she told Bev, "I'm thinking of rereading *The Long Winter* in Laura Ingalls Wilder's series, to put things in perspective. At least we're not starving."

"Quite the contrary," Bev said. "I'm craving carbs and indulging the craving. So I'd have to read *The Long Winter* on the treadmill."

Snowy realized Bev hadn't mentioned Roger in any recent conversation, not even just to complain about a retired husband underfoot. "Um," Snowy asked, "has Roger got cabin fever? Tom has, more than usual, knowing he's going to be cooped up with his knees."

"Roger?" Bev said. "He's hovering over the computer and investments." Then she seemed to swerve away from that subject, saying, "Remember our marshmallow-fluff-and-raspberry-jam sandwiches? I've begun fantasizing about them. Next time I'm buying groceries I won't be able to control myself, I'll buy the ingredients."

Eating was a symptom of stress, Snowy thought, as well as a symptom of seasonal affective disorder. SAD. Hell, it was a symptom of everything! She said, "What's got my attention is suet. When I cut it up for the suet feeder, I start thinking about the suet pudding in British novels. I'm afraid I'll find myself searching for recipes."

Bev retched, a noise she'd perfected in high school. They laughed, and Snowy suddenly remembered that the ingredients in both types of haggis recipes included suet. No. She would not make suet pudding or haggis. She wasn't going stir-crazy.

A one-day snow reprieve, then another snowstorm. When Snowy stepped off the back porch with her shovel, she startled a partridge sitting in a white pine—and it startled her as it shot past like a feathered torpedo. A partridge, so near the barn. Would it eat birdseed? She scattered extra.

More snow and more. On some houses, thick icicles on roof edges had lengthened down, down, down right into the snowbanks. The *Gunthwaite Herald* had a front-page photo of the latest roof collapse; the little roof over a gas station's pumps had fallen smack on top of two cars, the two drivers and one passenger all safe but standing there looking shell-shocked. Well, Snowy thought, at least this hadn't happened at the gas station that used to be Varney's.

In the store, people were now saying that they were ready to join the wimps and wusses in Florida, thanks to this goddamn winter.

Bev phoned and said, "I did buy marshmallow fluff and raspberry jam. But marshmallow fluff just looks like a snowstorm to me now. How is Ruhamah, any hints?"

"No," Snowy said. At the moment Ruhamah was in Oakhill, meeting with the Gunthwaite bookkeeper who did the books for the Woodcombe and Thetford stores and now would do Oakhill's. The third store. The worry of this third store would not lessen!

Valentine's Day, a Thursday, was a day of cleaning up after Wednesday's snow, sleet, freezing rain. A town plow went along Main Street filling in the ends of driveways as usual with hard-packed snow, but one of the town's road crew followed in a bucket loader, gallantly opening those ends so for once you didn't have to chew and chop them clear. A Valentine from the town, she thought.

Tom always acted offhand about Valentine's Days. She'd got the impression that Joanne had made a big deal out of it, so she herself was always offhand too, each year telling him lightly, "For God's sake, don't bother with flowers or candy, what would you like special for supper?" This year he suggested, "How about a risotto? Maybe with prosciutto?" So that's what she made, although it meant standing at the stove for twenty damn minutes, stirring, adding chardonnay to the rice, stirring, adding chicken stock, stirring, adding chicken stock . . .

Tom came into the kitchen, gave her a hug, kneaded her spine. "I've got something to show you."

"That's such a provocative statement."

He grinned. "After supper."

And after supper he took her hand and led her out to the stairway. She followed his slow descent into the workshop. He crossed to his rolltop desk. Beside it, a canvas tarp was draped over an object that wasn't coffin-shaped, unless the lid was up.

He whisked off the tarp. "Happy Valentine's Day."

A settee. She saw that he had built it from his supply of pine boards. Its sides were boards that reached to the floor, and into each he had cut out a big heart. A love seat.

He said, "For the garden. So you can sit and rest your back while you're working in the garden. Shit, you're going to cry, I was afraid of that."

She did so, hugging him. There *would* be spring and the garden after this long winter. Wouldn't there?

Next came sunny days. This year Roger's birthday occurred on Monday, Presidents' Day, and Bev had invited Snowy and Tom to Waterlight for lunch to celebrate his seventy-first, but the weather changed to fog, rain, and ice so treacherous she phoned Snowy and canceled. Shoveling ice away from the barn's front doors, Snowy saw a town sanding truck going *backward* up the incline at the end of Main Street, which was too icy for the normal procedure.

That evening Puddles phoned and said, "Have I got it right, tomorrow is the pre-op?"

"Yes," Snowy said. This was a meeting at Dartmouth-Hitchcock with one of the surgeons and the anesthesiologist.

"How's Tom?"

"The weather is a distraction."

"The fucking ice! I hope he's not being a chowderhead and traipsing around outdoors. For another distraction, ask him if he remembers rubbing cigarette ash into his white bucks to dull them. Blivit suddenly remembered doing that, isn't he adorable?"

Surprised, Snowy said, "Blivit smoked?" He seemed too ice-creamy to have been hooked on cigarettes.

"Didn't we all?" said Puddles. "Bye!"

The next day Snowy and Tom drove in sunshine across the state to Lebanon for the pre-op meeting. Many many details; even a bottle of antibacterial soap with which to wash his legs the night before the operation. But as the weather report had warned, the sun didn't last. They drove back in snow, made even more fun by occasional whiteouts.

Tom said, "Although I never ever would want to move to Florida, I don't blame everybody for saying they're ready to."

"Me neither. Aside from the warm weather, isn't there the need for any kind of a change of scenery?"

"The fire tower has been my change of scenery."

"It will be again, Tom."

"Remember how I once asked you if your desk was your change of scenery and you supposed it was?"

"Mmm," she said, and they fell silent.

When they reached home Snowy said, "No matter what the forecast is for the day of the operation, let's stay at that nearby Marriott the night before. You'll have to be at the hospital so early anyway."

"I hate spending money on a hotel because of an operation."

Not exactly a romantic getaway. She said, "We could go out to dinner. I'll ask Bev where."

Tom said, "The Last Supper." Then, continuing on a cheery note, he quoted Samuel Johnson: "'When a man knows he is to be hanged in a fortnight, it concentrates his mind wonderfully.'"

That evening, Snowy Googled "suet pudding" and to her astonishment found a slew of recipes.

3

"WHAT?" SNOWY SAID TO the doctor making the rounds. Her own knees went suddenly rubbery. "A blood transfusion?"

It was the morning after the operation. Yesterday when one of the surgeons had come into the waiting room and told her that everything had gone great, she had almost broken down into sobs. Then she had walked along hospital corridors, looking out the windows at the second of two mercifully sunny days, at the sky as blue as Tom's eyes. She'd found a window seat, taken her cell phone out of her shoulder bag, and phoned Ruhamah and David, asking David to phone Brandon, Tom's older son, in Alexandria, Virginia, and Tom's older brother, George, in Sarasota, Florida. Then she phoned Puddles and Bev, and then Harriet, home from the Galapagos Islands. Rejoicing, she told everybody exactly what the surgeon had told her: "It went great!"

But now this morning the doctor was saying, "His hemoglobin is low. My recommendation is a blood transfusion."

Yesterday, after seeing Tom in the recovery room and then in this room, a private room but very small, her main worry aside from his knees had been his appetite; he was queasy and a nurse had had to put an anti-nausea medication in his drip. This morning when Snowy had arrived from the Marriott he'd still felt ill, but otherwise he was progressing so well that Sean, the muscular physical-therapy guy with a purple tattoo snaking up a forearm, had suggested he try to move from the bed into the old blue plastic recliner pushed beside it. Tom had scooted over, and Sean said, "If this was the Olympics, I'd give you a ten!" Encouraged, on the day's menu Snowy had checked off a turkey sandwich and a brownie for Tom's lunch and comfort food for his supper, pot roast and tapioca pudding.

Now she was standing here staring up at this doctor. Blood transfusion. Should she phone Puddles? You no longer had to worry about AIDS in blood, did you? She and Tom looked at each other.

He nodded. "Guess we'd better go ahead."

After the doctor spoke to a nurse and they left, Snowy dropped into a straight-backed chair beside Tom in the recliner. Out the window snow was falling, but she had been planning to drive home in the storm, regroup, and come back tomorrow. She said, "I'm going to stay."

"No," he said. "I'll be okay."

She thought: Farewell forever to last night. The Gaelic poem. She had gone to bed and left Alan alone and he had died. Tom couldn't drive off and drown himself, but she wasn't leaving him alone, with strange blood about to be poured into him. She said, "I'm staying. Not at the hotel. Here. I'll see about spending the night here."

"No," he said again, but then the blood was delivered and she stepped out of the room.

She walked over to the nurses' station and said to a nurse, "May I spend the night in Tom's room? There doesn't seem to be enough space for a cot, but I could sleep in the recliner."

The nurse considered her. "That's a fine idea. I'll show you the linen supply, you could pick up yours this evening—oh, and the blanket-warmer, whenever Tom would like another blanket, and I'll show you the kitchen if he wants a drink or a snack."

How domestic! She followed the nurse on the little tour. The sign outside the kitchen didn't say Kitchen; it said: Nourishment.

The nurse checked her watch. "Lunchtime. Take something for yourself from this refrigerator and order a guest meal for your supper."

Nourishment.

Snowy chose a small container of peach yogurt. Returning to Tom's room, she found that he had moved back to the bed. He was gazing up at the ceiling, or through it, and he seemed absolutely alone. A bag of blood was seeping into him.

His lunch had arrived, and she looked quickly away from that bag, looked instead at the turkey sandwich and brownie on the tray, but it dominated the room. She whispered, "Tom?"

He turned his head toward her.

She said, "I got permission to stay here. Would you like your sandwich?"

"No."

"The brownie?" To try to amuse him she almost added the joke about life's being uncertain so eat dessert first, but she stopped.

"No. You have them." He closed his eyes.

Her yogurt no longer seemed like a comforting choice. She put it on the tray. Quietly she got a paperback out of her Woodcombe General Store tote bag of books, whose heft had made her see why e-books were handy. She had brought comfort reading for herself, books she'd reread a hundred times, and she'd chosen some of his favorites. Yesterday she'd read Agatha Christie's *Murder at the Vicarage*. Today she picked up the brownie, sat down in the recliner, which felt more like a torture rack than a bed, and began Dorothy L. Sayers's *Gaudy Night*.

Tom woke up roughly. "Hey. What? What's going on?"

"A nap," she said. "I hope it helped?"

Before he could answer, a nurse came in carrying a little tray. "The morphine has been stopped," she said. "This is oxycodone, five milligrams."

Eek, Snowy thought, isn't that what addicts rob pharmacies for?

Tom swallowed the pill, and the nurse left. In came another nurse, who asked him, "How are the knees?"

He paused, not giving an automatic answer. Then he said, "Hurting. Well, it isn't the old way of bone-on-bone. It's more like the stiffness of surprised flesh."

"Time for Cryo/Cuffs," the nurse said, and went out.

Snowy told him, "I'll go get my things from the car."

He said, "Snowy, you don't have to stay here overnight."

"I'm staying."

"But where, there's no room!"

"In the recliner."

"Sleep in that dilapidated recliner? No!"

"Yes. I'm staying." She picked up the phone and ordered a guest meal the same as Tom's supper.

The nurse returned carrying a blue plastic jug that rattled with ice and sloshed with water. "The gravity-feed model," she explained. A short hose was attached to the pads she wrapped around his legs. "Now, isn't this better?"

He smiled. "Cold as the knee-wraps I keep in the freezer, if not more so."

The nurse patted his shoulder and left again.

Snowy slung her yellow-and-black MacLeod wool scarf around her neck, a scarf she'd bought in a Stornoway shop, and pulled on her parka. Out of the tote bag she took Dick Francis's *To the Hilt* paperback and gave it to Tom. "How's this? Or shall I turn on the TV?"

He grabbed the remote off the bedside table. "I can do it." He clicked the TV on.

Leaning down, she kissed him. "Be right back."

The corridor led her into the long carpeted expanse called the mall, where there were little stores, such as Au Bon Pain with its breads and pastries, Sbarro with its pizza, and the Pink Smock Gift Shop. Outdoors, snowflakes on her face were a welcome astringent. In the parking lot she unlocked her car and opened the back. Beside her overnight bag a walker waited for Tom's discharge, folded up, borrowed from Fay and Martin Rollins who had actually bought one, instead of renting, when Martin had a knee replacement last year. They had offered the walker to Tom, and they'd even offered the raised toilet seat, with arms, which they'd also bought. That awaited Tom in the barn's apartment. Reality.

She lifted out her overnight bag. When she'd packed it Sunday morning, she'd added an extra day of clothing just in case, but if she stayed tomorrow night she'd be out of clean clothes. Yuck! This was something that hadn't even happened on backpacking hikes with Tom!

Going indoors, she dawdled in the mall. She could look for birthday cards in the Pink Smock, she could have a cookie at Au Bon Pain . . .

She didn't. She had told Tom she would be right back. She went on to his room.

The TV was off, and he was fuming. "I thought the blood was finished, but they brought another damn bag, do they think I'm Dracula? And some woman from the Concord rehab place just came in here and she claims they can't tell yet whether or not I can go there!"

During the pre-op session, it had been explained that patients might go to a rehab place to recuperate after the surgery before going home, but if you had somebody to look after you at home (such as Snowy), you might not qualify. Tom had got it into his head that he wanted to spare her, and besides, the staircase up to the apartment might be too much if he was fresh from the hospital. He was determined to go to the Capital City Rehabilitation Center.

Taking off her parka and scarf, Snowy said, "Today's Tuesday. The earliest you'll be released is Thursday. That's not long to wait to find out."

"I don't give a fuck, I want to know now!"

She yanked out the paperback, squashed and forgotten beside him in the bed. "Here's the Dick Francis. Or how about your *Whisky Galore?*"

He threw Dick Francis across the room. It bounced off the bathroom door.

She stood rooted, shocked. Trying to keep her voice steady, she said, "Do you want to turn on the TV again? Let's see what's on TV."

"There won't be a goddamn thing!"

She edged toward the door. "Then I'm going to phone Ruhamah and make sure everything's okay at the stores."

She fled. She roamed corridors, found the window seat she'd used yesterday, and phoned Puddles, picturing ocean waves cresting and receding, cresting and receding, on the shore below the farmhouse.

"Hi!" Puddles yelled, a crowd roaring behind her. "I've only got a moment, I'm at a basketball game! How's Tom doing?"

So Snowy switched the image to a high-school gym, Puddles with her cheerleaders rooting for the Long Harbor High School team, the Seafarers. She said, "His temper's getting short. They've given him oxycodone. He's acting like he's—I don't know, it's scaring me."

"Oh, shit. Ask them to decrease the dosage. Or ask them to switch him to Vicodin, that's what I had and I didn't lose my marbles."

"Thanks, Puddles, I will. Bye."

"Bye!"

Snowy stood up, rubbed her back, walked farther down the hall to a single-person restroom, locked herself in, and let herself cry. She remembered the presurgery dinner with Tom at one of the places recommended by Bev. Jesse's Restaurant and Tavern. Their nerves making the occasion precious, she and Tom created a good time in the log-cabin atmosphere. Tom had a perfect sirloin, and she had a plenitude of peel-and-eat shrimp from the salad bar. At the hotel, she helped him take his shower using the antibacterial liquid soap. Precious.

She dreaded returning to his room. But she found him looking calmer, reading Compton Mackenzie's *Whisky Galore*, the fictional version of the aftermath of a shipwreck in the Hebrides, when the islanders relieved the ship of its whisky cargo.

"Sorry," he said. "Everything okay at the stores?"

She hadn't been lying, she'd intended to call Ruhamah; she'd forgotten. She picked up Dick Francis. "Everything's fine."

Then a delivery man came in, Get Well balloons bobbing from one hand, flowers in his arms, and there were the gift cards to read. Puddles and Blivit had sent the balloons. The bouquet of dried lavender and lavender silk roses was of course from Lavender and David and daughters Elizabeth and Lilac. In a clear glass vase were flowers Snowy didn't recognize, unusual colors of dark red, mustard yellow. Tom read the little card aloud, "'These are the gas-station flowers we told you about, alstroemeria. Get well soon, Roger and Bev.'"

Snowy laughed. "Remember, on their second honeymoon, when they stopped at a gas station in the Cotswolds Bev couldn't believe her eyes, bouquets of flowers were for sale there, at a gas station! She hadn't a clue what they were. She bought a bouquet and pressed a blossom to bring home, and looked it up. Alstroemeria. But for Bev the name is still 'gas-station flowers.' Remember, Roger speculated about the likelihood of you guys selling flowers at Varney's."

Tom didn't laugh or start reminiscing about Varney's. Snowy tied the balloons to the head of the bed and set the bouquets on the windowsill. She sat back down in the recliner. They read. *Whisky Galore* was funny; usually he laughed while reading it, but not today. Then a nurse came in, checked the blood bag, and said, "Done!"

Whew, Snowy thought, isn't this cause for rejoicing?

Tom scowled into *Whisky Galore*.

Dinner was brought.

Tom said ferociously, "Pot roast! Yours is the only good kind. Why did you order this crap?"

"Try the tapioca pudding." She was desperate. "You know, eat dessert first."

"Ha-ha," he said, but he took a spoonful. "Christ, it tastes like it's been sitting in a fridge for months."

"Let's watch the evening news." She reached for the remote.

He seized it and switched the TV on.

She said, "I'd better go get my bed linen."

At the nurses' desk, she said to a nurse, "I think Tom is having a bad reaction to the oxycodone. Could the dosage be reduced or the medication be changed to Vicodin?"

"I'll make a note," the nurse said.

Snowy fetched her sheets and warm blankets for both of them and returned. Tom was asleep. She turned off the TV and read. Then she tiptoed out of the room and took a walk, finding the nightlife of the hospital under way. Night workers were cleaning the carpets in the mall, the chemical smell overwhelming.

IN THE RECLINER, her sleep was intermittent.

A nurse awoke Tom at three o'clock, saying, "More pain pills." Snowy started to ask for pill names and dosage details.

No. That could rile Tom up. He and she dozed with TV, and when the *Today* show began, she went into the bathroom and showered. Getting dressed, she suddenly heard real voices, not TV voices, and hurried out.

A different doctor from yesterday was doing the rounds and telling Tom in an unfortunate peremptory tone, "The decision about rehab won't be made until tomorrow."

Tom lit into him. "You might try being understanding! At medical school, did they teach you anything about sympathy, empathy? I'm in a helpless situation, you get that? I want to be able to plan! There's no need to have an attitude! The doctors' God syndrome!"

Snowy said, "Tom—"

But Tom had jolted the doctor into better behavior, into saying, "I do understand. You'll have the information as soon as possible."

Snowy asked, "The blood transfusion, is everything all right now?"

"Yes," the doctor said, and left.

Snowy stroked Tom's forehead. "Everything's all right."

"What a fucking asshole."

Breakfast arrived. Snowy ate her cranberry muffin. Tom ate half of his, staring at the television set, looking spacey. But when Sean, the PT guy, came in and showed him how to get to his feet using a walker and move to the recliner she'd vacated, Tom did it smoothly.

Sean said, "A natural athlete!"

"No," Tom said. "I'm scared of falling." Then he told Sean, "I work at the fire lookout tower on Mount Pascataquac. Come spring, I've got to be able to hike to it, a mile up, a mile down."

"Well," Sean said, "hang in there with the PT."

After Sean left, the nurse brought another tray with medication, announcing, "Oxycodone, five milligrams."

Snowy said, "Please, can't it be cut back? Or changed to Vicodin?"

"I'll see," said the nurse, but she waited until Tom had swallowed the pill before she left.

"You know," Tom said, "I'm feeling half-plastered. Maybe it's from reading *Whisky Galore*."

Snowy smiled at him, relieved by this small joke. Could the oxycodone now be causing him to mellow?

He dozed in the recliner. She sat beside him in the straight-backed chair, wanting to go for a walk through today's snow flurries, to breathe the ozone, wanting to phone Puddles. But she didn't dare leave him and she shouldn't keep pestering Puddles. She took *Wildfire at Midnight* out of the tote bag. This Mary Stewart novel was set on the Isle of Skye, so she would be joining Tom in Scotland. A nurse brought Cryo/Cuffs.

For lunch Snowy had ordered seafood-salad sandwiches. Tom was peering suspiciously under the top slice of bread when a woman entered the room and introduced herself as the discharge coordinator. This woman didn't mind hazarding guesses. She guessed that Tom would be discharged tomorrow and could go to the Concord rehab. But when she left, Tom said, "I'll believe it when I see it."

Sean reappeared. He taught Tom exercises in the recliner, then escorted him in the walker to the bathroom door and waited, admiring the windowsill bouquets, until Tom emerged, then guided him in the walker down the corridor. Snowy quickly phoned Bev and lied, "Tom sends his thanks for the gas-station flowers. They've lifted his spirits. Memories of Varney's!"

"How is he?"

"He'll be discharged tomorrow and I'll drive him down to the rehab place in Concord. I'll phone you when I get home. Bye."

Upon their return from this excursion, Sean said, "I'd judge that you need at the most three to seven days at the rehab."

Tom asked anxiously, "You'll put that in your report?"

Sean grinned. "Sure thing."

This afternoon a delivery man brought Tom more gifts, but he scarcely noticed. The back of the recliner wouldn't stay up, and, twisting in his seat, he was concentrating on trying to fix it. A dish garden had been sent from Brandon, Brandon's wife, Stephanie, and their two sons, eight-year-old Brandon, called Branny, and five-year-old Tommy. Harriet sent a creamy hydrangea plant in a rustic basket. Snowy added the dish and basket to the collection on the windowsill.

Then in came the occupational therapist. Tom turned from his repair attempts and sat upright. She observed, "Most people can't yet sit with their knees bent the way you can."

He looked confused. He snapped, "Does that mean I don't need rehab?"

"No," she said soothingly, "no, I'm sure you'll have your stay there."

When she left, he started raging at the recliner, clanging the back in frustration.

"Tom," Snowy said. "Please, Tom—"

He began hauling himself up by the walker.

"No!" Snowy said. "Wait, don't get up on your own, I'll get a nurse—"

"Goddamnit, I have to pee!"

Snowy ran to the door, leaned out, and cried, "Help! Help!"

Two nurses, female and male, rushed in.

Snowy said, "He wants the bathroom, but—"

"Okay," said the male nurse, holding the walker steady as Tom rose to his feet, "you're doing great."

"I've practiced with Sean!" Tom said. "I can stand up by myself, for God's sake!"

"Sure," the male nurse said quietly, stepping away.

Tom pushed the walker into the bathroom. The male nurse followed him in. Tom yelled, "I'm all grown up, get the hell out of here!"

The male nurse backed out. "Okay. Okay."

Snowy babbled, "I'm sorry, it's the oxycodone, can't he be taken off it, and the recliner seems to be falling apart, he's trying to fix it, he's used to fixing things, he can fix anything—"

The female nurse said, "I'll make a note about his medications."

The male nurse fiddled with the recliner until the back remained up, at least temporarily.

Tom shuffled out with the walker, muttering, "A hospital like this should be able to afford a decent recliner." He lowered himself into it. A feat, Snowy thought, but nobody applauded.

As the nurses left, the male said to Tom, "Take it easy, mate."

Snowy turned on the TV, and Tom glowered at some talk show on the screen. Dinner arrived. She had again chosen the same meal for both of them, grilled salmon with lemon-dill sauce and angel cake with strawberries. It looked really delicious. She lifted a forkful of salmon off her plate and realized she couldn't chew, much less swallow.

Tom wasn't touching his food at all.

She pleaded, "Tom. It'll be okay. It seems like you'll be discharged tomorrow, and probably I'll be taking you to the Concord place, but maybe we'll be going directly home and that'll be okay too. The way you're progressing, David can get you up the stairs. See? It'll be okay."

He looked at her. Something glittered in his eyes.

Madness.

HER GOAL WAS to get out of Concord before the five o'clock rush. Tom's wish for a stay at the Capital City Rehabilitation Center had indeed come true, and she'd driven him here this afternoon. The rehab place had itself been rehabbed from an old brick elementary school. After the admission procedures were concluded, Tom was given a double room on the second floor, where Snowy had now settled him into a plastic chair beside the window whose view was of a snow-covered expanse that must've once been the playground with swings and a jungle gym for youthful exercise. Next to him were his overnight bag, their tote bag of books, and the Cryo/Cuffs and empty gravity-feed jugs the hospital had sent with him. Snowy's wristwatch told her it was four-thirty. Time to leave.

But ever since he had reached this destination he had wanted, he had begun looking more and more rebellious. Time to leave him here. Time to leave him. Farewell forever to last night. She couldn't stay with him; the other bed was occupied, by a man who had trouble speaking, maybe from a stroke. But she could find a room at the closest of Concord's hotels and motels, to be nearer to Tom than their home in Woodcombe.

Home. The urge gripped her. She was deserting him, leaving a kid at summer camp miserable and homesick. She kissed him and said, "I'll call you tomorrow," and hurried to the elevator, down out the front door to the parking lot and her car. The balloons were tied tight to a backseat headrest; the lavender bouquet, dish garden, and hydrangea basket sat on the backseat; the gas-station flowers, stems wrapped in damp paper towels, stood in their drained vase behind the passenger seat. Her overnight bag was in the rear. She drove off.

Getting discharged from the hospital had taken ages, right through lunch, and while she and Tom had waited she'd gone outdoors into sunshine, brought the car's New Hampshire atlas back to his room, and refreshed her memory of the criss-crossing streets on the downtown Concord map. Tom in his despised recliner seemed better, more normal, though he was antsy, eager to get going, talking while she tried to concentrate on the map. She always navigated by the state house's gold dome when it could be seen above houses and stores, and she had other guideposts too, such as a coffee shop with a tempting sign in the window saying Dessert Break 2–4:30 p.m., a lovely idea, an afternoon dessert break like a morning coffee break, an idea that always reminded her how easily she had adopted the British teatime break (scones! treacle tarts!) when she was over there.

But she had never stopped at that coffee shop, and today when she spotted it she was too late. She could use some coffee to stay awake. On the next cross street she saw another guidepost, a house set between a Chinese restaurant and a tire-sales garage. The house had a sign saying The Second Time Around; it was an antiques store. She'd known it as the headquarters of the Association of New Hampshire Writers before the association acquired an old mansion on a hilltop. Up ahead an arrow pointed to I-93, to home. She should turn around, return to the Capital City Rehabilitation Center. No!

She followed the arrow and raced north on the turnpike. Even though she'd got ahead of the end-of-the-workday stampede, the traffic was heavy, Massachusetts license plates mingling with New Hampshire. A Thursday start to the weekend? Some cars had skis on their roofs. The car ahead of her displayed a proud bumper sticker that said: My Kid Beat Up Your Honor Student.

Now that she had fled Concord, she was awash with remorse. She should have stayed. And after two nights in a recliner, she was too exhausted to be driving home, so she should have stayed for that reason too. She could still change her mind, turn back at the next exit. She pressed the radio button for NPR.

Massachusetts license plates were white-red-blue. New Hampshire plates showed the profile of the Old Man of the Mountain, the ancient rock formation up in Franconia Notch. These white-and-green license plates were a constant reminder for her of Kenneth Collins, the crazy guy whom the newspapers had dubbed the Old Man Bomber, who in 1992 had tried to take her with him on his mission to blow up the Old Man. She had clouted him with a bottle of chardonnay, and he'd been arrested. When he eventually was released from jail, he had tried to kill Tom atop Mount Pascataquac, then had blown himself up.

A few years later, in 2003, Mother Nature had accomplished what Kenneth Collins hadn't. The rock formation collapsed. She still was shocked by the sight of that blank in the sky. Like the blank of Alan's absence.

She shivered, shook herself. Kenneth Collins's mad eyes glittering. The glitter in Tom's.

New Hampshire license plates sported the infamous state motto, "Live Free or Die," from the Revolutionary War General John Stark's toast, "Live free or die: Death is not the worst of evils." The appearance of the motto on license plates had led in the 1970s to a lawsuit ending with the U.S. Supreme Court's decision in favor of freedom from mottos. This meant that you couldn't be arrested for covering up the motto, and she remembered how Alan had gone through a phase of taping over it on their license plates.

At last, the Leicester/Gunthwaite exit. She swung off. The old highway took her to an area where homes were now businesses, including Weaverbird, Bev's daughter Mimi's farmhouse whose front rooms had been converted into a weaving shop. The Weaverbird van was parked in the driveway. I could, she thought, stop at Mimi's and ask for a cup of coffee. She drove past, on through what she thought of as an invasion or a mirage, the malls, Walmart, and Home Depot where there had been woods. She could stop at Applebee's. She kept going into town, taking side streets to get around Main Street, Gunthwaite native that she was, hometown girl.

On North Road, in her shoulder bag her phone began ringing. She pulled into the strip mall parking lot, punched off the radio, and grabbed it. Tom. Although the car's windows were closed, she could smell oregano wafting from the pizza joint.

She asked, "Are you okay?"

"Everyone's crazy here!" he said. "They won't let me go anywhere without someone with me, not even to the bathroom! What is it with these goddamn people and bathrooms?"

"They want to make sure you don't fall—"

"Where are you? Come get me."

The kid at summer camp. The college freshman phoning parents, begging to be allowed to return home (something she'd never done). She said, "I'm on North Road. Tom, you're there because they don't think you're ready to be home, especially with our staircase. Remember how Sean told you three to seven days of rehab?"

"Come get me!"

"What meds have they given you?"

"I don't know. Well, oxycodone."

"After I *warned* them about that?"

"Come get me!"

She leaned her head against the headrest and let tears run down her face but managed to keep her voice steady. "I'll come get you tomorrow."

"You're lying."

She sat bolt upright. "Tom. Listen to what you just said."

A silence.

She said, "I can't turn around and drive back, I'm too tired, it wouldn't be safe. I'll be there tomorrow morning."

Another silence. Then he asked, "You promise?"

"I promise."

He didn't reply. She heard a gulp and realized he was crying too. His phone clicked off.

She almost did turn around and drive back to spring him from the place. Yet, the paperwork he'd signed—he probably wouldn't be allowed to leave at this time of day, so soon after he'd arrived, would he? Complications, arguments, Tom's fury. Digging a Kleenex out of her shoulder bag, she blotted her eyes. She drove on.

But the sight of Bev's Subaru in front of the real-estate office caused her own Subaru to make a left turn into the plowed white parking lot. Nearly six o'clock, and Bev was still here. No other cars, none of Bev's salespeople, only Trulianne's pickup truck.

Snowy parked and clambered slowly out, stretching her back.

The original summer cottage, Bide-a-Wee, had been white with blue trim and over decades had been enlarged with ells and porches and dormers and sheds. When Bev bought it eight years ago, she'd kept the exterior colors the same and renovated the interior into her office in the front rooms, with the rest of the house Trulianne and Clem's apartment. Across the parking lot, Trulianne's small-engine repairs shop was closed for the day. Trulianne would be in the apartment with Clem, having supper. In the office, Bev would be working.

However, after Snowy opened the front door into the hall and tapped on the office door and opened that, she saw Bev not at her desk but curled up in the wing chair engrossed in a paper-back. For the upholstered chairs and the sofa and curtains Bev

79

had chosen a pattern of great big flowers, bright greens, blues, and purples. In her younger years, with her red hair Bev would have been just as colorful in this setting, and oddly enough with her white hair she still was, her clothes contrasting too, the old white sweater, her gray slacks (Bev not wearing dressier clothes on a workday?). Bev glanced up, swiftly slid the book between the cushion and the side of the chair, and stood, saying, "Snowy, is everything okay, did you get Tom to the rehab place?" She studied her and then rushed across the room. "You've been crying."

Bev had to bend down to hug her. Over Bev's shoulder Snowy could see the top of the paperback peeking up above the cushion. On the cover a man's familiar face smiled at her. Who?

Snowy said, "He hates the place and wants to come home." She started crying again; she could not stop the tears. "He's supposed to stay at least three days, I thought I'd have a reprieve, but now I promised I'll go back tomorrow for him, I hope he can sign himself out if there's a fuss."

Bev hugged tighter. "Hell and damn."

"They're giving him oxycodone after I told them not to!"

Bev led her over to the sofa, gently pushed her onto it, and brought a box of Kleenex from the desk. "I'll drive you down there tomorrow. You've been coping too much on your own."

Snowy blew her nose. "Henry Fonda! Is that Henry Fonda?"

With obvious reluctance, Bev drew the paperback out from behind the cushion. Then she cocked a hip and posed, with the cover facing Snowy.

Yes, it was Henry Fonda. Katharine Hepburn smiled at Snowy too, and so did Jane Fonda and a young boy. The paperback was faded, yellow. The cover said: *On Golden Pond*, a Play by Ernest Thompson.

Bev handed Snowy the book. "I bought it when the movie came out. Nineteen-eighty-one. Remember, the movie was made in our Lakes Region before either of us moved back here? If I'd been here, I hope I could have got brave and become one of the locals involved. Not like Camden."

Snowy held the book, remembering the movie and also remembering how Bev had been waitressing in Camden, Maine, in 1957 when the movie of *Peyton Place* was filmed there. Bev hadn't dared go to the auditions for extras.

Bev said, "Funny, isn't it. *Peyton Place* is set in New Hampshire and the movie was made in Maine, while *On Golden Pond* is set in Maine and filmed in New Hampshire. Um, have you heard, the summer theater is starting up again."

"Oh?" Snowy racked her brain. When Bev left Roger in 1987 and moved from their Ninfield, Connecticut, home to Gunthwaite, Bev hadn't got involved in the Gunthwaite Summer Theater, saying she was far too busy starting her real-estate career. In Ninfield she had acted with the Ninfield Players. With one leading man in particular. Snowy hadn't paid any attention to the Gunthwaite Summer Theater. She recalled, "It was in a barn."

Bev said fondly, "They almost always are."

"Oh, and you told me there were jokes about how it folded because there were bats flying around scaring the audience, but you thought the real problem was disorganization. You told Puddles and me that, and Puddles said the problem was you weren't the leading lady."

Bev gave a little laugh, took the book back, walked over to her desk, and put it in the top drawer. "You're coming home with me. We'll fetch Tom tomorrow. Tomorrow is February twenty-ninth, this is a Leap Year, did you realize that? Women can propose to men. Nowadays I suppose they can any day of anytime. Snowy, phone Ruhamah, tell her you're spending tonight at Waterlight."

81

Snowy hauled herself to her feet. "Thank you, Bev, but for one thing, I ran out of clothes, I'm re-wearing yesterday's, it's awful. For another, your schedule. And now I know what to do. I'll get David to drive me down tomorrow. Tom can stay with David and Lavender until he can climb the stairs to our apartment. They have a spare room downstairs."

"There's nothing urgent on my schedule. Nothing."

"But your work and your TV appearances—"

Bev said, "My TV segments have been canceled. Reason given? The economy, lack of interest in second homes." Then she hurried on, "Oh, guess what, the summer theater, they're planning their summer season and they're going to be doing an Agatha Christie, *Murder at the Vicarage*!"

"I've just been rereading the book! Are you joining the group? You should audition for Miss Marple!"

"I'd be lucky to get the role of the corpse. Except it's a man, isn't it. They're going to do *The Miracle Worker* too, and in Ninfield I played Anne Sullivan."

"Like Anne Bancroft on Broadway with Patty Duke!"

"Not quite." Bev touched the desk's crystal thistle paperweight, a present Snowy had brought from Scotland, and confessed, "I've been attending the planning meetings, I don't know why, and I didn't want to tell you until—well, no auditions yet, so I don't know if it'll all come to naught. But if I don't get a part, I'll paint scenery. Anything, for the smell of the greasepaint! The other plays they've decided on are *Barefoot in the Park*, *The Importance of Being Earnest*, *The Cherry Orchard*, and—oh, they didn't pick *Same Time, Next Year*, remember when I got the lead in Ninfield—"

With, Snowy thought, the leading man, what was his name? Brad?

"—the last play of the season is *On Golden Pond*," Bev said. "I'm not too old, I'll be the perfect age after my birthday. The character of Ethel is sixty-nine. Katharine Hepburn played her at age seventy-four. But I'm so very rusty!"

THE NEXT AFTERNOON, Snowy climbed out of the passenger seat of her Subaru, which David had driven to and from Concord and now had parked in the driveway of his and Lavender's house. The white Cape stood midway down the curve of Crescent Road, a wedge of woods separating it on either side from the neighboring houses. Within the house their dog was barking halfheartedly.

The temperature this morning had been twelve below zero and didn't seem to have risen much all day despite the sun. Although David had done the driving, she was so tired and punchy that she actually said to Tom, struggling with David's help out of the backseat, "Home again, home again, jiggety-jig."

He ignored her, watching while David unfolded the walker. At the rehab place he had glared at everyone, eyes glittering, but he hadn't said anything, not even when she told him, "See, I kept my promise!" He had remained silent during the entire drive back; most of the time he'd been dozing. She herself had dozed off, then awoke when tears spilled down her face. Exhaustion. At the wheel, David hadn't noticed or at least had pretended not to.

She hoisted her shoulder bag, collected Tom's overnight bag and the Cryo/Cuffs and jugs from the rear of the car, and followed David, who hovered as Tom maneuvered the walker along the snowblower-path from the driveway to the back door. The rehab place hadn't objected to Tom's early departure. Indeed, they seemed overjoyed to be rid of him. Sometime later, Snowy thought, I'll find this funny.

The inside door flew open inward and the storm door was pushed outward by Lilac, David and Lavender's younger daughter who would be fourteen in April, home this week of New Hampshire schools' February vacation. Her chestnut hair flowed straight down her flannel shirt; her jeans ended at scuff slippers each decorated with a silhouette of a dog. Tom had once mentioned that Joanne thought Lilac looked like Joanne's mother more than Lilac's older sister did, but to Snowy both Lilac and Elizabeth had luckily got the family beauty. Lilac squealed, "Welcome, Grandpa!" Then the reality of the walker suddenly drained excitement from her expression.

Not replying to Lilac, Tom concentrated on setting the walker on the granite doorstep.

Snowy said, "Hi, Lilac," wanting to beg Tom to be careful, be very careful, but knowing better. Thrawn. Anyway, David was there to catch him. And here came Lavender hurrying into the kitchen, light-brown hair curling bouncily around her rosy face. Home from work, Lavender was still in professional attire, scrubs patterned with *Peanuts* characters. Nowadays she worked mostly in the pediatric ward at the Gunthwaite hospital. Her arrangement with Snowy and David for next week—or until Tom could climb the apartment stairs—involved her looking after Tom before and after work and their looking after him in between.

Lavender didn't hesitate to tell Tom, "Be careful. Easy does it."

He heaved himself up onto the doorstep. Without taking a break he lifted the walker onto the threshold and pulled himself into the kitchen.

"Doing great," Lavender said. "David, help him off with his parka. Tom, why don't you sit by the stove and rest up, then we'll shift to the spare room. Which chair? The rocker is too low, let's use one from the table."

The kitchen always felt to Snowy like a Beatrix Potter illustration, low-ceilinged, snug. Floral cups and saucers bloomed on the open shelves that Snowy considered dust collectors, much as she loved the look. The tea cozy atop the teapot had been a present from Snowy and Tom, a Scottish souvenir, two lambs nestling against their mother ewe. The old white stove was part of Woodcombe's past, a Magee propane cooking range with a heater that supplemented the house's furnace. Many Woodcombe houses had once had Magees, but this was the only one that Snowy knew of that hadn't been replaced by a modern stove. Its oven behaved erratically; Lavender had to set it fifty degrees lower than the temperature she wanted. How, Snowy thought, can I get Lavender out of this kitchen and somewhere private so we can discuss Tom's meds? This morning, before leaving with David for Concord, Snowy had phoned Tom's doctor, asked for a phoned-in Vicodin prescription, and en route they'd stopped at the Gunthwaite CVS and picked it up.

David did help Tom take off his parka, but on his own Tom lowered himself into the chair that Lavender moved close to the stove. Snowy hung her shoulder bag over another chair. Off the kitchen was the downstairs bathroom and the small spare room, a catchall room usually used to fold laundry, do mending. She went in. The room had been tidied up for Tom's stay, the double bed cleared of everything except its white Bates Heirloom bedspread, like the one on her parents' bed long ago. She set the Cryo/Cuffs down on the bedside table, the jugs and overnight bag on the floor, and opened the bag, placed Tom's pajamas and bathrobe on the bed, slippers beneath the bed, his hairbrush, comb, toothbrush, and glasses case on the bureau. Remaining were the jeans, shirts, and underwear he'd worn last Sunday, Monday morning, and yesterday. She would take them home and bring back some clean clothes before work tomorrow morning. She carried the bag into the kitchen and saw that Lilac was looking scared by all the caution and care in Tom's arrival—and by his silence? So Snowy asked her, "Where's Swiss Miss? We could hear barking."

"Shut in my bedroom. Mom was worried she'd jump on Grandpa." Lilac added, "But Swiss Miss doesn't jump anymore. Much."

Swiss Miss, a mostly chocolate lab chosen in puppyhood from the Gunthwaite humane society, was getting on. Snowy said, "How old is she now?"

"Thirteen." Lilac reached into a cupboard for a dog biscuit and headed for the living room. "Let's go upstairs and tell her she's totally a good girl."

"Sure," Snowy said, taking off her parka and throwing it over her shoulder-bag chair, wondering if she could summon up the strength to climb those stairs, as Tom had for his two steps into the kitchen.

The living room was also low-ceilinged, with braided rugs on the crooked floor and a woodstove piped into the brick fireplace. Near the fireplace was Swiss Miss's doggy bed. Snowy remembered Lavender and David's wedding ceremony here in 1990, when they'd stood at this fireplace with a justice of the peace and exchanged vows, Lavender speaking of love and the harmony of souls, David reading Robert Frost's poem about cleaning the pasture spring—a poem, David had told the guests, that Tom had helped him choose. Although divorced three years, Tom and Joanne had attended the wedding together. That June, after their daughter, Libby, had died on Mount Daybreak, Tom had built her coffin and driven north with it to Newburgh, to the farmhouse in which he and Joanne had lived and raised their kids. After the funeral he had stayed in Newburgh, with Joanne, to have arthroscopic surgery done on the knee that had caused Libby's death. Then he and Joanne had come to Woodcombe for the wedding. Snowy remembered seeing them here, sitting on that very sofa across the room, Tom's walking stick leaning against it. Both he and Joanne had looked lost. Tom seemed much older, and Joanne's face had gone gaunt, the skin stretched taut over her lovely cheekbones. Snowy's heart had broken for them both.

After the ceremony, Tom had remained in Woodcombe. And eventually Joanne married a high-school classmate, Victor, and moved from Newburgh down to Nashua.

Going into the hall with Lilac, Snowy asked, "Elizabeth must be at the away game?" Named after Libby, Elizabeth was three years older than Lilac. God, these grandchildren of Tom's were ancient in comparison if Ruhamah was really—

"Yup," Lilac said, climbing the hall stairs, Snowy following but hanging onto the banister.

Elizabeth was a junior and a cheerleader at Woodcombe High School, which was too small to have a football team but did have soccer, basketball, and baseball teams, loyally supported by the town. This afternoon the basketball team had gone to Piperville for a game. Joanne had been a cheer-leader at Gunthwaite High School, and sometimes she went to Woodcombe games to see her granddaughter cheer. Reliving glory?

Swiss Miss began barking again, but this time happily.

In the upstairs hallway Lilac opened the door into her bedroom. Wagging, Swiss Miss staggered up from the braided rug, and Lilac dropped down, hugged her, gave her the biscuit. As Swiss Miss crunched, Lilac asked, "Is Grandpa okay?"

"Yes," Snowy said, trying to sound reassuring, "yes. And he'll be more okay now that he's got your mother taking care of him." On the bed was a patchwork quilt, on one wall was an enlarged printout of a New Hampshire map showing the location of the sixteen fire towers around the state, and against another wall stood an upright coffin masquerading as a bookcase. What Lilac had inherited from David and Tom was woodworking skill, and under their supervision she had advanced from building birdhouses and such to building this coffin, which had replaced a little-girl pink bookcase. On one shelf, in a "That's My Grandpa!" picture frame, Tom waved from a window of his room (called a cab) atop his fire tower. Lilac aspired to be a fire warden as well as the next generation making North Country Coffins.

Lilac said to Swiss Miss, "Ask Snowy if Kaylie is herding Ruhamah's chickens again."

Lavender's voice downstairs called, "Snowy?"

Snowy informed Swiss Miss, "Kaylie even tries to herd snowflakes," and went out into the hallway. The open door to Lavender and David's bedroom showed the one place in the house in which Lavender had given full rein to her name, the color scheme consisting of white walls and lavender everything else. Lavender stood at the foot of the staircase and beckoned, then put finger to lips.

Hastening down, Snowy whispered, "Has he begun talking yet?"

"He told David not to go into the bathroom with him. David hadn't intended to."

"The bathroom—I forgot, the Rollinses lent us a raised toilet seat, it's at the apartment."

"David'll come over and get it." Lavender patted a pocket of her *Peanuts* scrubs; on this pocket, Linus sat clutching his security blanket and sucking his thumb. "David gave me the Vicodin you picked up. Don't worry, Snowy, we'll sort the meds out. A visiting nurse will be here from Gunthwaite tomorrow, mainly to start keeping track of his Coumadin, the blood thinner. It'll probably be Janet, and when she arrives I could give you a call and you could come over and meet her."

"Thank you," Snowy said. "Thank you." She stared at Linus, at all the characters, and remembered playing Pig-Pen in a skit at Bennington. God, she was going to start crying again. "He's still hardly eating. At the rehab place, they said he'd barely touched his meals."

"It's a common side effect. And some patients get very nauseated." Lavender put an arm around her, leading her toward the kitchen. "Don't go to work. Let Ruhamah and Rita handle the store the rest of the day. Go home, get some rest."

Tom wasn't in the kitchen. While Lavender spoke with David, Snowy heard the thump of the walker and went to the spare room's doorway. If you could pace with a walker, that's what Tom was doing, up and down the room. She didn't dare go in to try to kiss him good-bye. She called, "I'll bring clean clothes tomorrow."

No answer.

Outdoors, she backed the Subaru down the driveway. David followed in his pickup. At North Country Coffins she unlocked the barn, and as they climbed the stairs to the apartment, he said, "You know what they say about airplane emergencies. You have to put an oxygen mask on yourself before you put one on your kid."

"Oh, David," she said.

The phone was ringing. In the kitchen, caller ID told her it was the Woodcombe General Store, and she picked up the receiver. "Ruhamah? We're home. That is, Tom is at Lavender and David's."

"Whew," Ruhamah said. "How is he?"

David went on into the bathroom.

89

Snowy said, "Still not himself. Lavender will be switching him to Vicodin now. She's ordered me to have a rest, but——"

"Good for her. After closing time, I'll bring some supper."

Last evening when Snowy had phoned her at the farm to say she was home, Ruhamah had asked what she'd be having for supper. Snowy had claimed she would dine healthily on Progresso's Chicken & Wild Rice soup and a salad, but Ruhamah had made skeptical noises. And actually, heating up soup seemed too much bother and in the fridge the bagged California organic baby romaine had gone slimy, so Snowy's supper consisted of Pepperidge Farm Milano cookies. Nourishment. She now said to Ruhamah. "You're so busy, please don't bother——"

David went past carrying the big toilet-seat armchair and waved.

Ruhamah said, "Shush. I'll be there at six-fifteen, and I'll bring supper for both of us."

"That will be wonderful."

But though she was home again, home again, jiggety-jig, Snowy couldn't rest. She went into the bathroom to get the hamper's contents to add to Tom's overnight-bag clothes, and suddenly she remembered how, after she'd learned of Alan's death, she had upended the wicker hamper, pawed through the clothes, and snatched up Alan's, snuffling big breaths but only getting a hamper smell.

She resisted the urge to smell Tom's. In the kitchen, she loaded the washing machine and set it off. He wasn't dead. He wasn't gone; he was over there on Crescent Road, under the care of certified nurse's aide Lavender. But wasn't he gone in another way? Was this like seeing Alzheimer's steal a person? If he did return to his real self, could the damage done by oxycodone eventually cause Alzheimer's? She wanted to phone Puddles. She resisted this urge, too. She opened the broom closet, grabbed her lamb's-wool duster off a hook, and carried it into the living room, where Puddles's balloons drifted, tethered to a rocking chair. Into the DVD player she put the movie of *A Prairie Home Companion*, which she had given Tom for his birthday last year; they'd taken out the library's DVD so often she'd decided they'd better have one of their own. Tomorrow, she thought, as Meryl Streep and Lily Tomlin harmonized on a version of "Go Tell Aunt Rhody," tomorrow she would add this DVD to the clothes she'd be bringing him.

She was carefully dusting the portrait of Ruhamah Reed, painted by Harriet from a frontispiece portrait in a collection of Ruhamah Reed's poems, when Meryl began singing a duet with Garrison Keillor. It was the Carter Family song about pawning a gold watch and chain. Snowy shakily joined in the chorus, "'Only say that you'll love me again,'"and then heard Ruhamah call from the kitchen, "It's me!"

Snowy abandoned the duster, shut off the DVD, and hurried into the kitchen, looking at the rooster clock. "I lost track of time."

Ruhamah had put a big paper bag on the trestle table. She lifted out one of the store's Styrofoam containers for take-out soups. On Fridays the lunch menu usually featured vegetable soup and tuna-fish rolls or egg-salad sandwiches; it had amused Snowy to carry on a Gunthwaite High School cafeteria lunch policy from the past, no meat on Fridays. She had planned this week's menu last Saturday, so she knew the container held the soup she'd named Greens and Garlic Soup, made with kale and potatoes. Very healthy. But instead of setting the container down on the table, Ruhamah stood there holding it, staring at Snowy.

Ruhamah blurted, "I'm pregnant." Then she said, "I wasn't going to tell you until I was sure, and then not until you'd got over the truck crash—I've seen you avoid the front of the store, Snowy, it was PTSD. Then when you were seeming better, I decided to wait until Tom's knees had been done, but now you have the oxycodone worry—well, if I keep waiting until worries are over, I'll be trying to keep a secret in maternity clothes."

4

"A baby!" Snowy shrieked to Bev over the phone in her office when Ruhamah had left after supper. "Ruhamah *is* pregnant! As of Thanksgiving, so she's fourteen weeks pregnant, she'll have the ultrasound at twenty weeks, I want to go shopping right now, but I can't buy pink or blue!"

Bev said, "Oh, this is so exciting. Then the baby is due— I'm too excited to do math!"

"The estimated date is August seventeenth. She says she and D. J. simply stopped thinking about when there'd be time for a baby and just, er, plunged into it. They've waited so long, she's in the 'advanced maternal age' category. I'll phone Puddles tomorrow, when I've pulled myself together. I'll tell Tom tomorrow, but . . ." Would Tom comprehend or care?

Bev asked, "You and David got Tom to their house? How long will he be there?"

"I don't know." How long, Snowy wondered, could Lavender cope with Tom? "I'll phone Dudley and Charl tomorrow. Ruhamah and D. J. agreed to tell me and his parents this evening, but she wasn't quite sure what time he'd be calling them from Washington."

Bev asked, "How is she feeling?"

"You were right, morning sickness. I mentioned how tired I got, but she won't admit to fatigue. She's so busy, Bev. She said that she and Cindy have decided to reopen the Oakhill store on Saint Patrick's Day—green decorations, free green scones."

"Well, green means nature, rebirth, fertility," said green-eyed Bev. "Have Ruhamah and D. J. decided on names for the baby?"

Snowy paused, hoping she wouldn't start crying again, as she had when Ruhamah told her this. She said, "If it's a boy, they're going to name him Alan."

"Ah, Snowy. His grandfather." Bev sounded as though she herself might start crying.

Richard, Snowy thought. Bev had named her older son Richard after her father, who had been killed on Iwo Jima. Her father had been named for his father, who had outlived him down in Bedford, Massachusetts.

Bev said, "You know how my grandfather was a stockbroker in Boston? I've been remembering my grandmother telling me about the stock-market crash in nineteen-twenty-nine. They managed to come through it, but some didn't, of course. She talked about it, but Grandfather never did."

On TV news, you were beginning to hear the word "recession." Not "depression." The Great Depression had followed the crash, and Snowy was following Bev's thoughts. Financial worries. Roger, Bev had said, was hovering over the computer and investments. Real estate wasn't completely occupying Bev's time; she had joined the Gunthwaite Summer Theater. Snowy said, "Bev, the scary economic news——"

Bev gave a little laugh. "Will history repeat itself? Let's not think about that now. Let's think about Ruhamah's wonderful news. If it's a girl, what will the name be?"

And this did start Snowy's tears. "Charlotte. My mother's name. Ruhamah was so young when Mother died, Ruhamah hardly remembers her, but she chose it, Bev, and it's like Charl's name so both sides of the family are represented. I need Kleenex, tears of joy, bye!"

She reached for a Kleenex and leaned back in her desk chair.

After Libby had died and Tom had returned to Woodcombe from Newburgh, he'd asked her, "After Alan died, did you ever feel like saying to him, 'Okay, we've been through that; you can come back now'?" She'd replied, "Yes." Tom had said, "It's what I want to say to Libby."

She looked up at, framed on the wall, the pen-and-ink sketch that Alan had drawn of the Ruhamah Reed House in Eastbourne. She said aloud, "We're going to be grandparents. Come back now."

As she folded laundry on the bed she would sleep in alone again tonight, she was barraged by questions. She thought of her mother's history of miscarriages, which were the reason she was an only child. What if Ruhamah had inherited this? And was Ruhamah's story about deciding on a whim the real reason? Was her decision a form of site fidelity? Was Ruhamah permanently avoiding a Washington life by tying herself to this area with the baby and a third store? D. J.'s constituents would enjoy the baby. The baby might actually ensure his reelection! The constituents would understand if Ruhamah continued to stay in Woodcombe while D. J. commuted.

The phone rang. She saw that her roommate was calling. "Hello, Harriet, thank you for the hydrangeas, they're beautiful."

"Well, you once remarked that they're the only flower Tom knows because there were some bushes at the house he grew up in. How is he?"

Not getting complicated, Snowy said, "He's home from the rehab place. You're still in New York?"

"Yes, but I thought I'd come up in about three weeks. Your birthday is on a Wednesday. Will you and Tom take the day off? Come here for lunch."

Snowy pictured the contrast, Harriet's Fifth Avenue apartment, which she hadn't visited but Ruhamah had, and Harriet's New Hampshire farmhouse that had once belonged to Bev's mother and stepfather. She pictured Harriet looking both arty and distinguished, with her now totally gray hair cut in a classy short swirl. "A birthday lunch would be lovely. Harriet, Ruhamah just announced she and D. J. are having a baby."

"Wow," said Harriet, who had never married, never had a child, and was, Snowy knew, content with those decisions. "That's a surprise!"

"Isn't it!"

"When's the baby due?"

"August seventeenth."

"A Leo! Ruhamah will have her hands full. Give her my love. I'll phone you when I arrive."

Later that night another snowstorm began. Saturday morning it was still coming down in a determined fashion as Snowy shoveled a path to the bird feeders. She paused to rest her back, listening to the white whisking of the snow against her parka. In Lavender and David's house, was Tom ranting about not being able to shovel or use the snowblower? When she bent to resume, she heard herself singing in her head, pleading, "'Only say that you'll love me again.'"

Then there was the sound of David's pickup arriving, plowing the driveway. She reached the feeders, returned to the workshop for a scoopful of sunflower seeds and filled them, then went back through the workshop to the driveway and saw that David had finished. He waved as he drove off. The street was plowed but not the sidewalk. Feeling slightly lawless, she walked down the middle of the street past the post office, where Ryan Hopkins was plowing the parking lot. David had already plowed the store's parking lot and shoveled the sidewalk in front of the store. She unlocked the door and had started a pot of coffee when Ruhamah made an entrance accompanied by Kaylie, who ran wagging to greet Snowy.

Ruhamah beamed. "D. J. phoned his folks. His mother is over the moon."

"Aren't we all! I'm going to do some more phoning right now." Snowy rubbed Kaylie's snowflaked fur and inquired, "Kaylie, will your nose be out of joint about a baby brother or sister?"

Ruhamah laughed.

Snowy poured herself a mug of coffee, clambered up onto a counter stool, and, using her cell phone, tapped Puddles and Blivit's number. Kaylie settled down on the floor beside her.

Blivit's nice baritone said, "Hello, Snowy."

"I'm sorry if this is too early, but—"

"No, no, Puddles is right here but her hands are gloved, I'll hold the phone to her ear."

"Snowy?" Puddles said. "How's Tom?"

"Gloves?"

"I'm working with turkey sausage patties, and I sure the hell won't risk Campy poisoning. Is Tom off the oxycodone?"

"Campy?"

"Campylobacter. Snowy, don't you wear gloves when you handle raw poultry?"

"Well, in recent years at the store we wear gloves, but—" Snowy reached down and patted Kaylie. Unhygienic! Gloves, latex or otherwise, reminded her to say, "Tom sends many thanks for the balloons." Did Tom even remember them?

"They were Mylar, of course," Puddles said. "I wanted to buy some condoms and blow them up and send them, to remind him of Gunthwaite High School days, but it wasn't practical. Blivit, stop laughing, keep the phone steady! What about the oxycodone?"

"He's just been switched to Vicodin. He's in Lavender and David's downstairs bedroom until he can manage our stairs. He was sent to the rehab place in Concord but he only lasted a day there."

Puddles hooted. "I could've predicted that!"

"The other news is—Ruhamah is pregnant!"

A silence while Puddles absorbed this. Then Puddles said, "Holy shit. You're going to be a grandmother at last!"

Snowy said, "I'll supply the details later, you continue making your breakfast."

"When's the due date?"

"August seventeenth."

"Let's hope June and July aren't full of heat waves. Give her my love! And Tom, too. Is he wearing TEDs, compression stockings? Blivit, remember how scared you were when you wrestled them onto me and how I kept laughing? Snowy, tell Tom that when he is able he's got to haul his ass to Hilton Head. You and he have got to take a break from this wicked never-ending winter."

After they said good-bye, Snowy realized that Ruhamah's pregnancy was a perfect excuse to decline Puddles's offer. Snowy must stay here in Woodcombe to look after Ruhamah.

Out the windows the snow was still coming down; not one customer had yet ventured in. Last evening Ruhamah had said that she'd be telling her best friend, Kim. Snowy suspected she already had told Kim, sworn Kim to secrecy, and was using a white lie to spare Snowy's feelings about not being told first. In any case, Kim now would tell her mother, and her mother would tell people and on and on, so soon the whole town would know about the upcoming great event. Customers would savor a new topic! Snowy tapped the phone number for Charl and Dudley's home, the Victorian painted-lady house on Water Street, on the river, in her old neighborhood.

Dudley answered the phone. "Isn't it splendid? Charl and I already have a million grandchildren, Snowy, but this is extra-special."

Yes, she thought. After becoming friends in their sandbox days, she and Dudley had dated in high school, then returned to being friends though Snowy knew his feelings toward her weren't so platonic as hers were toward him. Her connection to him had always been a strong one, but now he and she would be even closer, co-grandparents. She also knew how proud he was of D. J. In high school Dudley's ambition had been to become a Red Sox player and president of the United States. Well, he'd become Gunthwaite's mayor, and in recent years he was the campaign manager for Dudley Washburn Jr. He and Charl would be spreading the news of the baby to all the constituents in the district.

Dudley said, "D. J. told us the names they've chosen. We're very happy about both."

If a boy, the baby wouldn't be named after D. J. or Grandfather Dudley. Snowy said, "I'm happy you are."

"The world certainly doesn't need a Dudley the Third." He paused. "How's Tom doing?" He and Tom had never been exactly fond of each other.

Kaylie scrambled upright, and a customer came in, Nelson Fletcher. Snowy said, "He's fine. My love to Charl. Bye." She followed Kaylie to the front of the store, where Ruhamah was laughing and telling him the news.

Midmorning, there was a phone call from Lavender saying that Janet, the visiting nurse, had arrived. Snowy pulled on her parka. The snow seemed to be tapering off as she hurried back to the barn for Tom's overnight bag she'd packed with clean clothes. She drove to Crescent Road, knocked, and let herself into the kitchen. Lavender and a comfortable woman in her fifties looked up from conferring at the kitchen table.

Snowy said to the woman, who must be Janet, "Thank you for coming in this weather."

"Oh," Janet said, "I never pay attention to weather reports. If I did, I'd never accomplish anything. So I just go, no matter what. My husband thinks I'm crazy."

Lavender said, "Snowy, Tom had a bad night. He's hurting a lot. The Vicodin isn't doing the trick the way oxycodone did, and Janet thinks he should be back on it."

"No," Snowy said.

"A lesser dose," Lavender said.

Snowy set down the overnight bag, untied her boots, kicked them off, picked up the bag, and in her Ragg wool socks padded to the closed door of the spare room. She opened it. Tom was sitting propped up by pillows in bed, Cryo/Cuffs wrapped around his pajama knees, layers of afghan and quilt around his shoulders. He held Dick Francis, unopened.

"Guess what," Snowy said, smiling. "You're sleeping with a grandmother-to-be. That is, when you're back home in our bed."

"Huh?"

"Ruhamah and D. J. are going to have a baby."

"I thought they were smarter than that."

Snowy dropped the overnight bag. She knew what he meant. However, saying it wasn't necessary. She unzipped her parka, sat down on the edge of the bed, and asked, "A bad night?"

"Very." He looked out the window at the snow. "The storm letting up? Could David get the plowing done? The snow-banks—he should borrow a goddamn bucket loader!" Then his voice became bewildered. "The orders. He said he and Jared will work tomorrow to catch up. I can't remember our schedule. Sales down. People always need coffins but they don't need coffins ahead of time. What a fucking mess I've made of everything." He lifted a hand and once again Dick Francis went sailing across a room.

Carefully she lowered herself onto the bed, curling beside him. He turned his face away, but she saw tears dammed up behind his glasses. She went cold with fear. Depression. Like Alan. The Great Depression. When she and Alan had started dating, she had been nonplussed to notice similarities between him and Tom. But not depression. Behind Tom's easygoing façade, he could be distant, aloof, detached, and he was always ironic. But he never was enveloped in Alan's thundercloud.

He ripped off his glasses. She put an arm across him and curled closer. He exhaled deeply and fell asleep.

When she returned to the kitchen, she said to Lavender and Janet, "He needs his rest in order to recover, doesn't he. Okay, oxycodone, but only for a few days."

ON TUESDAY, MARCH 4, Hillary won primaries in Texas, Ohio, and Rhode Island.

Although Obama remained ahead in delegates, Bev phoned Wednesday evening to rejoice and then said, "The summer theater, we're having the next meeting here at Waterlight, Saturday afternoon."

Of course, Snowy thought, sitting in her office unable to work on the poem on her desk, hearing the freezing rain assail the roof, her mind shattered to pieces, the mornings at Lavender and David's looking after Tom while David worked with Jared, the afternoons joining Rita at the store while Ruhamah was in Oakhill and David took care of Tom until Lavender's return from the Gunthwaite hospital. Of course, Waterlight! The theater's barn would be unheated, winter meetings would be held in homes, and Waterlight was perfect.

Bev continued, "Um, it's the auditions. We have to do a short monologue. I can't decide. I'm too old for everything! I could do Emily's speech in *Our Town*, the one she does after she dies, but I'm even too old for that. Emily died young."

103

"You mean the speech about 'Oh, earth, you're too wonderful for anybody to realize you'? Bev, it's a classic and it's New Hampshire."

After a silence, Bev said, "Well. Maybe." Then she said, "How's Tom?"

"Still no appetite. And his thermostat has gone awry, he's always feeling the cold. He's spacey, short-tempered, befuddled." Then Snowy said the worst word: "Depressed." To accentuate the positive, she continued, "However, his knees are improving. He isn't saying anymore that he hopes he really can return to the fire tower this spring, but I know he does hope. Angela, his visiting physical therapist, acts impressed with his exercises. And this morning she escorted him halfway up Lavender and David's hall stairs, old and steep. He wanted to go to the top; she said he could practice the halfway climb under David's supervision." She sensed that Bev had stopped listening.

Bev said, "The summer theater is planning a yard sale for Memorial Day weekend. If you and Ruhamah do any spring cleaning, don't discard things. Donate them to us! Got to go make the monologue decision, bye."

"Bye," Snowy said, thinking: Memorial Day. This was a difficult holiday for Bev, because of her father.

On Thursday came news of another roof collapse, this time the flat roof of an auto-supply outlet in Gunthwaite. On Friday, Angela oversaw Tom's exercises and then his climb to the top of the stairs.

Snowy phoned Bev that evening. "Angela pronounced Tom ready to return here Sunday afternoon."

"That's great! Isn't it?"

Snowy thought of how, after Lavender had got home and learned the glad tidings from David, Lavender had phoned her to arrange the details of Tom's return and couldn't quite conceal her relief. Tom had managed to tax even Lavender's professional patience.

Bev said, "Or will it be too much for you?"

Snowy replied, "When that maneuver is done, we'll switch to Vicodin again. Have you decided on your monologue for tomorrow?"

"I'm going to do Emily. My mother loved that play."

Saturday afternoon, with Ruhamah minding the store, Snowy went to the Village Beauty Salon in the ell of Marge Ames's Cape and had her hair highlighted and trimmed.

Daylight Saving Time always used to start in April and end in October. Snowy couldn't adjust to the new dates. This year, March 9 was the start, that very Sunday, so before she went to bed Saturday night she walked through the apartment turning clocks ahead. Today's heavy rain was still coming down hard. But it wasn't freezing, so could that be a sign of spring, as the April Daylight Saving used to be?

When the phone rang in what seemed the middle of the night, she sat up, switched on the bedside table's lamp, and grabbed the phone, as confused by the time on the bedside clock as by this phone call. Two o'clock. Thus it was really one o'clock, in Standard Time. Then she thought: Tom. Ruhamah.

But an automated voice intoned, "Alarm Code Two, back door open."

The store! She struggled out of bed. Years ago, she and Ruhamah had decided that even a little general store should have an alarm system. Ruhamah would be getting this phone call too, and so would Kyle Granville, the police chief, who lived in a converted hunting camp on Fifield Road.

She heard overhead that the rain's pummeling of the roof was slowing down. Was she also hearing the alarm, or imagining it? Could the wind and rain have blown that locked back door open, protected by the back porch though it was? She *had* locked it last evening, hadn't she?

Or was the store being burgled? With young Kelsea and Cody Crowley in the apartment upstairs!

As she yanked on underwear, jeans, sweatshirt, boots, parka, and snatched the store's keys off the kitchen counter, she remembered awaking that May morning in the Hurricane Farm bedroom without Alan in bed and searching the house for him, then wondering about the store. A fire? A burglary? Those were pre-alarm days, so she thought he might've got a phone call from Bill Danforth, the police chief at that time, a call she'd slept through. She had phoned the store, no answer, so she'd driven there. It hadn't been broken into, but Chief Danforth had arrived in his police cruiser, a Jeep Wagoneer, to tell her Alan had drowned.

The phone rang again. Ruhamah said, "Don't you go to the store. Let Kyle check it and report to us."

"I won't," Snowy said, but she didn't put the store's keys back on the counter.

Ruhamah said, "I'll phone the Crowleys and tell them not to go investigating."

Snowy only meant to walk down the driveway and wait for Kyle. Yet when she stepped outdoors, she could definitely hear the screech of the alarm. The rain was indeed letting up, and under the streetlights the town looked washed out, winter-weary. The alarm wouldn't disturb the Ramseys across the street, they were in Florida, but the other neighbors—and Kelsea and Cody—

She had to shut off that alarm.

Down the sidewalk she ran, past the post office, onto the store's front porch. In a few hours, life would be back to normal and the Sunday newspapers would be delivered, dropped off on this porch, and she would begin the heavy work of lugging them indoors. Wouldn't she? She unlocked the door, covered her ears, and darted in. The night-light glowed. At the alarm she tapped the code number (125, the Ruhamah Reed House's street number in Eastbourne). Oh, the relief from that racket!

The store smelled of pickle brine, coffee, and yesterday's lunch special, grilled hot dogs, and of rain soaking into old wood. As she switched on the main light, she noticed something wrong about the shelves nearest the checkout counter. The fudge was missing. Amongst the impulse purchases on these shelves, such as plastic-wrapped homemade brownies, Woodcombe General Store coffee mugs and tote bags, jugs of last year's maple syrup soon to be replaced with this March's, there was a gap where there should be Irene's plastic-wrapped fudge. Irene Mason, who until her retirement had helped run the store ever since Alan and Snowy bought it, still made her fudge for the store.

Mice? Thanks to Ruhamah's thorough trapping, not to mention Kaylie's patrols, there wasn't a mouse problem. Anyway, a mouse couldn't drag off packets of fudge, could it?

She shivered. Chilly, the room felt too chilly. She went cautiously farther into the store. The glass doors of the tall beer cooler showed that its usually crammed shelves were empty. Gone too were the unrefrigerated six-packs stacked nearby, and so was the store's small assortment of wines. Beyond, the back door was slightly open, the door jamb splintered.

She whirled around. The broom closet's door stood ajar. Years ago during renovations, she and Ruhamah had moved the store's office upstairs into their apartment, and after Ruhamah's marriage their office work was done at Ruhamah and D. J.'s house. The old office had also served as a broom closet, so a new broom closet had been tucked into a corner of the store and a safe installed. After she and Ruhamah closed last evening, Snowy had put the till in the safe. She yanked the door wider. The broom and mop were toppled, a bucket overturned, but the burglars hadn't been able to open the safe.

Burglars. There must have been more than one, to move all that beer that fast.

She went on to the door to the cellar storeroom, which she had locked last evening. It remained locked, with no splintering, no indications that they'd tried to bash it open. They hadn't had time, with that alarm.

A man's voice said, "Snowy?"

She jumped.

On the front porch, Cody Crowley peered around the door. He'd disobeyed Ruhamah and come down the outside staircase from the apartment. "Are you okay?"

Out the store's windows she saw Kyle Granville's Jeep Wagoneer jounce to a stop, its red light spinning.

Shakily Snowy told Cody, "Beer bandits. With a sweet tooth, for fudge."

Throughout the morning the sun emerged and a March wind picked up, to welcome Tom's return that afternoon.

AS THEY NEARED Cowshit Corner and the Pike farm, Tom gradually braked his pickup. In the passenger seat, Snowy tried harder than ever not to clench her fists or otherwise act nervous about his driving, though he might think she was just braced against all the frost heaves on the road from Woodcombe.

This morning he was making his maiden voyage with his new knees, driving farther than Main Street. It was a Monday,

Saint Patrick's Day, sunny and windy, and he had insisted on driving her to the grand reopening of the Oakhill General Store, to join Ruhamah there while Rita minded the Woodcombe store. She wasn't taking this Monday off; she would return to the Woodcombe store to help Rita, while Ruhamah stayed in Oakhill. Under her parka she wore a green V-neck sweater over a green shirt in honor of her Higgins ancestors. Although he must have some Irish ancestors (didn't everybody?), Tom was defiantly wearing not only the Forbes tam she'd bought him in Edinburgh during the trip with Ruhamah but also a Forbes scarf he'd bought during their own trip. He still felt cold all the time so maybe he needed both to keep warm, and anyway, the Forbes tartan was predominantly green so maybe nobody would guess.

The cows were gathered in the barnyard, concentrating on a hay breakfast. The cows were *not* crossing the road and hadn't recently. Without any slipping or sliding, Tom rounded the curve.

Ever since the end of Angela's visits and his return home, she had been driving him three times a week to the rehabilitation section of Gunthwaite Orthopaedics, where under the supervision of Bryce, a physical therapist, he did exercises in a little swimming pool and on dry land. Tom, who had worked one summer as a lifeguard at the Gunthwaite town beach, was paddling in a pool. He'd said after the latest session, "It's too slow. Christ, no matter how fast I improve, I won't be hiking up to the fire tower this spring." During his PT, she read in the waiting room, her days scrambled by all this to-ing and fro-ing. But he had announced that after today's drive to Oakhill he would henceforth drive himself to rehab. He sounded belligerent. Mostly he remained silent, but when he spoke his statements were apt to have an antagonistic overtone, as if he expected vehement objections. Other statements were uncertain, as if his confidence had been undermined by—what? By Vicodin? He had tapered off to one each day. By the oxycodone before? Or simply by his knees? (And was worry about his knees keeping him from kissing her, afraid of starting something he wasn't supposed to finish until further recovered?)

Now came the descent downhill, the moment when the driver of the Landry Lumber Company truck had had the sickening realization that his foot had slammed to the floorboard without brakes. Tom must know that this was the first time she'd been back to Oakhill since the accident because Ruhamah had been handling everything, and normally he would've said something soothing or funny about the plunge down into the village. Today he just drove, slowly. She imagined the pressure on his right knee as the pickup proceeded down to the town hall, the church, the fire station, and Buddy's Auto Service. The village scene reminded her of Bev and *Our Town*, of Bev now awaiting her audition's results.

Then she stared at the general store as Tom pulled into the small parking lot nearly full of cars and pickups.

"Wow," she said. The new clapboards on the rebuilt front of the store were crisp white. The new front window was bigger than the old and so shiny clean you could actually see the interior, which in turn looked clean. But, climbing down out of the pickup, stretching her back, and walking around to the driver's side in case Tom should fall getting out, Snowy perversely missed Moose's signs in the old dingy window. She was, however, pleased that the unreadable overhead sign had been replaced with a fresh new white sign clearly identifying the store and then making a cozy joke:

OAKHILL GENERAL STORE
Your One-Shop Stopping Center

110

Ruhamah and Cindy had festooned the store's front door with green bunting and stuck shamrock stickers on its windows.

Tom hung onto the steering wheel and lowered himself down. When he opened the store's door for her, Snowy remembered how he had held her in his arms in his workshop when she'd told him about the truck crashing in. But later she hadn't mentioned the PTSD to him. He wouldn't know about this fear. Deep breath in, deep breath out. She stepped inside.

Voices, warmth, coffee, people standing around in parkas and heavy jackets. The store wasn't big enough for a lunch counter, but at the little self-service coffee counter Ruhamah, in a new oversize green flannel shirt and her black knit leggings that had some waistline leeway, was doing the serving today, with a coffee carafe and the free green scones, green doughnuts, green cookies.

"Snowy!" Cindy cried, in jeans and a lacy green sweater and those incongruous cat-eye glasses, running to hug her. "Everybody, here's our other owner from the Woodcombe store!"

A nearby guy said, "You're the one who beaned the Old Man Bomber with a bottle of wine."

"Um, yes," Snowy said, acknowledging fame. She said to Cindy, "You remember Tom." Cindy would remember him from the times they came here from Buddy's garage when Cindy happened to be working for Moose.

Cindy said, "I sure do remember Tom, and that's some tam! But wow, Tom, you've lost weight." She hugged him too. "Isn't this a great day? The town is the town again, now the store is open again!"

Wayne O'Donnell, her husband the road agent, sauntered over from Ruhamah's counter, coffee container aloft. His green sweater was of the Irish fisherman variety. It dawned on Snowy that Cindy had knitted their sweaters. Wayne said, "If this was summer, we'd be out on the back porch."

"Cindy's Porch," said Snowy.

Cindy laughed. "That's such an honor. When it's all finished, Ruhamah says the name will be painted on it. Wayne, show Tom how the porch is coming along. Snowy, have a cup of coffee and a scone, I made the scones, Wayne's grandmother's recipe though she didn't ever use green food coloring—"

Rattling on, Cindy led Snowy to Ruhamah's coffee counter, where people were talking about the Woodcombe store burglary, speculating with amusement about why the burglars hadn't been caught.

"They drank the evidence!"

"What did they do with the empties?"

"They could hide them in a shed and take a few to the dump with the trash once a week."

Ruhamah handed Snowy a Styrofoam cup of coffee and a paper plate holding a green scone and a shamrock napkin as Cindy chimed in, "With the bottles, they could smash the glass and make a stained-glass window or a mosaic walkway—"

Evidently Cindy knew more crafts than knitting and chair caning.

Someone said, "It'd have to be a mosaic turnpike. That was a *lot* of beer."

Someone else said, "Must've had a van. Must've had an army. They're probably in Massachusetts."

"—or make jewelry," Cindy continued.

Like Puddles's engagement ring, Snowy thought, the sea-glass ring that Puddles had requested from Blivit instead of a diamond. She and Ruhamah exchanged a look about this conversation, versions of which they'd listened to in the

Woodcombe store. Levity was understandable, burglarizing for booze and fudge. But to have your store broken into, a store that was still your home although you no longer lived in it—

Someone asked, "What to do with empty beer cans?"

Several people answered, "Stomp 'em."

Funny. As *Whisky Galore* was funny, with the islanders hiding the salvaged bottles down wells and in outbuildings and such. She looked around for Tom, wondering if he had come indoors from the porch and overheard all this, and then she heard his voice. From beyond the back door, out on the porch, but loud and clear.

"—a fucking hazard, nobody can see the road with all the goddamn manure on it, last year I went sliding straight across into the fence! Can't a road agent control cowshit?"

Snowy thrust her coffee and paper plate at Ruhamah and rushed to the back door, yanking it open onto the porch, a roofed platform lacking screening. Wayne stood holding his coffee, a tolerant expression on his face. Was he used to being yelled at by taxpayers about unplowed roads and frost heaves and potholes? But Tom didn't pay taxes in Oakhill. Beyond the porch, the brook flickered through a sunny field scattered with dregs of snow.

"—and then," Tom was shouting, "I had to tell the insurance company what caused me to dent and scratch my pickup on a barbed-wire fence, and you can bet your ass they didn't want to take it seriously!"

"Tom," Snowy said. "I've got to get back. Let's go."

Cindy came running out. She gasped, "The Pike farm has always been a problem—"

Wayne said calmly, "Cindy, let me handle this."

There was a roar overhead. Ice slid off the porch roof and landed like a thunderclap.

113

After a moment of stunned silence indoors and out, some of the customers looked through the back door's window, then emerged onto the porch. Snowy yanked at Tom's hand and pulled him against the flow, into the store, where Ruhamah was standing rooted, clutching the coffee carafe.

Snowy said, "Everything's okay, just some ice off the roof."

Ruhamah set down the carafe. "This isn't an unlucky store. Is it?"

"No, it isn't," Snowy said. "Everything's fine. Time for me to get back to the Woodcombe store, though."

Ruhamah looked at Tom, now quiet but sullen. When she returned her gaze to Snowy, her frightened expression held unspoken words: Oh my God. Will you be safe with him?

SNOWY DIDN'T DARE suggest that she herself drive them home. Fists clenched, she sat braced in the passenger seat as Tom drove back up the hill. The cows were still breakfasting in the barnyard. She'd feared he might stop here, find Mr. Pike and make another scene, but he kept on driving past.

As they came to the stretch of road that ran alongside this brook that reminded her of her first grown-up Christmas cards, she suddenly thought: I'm a grown-up; I should know what to do. But she didn't. Alan had refused to get professional help. But wasn't Tom's a short-term problem, until he was off Vicodin?

On they went, Tom not speaking. In the woods, maple trees were tapped and loops of tubing carried off the sap; you hardly ever saw pails on trees anymore. Woodcombe Lake's icy surface looked honeycombed. With Alan, she had realized that depression could be contagious and that she mustn't catch it. Nonetheless, she hadn't saved him.

114

Tom parked beside David's pickup in front of the barn and made his slow descent from the driver's seat. She followed him into the barn.

"No Jared?" he said sharply to David.

David looked at Snowy. "He's at Harriet's house, opening up. She's arriving tomorrow, as I guess you know."

"We'll be having lunch there Wednesday." She asked Tom, "Are you coming upstairs?"

He shook his head.

She said in a sprightly tone, "Then I'll go up, then over to the store to help Rita, and I'll be back with some lunch. Corned-beef sandwiches are on our menu, natch!"

David laughed, but Tom said, "Don't bother. I'll make myself something."

So that would be another milestone, like the drive to Oakhill. She said, "Great," and went up the stairs into the prison of the apartment. After using the bathroom, she was about to leave but stopped in her tracks. A thought struck: his rifle.

On his sixtieth birthday they had done a backpack up north in the Kilkenny, reeking of fly dope. They'd sat at the shore of Unknown Pond and watched the sunset and talked about the future. Tom had said, "I can't picture life ten years from now. If I get lucky with my health, I'll work until I drop. But it's heavy work, and how long can I keep manhandling lumber, into my seventies, eighties? If I get sick, I won't stick around—oh Christ, Snowy, I know it's a terrible subject, but—"

Breaking out in a sweat, she ran into the bedroom, opened the closet, pushed aside clothes. The .22 was there where he kept it, leaning against the back wall, forgotten except when he or she spotted a woodchuck in the garden.

Forgotten?

She stood on tiptoe, patting the top shelf where plastic bags held old pocketbooks that might someday match some outfit and shoeboxes held shoes she might someday wear again. Her fingers touched the box of cartridges, where it should be. She left the box there, but very gingerly she lifted the .22 out of the closet. Where to hide a rifle?

Sweating more, in her office she moved all the books off the bottom shelf of her bookcase, discovering an embarrassing layer of dust behind them. When had she last thoroughly cleaned her office? When the hell did she have time to do anything thoroughly? She set the rifle on its side and put the books back, thinking about the summer of 1956, between her junior and senior year in high school. Tom had broken up with her one night at the drive-in theater. After he'd brought her home to her folks' house, she had gone into the bathroom and almost drunk a bottle of iodine. Two years later, after she'd happened to see Tom and Joanne leaving the Congregational church as bride and groom, she had gone home into that same bathroom and contemplated razor blades and her wrists. She had never told Tom—or Alan—about these teenage close calls with suicide.

Down in the workshop, Tom and David were conferring. She waved without interrupting and went outdoors. Instead of walking to the store, she got in her car and drove. Rita was at the cash register, checking out groceries for centenarian Gladys Stanton, who noticed Snowy coming in and said, "Hillary and Obama, neck and neck. We've done what we could, we just have to wait and hope. Hope springs eternal."

"Yes," Snowy said, "here's hoping," and to Rita she said, "I'm sorry, I've got some errands to do first, I'll be back this afternoon, is that okay?" She knew that Rita preferred working alone, ruling the roost. God, all this overtime Rita was getting paid, thanks to Tom's knees, cutting into already slim profits!

"Fine with me," Rita said.

Snowy drove to the Abnaki Mall and went browsing for baby clothes. Just browsing, she vowed; she mustn't buy anything yet, not yet or it would be bad luck. Miscarriages. But of course she couldn't resist. She bought a pale yellow onesie that said: Hello, World!

The next evening Harriet phoned. "I've arrived. Have you noticed, you've had quite a winter since I was here at Christmas."

In the kitchen, Snowy laughed. "It escaped my notice."

"Jared says the forecast is light snow tomorrow morning, becoming rain."

"Harriet, as you know, on my birthday I expect blizzards and I very often get them. Tomorrow's weather will seem like spring. It won't keep Tom and me from driving to Gunthwaite. He has PT there tomorrow morning, and then we'll head for your place."

The next day arrived with the predicted snow out the apartment windows. Her sixty-ninth birthday. A day off from the store; a day to put on, with her best jeans, the long-sleeved black Bennington College T-shirt that Harriet had given her at Christmastime and over it her pink fleece vest. A day to find, when in her office she checked her e-mail, an e-card from Ruhamah with a dancing springtime flowerbed and a message from Kara, her editor, saying "Happy Birthday!"

Then Bev phoned, her voice rushed and excited. "Happy birthday! And guess what, I'll be in three plays! First, I'm Mrs. Price Ridley in *Murder at the Vicarage*, next I'm Lady Bracknell in *The Importance of Being Earnest,* and then"—she paused, and Snowy stopped trying to remember who Mrs. Price Ridley was in the book and waited for the biggest news—"I'm Ethel in *On Golden Pond!*"

"Oh, Bev! Congratulations, congratulations!"

"Hope you get a scrumptious birthday cake at Harriet's, bye!"

Mrs. Price Ridley, Snowy remembered, was a matronly parishioner who wore matronly hats. Thank heavens that Bev didn't seem insulted by the casting.

117

Tom either forgot to wish her happy birthday or couldn't be bothered. After his shower he had got dressed in his rehab outfit of sweatshirt and sweatpants and she didn't dare suggest he bring something nicer to change into. But, hoping he would agree, she said, "The Subaru is safer in the snow than the pickup, isn't it? Why don't I drive us."

"We'll take the Subaru. I'll drive."

"Okay. Oops, I just had a thought, should I bring a hostess gift even though I'm the birthday girl?"

This was an opening for Tom to wish her happy birthday. He didn't.

She'd planned to ask him to fill the Subaru's tank at the store's gas pumps, but she was sidetracked by the problem of the hostess gift, hurrying into the store, grabbing a quart of the new maple syrup just arrived from a Woodcombe sap house, and she completely forgot. However, after his PT session at Gunthwaite Orthopaedics, as in silence and the falling snow he drove along State Avenue, she said, "The gas gauge, it's down below half. Would you like to fill up at Varney's?"

He said, "Today Bryce finally told me in no uncertain terms that I'd better not overwork my knees by trying to climb Pascataquac this season."

"Oh, Tom."

Silent again, he pulled into Varney's. He didn't as usual complain about the self-service pumps that had replaced the old pumps; he just parked at one.

At the next pump was a station wagon approximately the size of the *Queen Mary*, its gas tank being filled by an old man, slight with thin silver hair, wearing silver-rimmed glasses, his parka neatly buttoned to his chin. Ralph Pond! Snowy exclaimed, "That's Puddles's father!"

Startled, Tom said, "Jesus H. Christ, he's still driving? How old *is* he?"

"He turned ninety-two last month. Puddles says she won't badger him about stopping driving because she herself couldn't live without driving."

"And that's a Ford LTD. How the hell old is *it?*"

"Remember? Mr. Pond always buys LTDs." Snowy knew Tom must remember his enjoyment of Mr. Pond's station wagons.

Tom's face went confused. "It's got to be secondhand, but it's in good shape."

Fright nudged Snowy's stomach, sickeningly. "You remember, Tom, you remember. When one LTD finally wears out, he locates another. Oh, there's Ginny in the passenger seat." Snowy hadn't spotted Ginny Barnes right away because Ginny's height had diminished enough to lower her almost below her headrest. (A preview of coming attractions?) Ginny was eighty-nine. After Mr. Pond had had enough of widower-life in an Ivythorpe apartment, at Ginny's invitation he'd moved into her house on Worm Hill. They were shacking up, just like Snowy and Tom. Luckily, Puddles found this funny.

Snowy unbuckled her seat belt and got out. "Hello, Mr. Pond, I haven't seen you since we bumped into each other at the Abnaki Mall last fall. How are you?"

"Well, now, Snowy." With his free hand, Mr. Pond tapped on the passenger window. "Ginny, it's Snowy!"

Still a pretty woman whose eyes were usually humorous, Ginny glanced up, then stepped out of the car. Her expression was concerned. She opened her arms and said to Snowy, "You look like you need a hug."

What, Snowy wondered, did *that* mean? What on earth did she look like? Stooping, she walked into Ginny's comforting arms.

The gas nozzle snapped and stopped. Carefully hanging it back on the pump, Mr. Pond said across the LTD's hood to Tom, "Puddles told us you've got yourself two new knees. I could use a couple myself, but I've waited too long."

And Ginny said softly to Snowy, "Puddles also told us that you're going to be a grandmother. Is everything all right?"

"Yes. Yes, everything's fine." Snowy wished for wood to knock on.

Tom hung up his gas nozzle and yanked the credit-card slip out of the pump. "Snowy, let's get a move on."

"A lunch," Snowy explained quickly. "We're going to a birthday lunch. Today's my birthday."

"Happy birthday!" said Mr. Pond and Ginny.

Tom drove to Main Street, then out past the snow-softened mobile-home park where Bev's son Leon lived with Miranda Flack. Snowy wondered if Tom was remembering that this was the route he'd driven her on their first date in March 1955. After the movies, after coffee and English muffins (so adult!) at Hooper's Dairy Bar, he'd driven to a little dirt road, a lovers' lane unidentified except by its nickname, the Cat Path. Which he was driving past now. He didn't turn his head to look. He didn't even scoff at the present-day residential-street sign.

After their parking session, he had driven her onward to Bev's house, where she was spending the night. These same roads, the turnoff onto another dirt road, one that had remained unpaved and still twisted uphill and down through the woods, crossing a brook, climbing uphill to a field and a driveway with a mailbox that used to say Miller, Bev's stepfather's last name, and now said Blumburg. Harriet's.

Up the driveway to a shutterless white Cape and a gray barn, a field, a bare apple orchard, and, far below, a snow-veiled view of the white lake guarded by mountains. Tom followed the driveway around to the back of the house. Instead of Bev's stepfather's Jeep parked here, Snowy saw a Lexus SUV. At Bennington Harriet had had the first of her Jaguars; after the purchase of this place Harriet had switched to a vehicle in which she could carry lots of stuff back and forth between New York City and New Hampshire. Beside it was Jared's Dodge pickup.

Snowy got out of the car, overwhelmed by the desire to see Julia, Bev's mother, opening the back door, tall, gaunt, gawky, her white hair in a practical short straight Dutch bob around her sharp-featured face. But the inside door and the storm door were opened by Harriet, looking elegant even though she was wearing items from what she considered her New Hampshire wardrobe, a plaid shirt and jeans. She called, "Happy birthday!"

Quickly Snowy straightened her parka, her shoulder bag, and hooked a finger through the jug of maple syrup. "Welcome back to New Hampshire!"

And in the doorway, she was once again hugged as though she needed one. Harriet pulled her into the kitchen, where Jared was standing at a Keurig coffee machine. Harriet took the jug, said, "Thank you," and called out to Tom, "Hi there!" She whispered to Snowy, "Can he manage the step?"

It was a plain granite doorstep. "Oh, sure." But Snowy hovered by the door until he had.

Both Julia and Harriet were artists, Julia with her weaving, Harriet with her canvases. However, Julia hadn't paid much attention to décor; in the old days in this kitchen there'd been worn linoleum and old yellow wallpaper of faded teapots. Snowy had watched Harriet being cautious about renovations, not for fear of upsetting Bev, who had detached herself from the place after her mother and stepfather left, but because of Snowy's continuing attachment. So the kitchen didn't resemble the photos in makeover articles in magazines. Appliances were simply newer, and furniture came from antiques stores instead of family attics. Harriet set the jug down on the small round kitchen table. Beyond, in the dining room that Julia had used as a workroom for her looms, Snowy saw the long farmhouse-style dining table all ready for lunch for four, with a birthday-wrapped present beside one place setting.

Jared asked, "Coffee? Tea? Hot chocolate?"

Tom said to him, "How about my hammer?"

Jared looked at him. "What?"

"I can't find my hammer. The one I've had since high school. You know the one. It's not in my toolbox. David hasn't seen it around."

"Your hammer?" Jared said.

Tom yelled, "What the fuck have you done with it?"

Snowy said, "Tom."

Harriet stared at him. "Tom, are you all right? Come sit down."

Tom roared, "Where the hell is my hammer?"

"I'm sorry," Snowy babbled to Harriet and Jared, "we'd better go, I'm sorry, I'll phone you. Tom, let's go home."

"Yes, you bet we're not staying here!" He hauled open the inside door, then the storm door, put his right foot on the granite doorstep, slipped, and fell forward onto his hands and knees in the snow. Knees.

Jared leapt outside, bent down to insert his hands under the armpits of Tom's parka, and dragged him upright.

Tom said, "For Christ's sake, I can get up! Let go!"

Jared didn't. He looked at Snowy, mouthing, "What should I do?"

Snowy repeated to Harriet, "I'll phone you," and ran outdoors to the Subaru. Tom had left the keys in the ignition, so she didn't have to try to take them from him. She started the car, pulled up beside Tom and Jared, leaned across and opened the passenger door. Jared let go of Tom but stood beside him until Tom collapsed on the seat, then helped him lift his feet in.

"Thank you," Snowy said. "Thank you."

As she drove away, the snow began to change to the predicted rain. She couldn't think what to say to Tom, so she just concentrated on the difficult sloppy drive back. She remembered a phrase she'd learned from Harriet: *ein milim*. It meant, "There are no words." No words to say what you are feeling.

Tom didn't speak until they reached Woodcombe and she parked in the barn's driveway, noticing that David's pickup wasn't here.

He said, "I found where you've moved the rifle."

Sweat sprang hot again, as when she'd hidden the .22. How should she reply? Should she spell out her worries, should she be forceful or casual? Again she thought: I'm a grown-up, I should know what to do. She said, "Tom—"

"Fuck it." He lunged out of the car and staggered into the barn.

Her heart thundering, she ran after him.

The workshop was empty. Of David. It was full of lethal weapons in the form of machinery. She said, "David must've gone home for lunch. Let's get the Cryo/Cuffs on your knees, and I'll make lunch."

"I don't want the goddamn Cryo/Cuffs and I don't want lunch." He hobbled over to his rolltop desk, sat down, and looked at the papers spread across it.

She rushed upstairs into the apartment, the small apartment, too small, suffocating her and Tom. In her office, the rifle remained behind the row of books. He hadn't moved it to a new hiding place. What should she do, what should she do? She looked at Alan's sketch of Ruhamah Reed's home by the sea.

Ruhamah, her own Ruhamah. Tom. Who needed her most? Ruhamah had a baby on the way, three stores to take care of, D. J.'s campaign. For support, Ruhamah had D. J.,

123

also Kim and other friends, and in-laws Dudley and Charl. When agoraphobia had struck Ruhamah, she had sensibly sought help and found it from Pamela Keach, a Concord psychiatrist.

Could Tom be convinced to see Pamela? No. He would kill himself first.

Ruhamah needed her less.

Tom was alone, drowning.

Snowy grabbed the phone, tapped the Maine number.

Puddles said somewhat indistinctly, "Happy birthday!" She swallowed. "Lunchtime. Talking with my mouth full. Speaking of that, how do you like being sixty-nine?"

Snowy didn't laugh. "Puddles, could we borrow a house? Not your Hilton Head house. Could we rent something on Quarry Island for a couple of weeks? We've got to get away from here."

5

PEOPLE KEPT REMINDING SNOWY that April is considered a winter month in northern New England. And on the morning of Friday, April 4, the day before she and Tom were to leave, snow began. She kept on packing, consulting the lengthy list she'd made. Puddles always said that islands meant tote bags, and during her trips with Puddles and Blivit she had learned the truth of this, so after putting clothes into an overnight bag, a suitcase, and Tom's backpack and her own, she stuffed Woodcombe General Store tote bags with warm hats and gloves, baseball caps, slickers, L.L.Bean boots, hiking boots, trekking poles telescoped as short as possible, books, magazines, camera, first-aid kit, and Cryo/Cuffs. More tote bags held groceries to supplement the island store's supplies. During this visit to the island, she and Tom wouldn't be guests at the castle, though Puddles and Blivit had tried to insist at first, with an invitation from Isabella Hutchinson Thompson, Blivit's father's sister. Eighty-seven-year-old Aunt Izzy.

During her packing, the snow changed to a sleety soup, then to rain. And Tom stayed down in the workshop with David. Two weeks ago, when Puddles had phoned with the news of a cottage to rent, Snowy had suggested a getaway to him, saying she needed a vacation before the busy season began. To her great relief, he hadn't violently objected. He hadn't objected at all; he had simply behaved as if this were not happening. Would he balk now, would she have to unpack?

She went out to the landing and called, "It's ready."

David drove the Subaru into the barn, came upstairs, helped her lug everything down. She had plotted the loading procedure. First she and David put in the items for the island. Last was a small tote bag containing Puddles's hostess gift (repeating Harriet's, a jug of Woodcombe maple syrup, though Maine produced more than New Hampshire) and the overnight bag, which she and Tom would use when they spent tomorrow night with Puddles and Blivit at the farmhouse.

The rain ended that evening. Ruhamah phoned to say bon voyage, but in her nervous tone was the question she hadn't asked aloud at the Oakhill store: "Will you be safe with him?"

The next morning, out the apartment windows the day was dank. Snowy had given Puddles an estimated time of arrival of four o'clock, so that she and Tom could be leisurely about departure and feel like they were already on vacation. After her shower she dressed in L.L.Bean clothes for a Maine trip, black knit pants, ocean-aqua sweater. While Tom was in the shower, she set out two tea bags instead of making a pot of coffee, filled the teakettle, and toasted an English muffin for herself. Eating it, she thought of cake. On her birthday, after phoning Puddles she had phoned Harriet to apologize. Harriet asked, "His meds are causing this behavior?"

"They must be," Snowy had said, "but he's tapering off on schedule, so maybe it's also the too-familiar situation here and not being able to do what he used to do."

Harriet said, "We're all facing limitations, aren't we?" Then she said, "Jared didn't take Tom's hammer."

"Of course he didn't. Tom gets—confused."

Harriet said, "I'll stop by your store tomorrow with what we haven't eaten of your birthday cake."

So Harriet had arrived with a chunk of butter-cream-frosted chocolate cake that wished Snowy in pink lettering a HAPPY BIR. Harriet also brought the abandoned birthday present, which turned out to be another cake, this one untouched, a genuine New York-style sour cream crumb coffee cake from a Manhattan bakery.

Tom now emerged from the bathroom shivering in his summer bathrobe; she had packed his winter one, L.L.Bean Royal Stewart flannel. He went into the bedroom. Snowy put a Tylenol caplet on the counter. Hooray, as of last week he had graduated from Vicodin to Tylenol! But this didn't seem to have lifted his spirits.

Their freshman year, she and Harriet had greatly valued the rare occasions when coffee cake was served for breakfast, and Harriet had come up with a theory about Coffee Cake Therapy: any deviation from the norm of studying was extremely important to your mental health, since small pleasures helped keep things in perspective. After Tom's making that scene at Harriet's house, the coffee-cake present had new significance. As Harriet left the store, she asked Snowy, "Are you going to be all right?"

"Yes," Snowy had said. The next day, while Tom was in Gunthwaite at PT, she had told David about the hammer and together they searched the workshop. She found it in the bottom drawer of his rolltop desk. "Why," she asked David, "would he have put a hammer there?"

David shrugged. "For safekeeping? It's special to him. But he forgot." Then David said what she'd said to Harriet. "He gets confused."

"What do we do with it? Do we tell him we found it?"

"Give it to me. I'll tell him that I ran across it at home, that I'd taken it home by mistake and forgotten."

She now saw Tom leaving the bedroom, stepping into the living room. He'd docilely donned the clothes she'd set out for him, L.L.Bean jeans and navy-blue fleece Henley shirt. They hung loose on him. She'd warned Puddles not to be startled by his weight loss. The blue of the shirt intensified the blue of his eyes in his thin face.

She said, "Here's your breakfast," and dropped an English muffin into the toaster.

In the bathroom, she brushed her teeth and packed her vanity case. She went to her office and slid the laptop into its carrying case. She opened her leather briefcase, which she'd bought in London during the trip with Alan before Ruhamah was born, and checked the contents. Yesterday she had arranged in it legal pads, pencils, a little pencil sharpener, pens, and a folder holding copies of her latest poems.

Back in the kitchen, she saw that Tom, standing at the counter sipping tea, had only eaten half his muffin. She said, "I guess I've packed all the last-minute things except your toothbrush."

He said, "What the hell are you getting us into."

A statement, not a question, but she answered, "I told you, a change of scenery. Rest and recuperation. Remember that saying, 'A change is as good as a rest'?"

"A batch of bullshit." But he went into the bathroom.

She tossed his uneaten half muffin into the wastebasket. The dump was open this weekend, and David would be taking their garbage with his. Had she forgotten any other necessary arrangements? As she washed the dishes, she looked out the sink window at the wet branches of a beech tree. Bev's mother used to claim that there had to be a window over a kitchen sink or you'd go mad doing dishes. She tried to imagine an ocean view. Puddles said there was one from the cottage's kitchen-sink window.

Tom came out of the bathroom carrying his toothbrush in its travel case. He stuck it into the vanity case. Then he just stood there.

She put on her parka and said, "Let's head 'em up and move 'em on." Oh God, where was her brain, this was a line from the old TV Western *Rawhide* that she and Alan were apt to quote! She'd never used it with Tom. During the late 1950s into the mid-1960s, had Tom and Joanne watched the Western in their apartment in the married students' barracks in Rumford or in their house in Newburgh?

He didn't react to the line, and he didn't move. He was balking.

There were noises downstairs. Yesterday she'd said good-bye to everybody, including David, who wasn't supposed to be working on Saturday, but it must be David unlocking the barn door, coming in, stamping slush off his boots. She opened the apartment door. Yes, David, climbing the stairs. Arriving early on his dump errand?

David said, "All set?" He stepped past her, taking Tom's parka off a peg, handing it to him, lifting the laptop case and the briefcase. "Is this everything?"

Snowy nodded, picking up her vanity case and shoulder bag.

Kaylie would have admired the way David herded Tom down the stairs. Snowy followed. As they went outdoors, she suddenly heard a phoebe's call, the first time this spring. Was it the phoebe who nested under one of the barn's eaves, returning once again? Then a honking sound overhead made her look higher. In the gray sky was the V of Canada geese returning, heading north. In order to return, she thought, you have to go away. But what if you want to stay away?

As David carefully placed the laptop and briefcase on the Subaru's backseat, Tom maneuvered himself into the driver's seat. Although Tom hadn't acknowledged the trip, she had expected that if he did allow himself to go, he would want to do most of the driving, as he had on the other trips to Maine. Usually they swapped at Moody's Diner in Waldoboro. Could his new knees drive that far? David took her vanity case, put it too on the backseat, and opened the passenger door for her.

She got in, saying, "David, thank you. Love to Lavender and the girls."

David said, "Safe travels," and closed the door.

Tom backed down the driveway and off they went past the post office, the store, the village houses. Her mind began saying,

"Good-bye, good-bye, to everything!" She realized it was reciting Robert Louis Stevenson's "Farewell to the Farm." But this departure didn't need a farewell. They were simply leaving for a two-week vacation. But still she almost wept. Good-bye, good-bye, to everything.

Up out of the mountain valley, onto the main highway, like the arrow of the geese.

Usually on trips she and Tom talked; they'd been known to sing. This time, there was silence. Oh, look—a robin, the first robin, bouncing across a bare patch of lawn amid snow! She didn't point it out.

Poems. April was Poetry Month. Amongst the appointments and commitments she'd postponed or canceled had been two poetry readings. She would *not* feel guilty about this, nor about leaving Ruhamah. Nor would she think about the dreams she'd been having since she made this decision. For years and years she had been a jogger, not a runner, and now thanks to age and scoliosis she was a walker; yet in these dreams she was running more smoothly than she ever could have even in her youth, sometimes through woods, once up an endless length of red velvet carpet, and last night through open doorway after doorway. She was running away.

Puddles had e-mailed a photo she'd taken of the cottage that Blivit had found, but unfortunately the photo wasn't exactly helpful because Puddles hadn't waited for a clear day and had snapped it in a snow squall. The cottage appeared to be a small reddish ranch-style house with a vague haze behind it that Puddles had said was Dark Cove. Snowy had asked worriedly, "Why is it called 'dark'?" Puddles replied, "Oh, it's just another little cove surrounded by firs, spruces, a dime a dozen on the island," and had then launched into a genealogical description of the cottage's ownership. If Snowy had grasped this correctly, the cottage belonged to Blivit's aunt's granddaughter's husband's Great-Aunt Mildred Cotter, who had been born and brought up on Quarry Island, attended the one-room schoolhouse, and then, as island teenagers still did, had boarded on the mainland while going to Long Harbor High School (the old high school, Puddles explained, not the newer one at which Puddles coached). Mildred had taken typing and shorthand classes and upon graduation had stayed with Portland relatives and gone on a job hunt that resulted in a long career as a secretary in a Portland law firm. Because the Cotter family home on Quarry Island was now lived in by another branch of the family, Mildred had bought this cottage for her summer vacations. She planned to retire there and had had it winterized. And after she retired she did sell her Portland house and live year-round in what had become known as Cotter Cottage. But this past November at age eighty-eight she had fallen, breaking her right leg—"her right tibia," Nurse Puddles had said precisely. After the hospital stay she had been moved to a room in a rehabilitation center near her Portland relatives. She intended to return to the cottage this summer.

Puddles had explained, "Blivit says she's frugal. As usual, he's being tactful. She's always refused to spend money on more than basic maintenance, so the cottage needs some upkeep, but it's livable, and, as you want, it's right on the ocean. With an ocean view from the kitchen-sink window. There's a little dock but no boat. She used to have one, what Blivit calls a peapod, but now she's sold it. Money. Blivit says she's very pleased about the opportunity to rent the cottage off-season, before she returns." Puddles added, "*If* she returns. Surgery at that age . . . " Then she said, "You and Tom, don't forget your cell phones. Blivit says she's had her island phone turned off for the winter. She was one of those who weren't too thrilled when the island got private phone service. Remember Blivit telling how for years the only telephone on the island was a phone booth outside the town hall? You don't want to have to use that in a gale."

Mildred charged five hundred dollars a week, so Snowy had sent a check for a thousand dollars to her at the Pines Manor Rehabilitation and Retirement Center.

And now they were crossing into Maine. A grocery store's sign said: Buy 1 Italian, Get 1 Half-Price. She and Tom had always laughed over that. In New Hampshire you also called them Italian sandwiches or Italian grinders, but this sign seemed to signify definite arrival in Maine, land of Italians and whoopie pies and Moxie, where a Moxie festival was held every year— and every year she and Tom had talked of attending.

After they passed Portland, there was a view of the ocean in Yarmouth, tantalizing. Usually on I-95, if they weren't getting off at the Freeport exit to go to L.L.Bean she would make a joke of waving wistfully in that direction, but she didn't today.

Next, the exit to Route 1 and Brunswick, where Harriet Beecher Stowe had written *Uncle Tom's Cabin* while her husband taught at Bowdoin College. The bridges: the Bath bridge over the Kennebec River, and in Wiscasset the long bridge over the Sheepscot River. This Wiscasset bridge was such a bottleneck that during tourist season Puddles timed any trips to Portland for the less-busy early hours and made sure she brought audiobooks to listen to in case she got trapped in a traffic jam on her return.

Route 1 bypassed Damariscotta and reached Waldoboro.

Snowy said, "Shall we stop at Moody's? Bathroom break and a late lunch?" He could say no to lunch, but to a bathroom? She didn't mention her screaming spine, because his knees must be hurting worse than that.

He said, "Okay," and when they reached the diner he pulled into the parking lot.

She remembered how, when she'd first seen the plain low building, she wouldn't have known it was a famous landmark if Bev hadn't told her so. She and Bev had had lunch here in 1988 on their way to Camden to meet Puddles, who was up from South Carolina to visit Portland relatives. Bev's parents had stopped at Moody's on their Maine honeymoon, and Bev and her mother had also lunched here when her mother took her to Camden the two summers Bev waitressed at the Grand View Hotel, the very hotel where later Bev and Roger honeymooned, stopping at Moody's on their way back to their Boston apartment.

Out of the car, Snowy stretched, watchful. Tom didn't totter but he held onto the hood of the car until his legs got working. As she and Tom went slowly up the steps into the diner, she thought how young she and Bev had been that time, while they thought they were getting ancient, age forty-nine, almost *fifty*.

In a wooden booth, while Tom was in the men's room she took off her parka, put on her glasses, skimmed the menu, and ordered what they always did, what she'd first had with Bev, crabmeat rolls and iced tea. She postponed a dessert order. She and Bev had had strawberry pie for dessert, but Tom preferred Moody's walnut pie, and she varied her choices. Today she felt like lemon meringue. But would he want dessert? Those previous Moody's lunches with Tom had always been giddy with adventure, with anticipation of the ocean. Would this lunch today be—moody?

When he returned to the table, she removed her glasses and said, "I've ordered, be right back," and went to the women's room. Two small pretty women about her age were conversing in French, one washing her hands, the other primping. They must be down from Canada, maybe in search of some early spring.

In English Snowy ventured, "I saw a robin this morning. The first I've seen this year."

135

French exclamations at this news, and in English the hand-washer said, "It has been a very long winter."

Snowy said, "The weather forecast predicted some sun this afternoon. Let's hope it melts all the snow."

"*Oui*, yes!" they said, and she went into a stall.

They were gone when she came out. In the unfamiliar mirror, her face startled her by its tenseness, its strained expression. She'd got used to the dark circles she had under her eyes lately, but she remembered how, if she'd been studying too hard, her mother would sometimes tsk-tsk and say, "You have circles under your eyes, Henrietta." As she walked back to Tom she saw the women in a booth with their husbands (presumably); they waved, and she waved back. She sat down and said to Tom, "Tourists from Canada. Another sign of spring."

The two glasses of iced tea had been brought. He sat looking out the window, shredding a paper napkin, not drinking his.

She squeezed lemon into hers. "I've been remembering that time Bev and I stopped here on our way to Camden. I couldn't resist buying a Moody's mug to take home to you. And remember the time you bought me my Moody's T-shirt as a surprise? I'd gone outdoors while you were paying the bill, and you came out with it." A pink one. She reached across the table and touched his hand. "I do believe I got tearful and called you a honeybunch."

He looked at her, then back out the window. "I'm not much of a honeybunch these days."

The waitress set down their plates. "Enjoy."

Snowy said, "Thank you, we shall."

Usually when they ate crabmeat rolls, they reminisced about the first time they'd seen crab-picking done. They had gone for a walk on Quarry Island, and beside a house they saw two women sitting at a picnic table, talking and talking and picking meat out of shells. Today Tom took a morose bite. Snowy glanced

136

over at the two Canadian couples tucking into fried clams and talking, talking. She clenched her iced-tea glass, envying that simple conversation.

Finally, the crabmeat rolls eaten, she asked, "Do you want walnut pie?"

"I guess not."

She gathered up her parka.

He said, "You have something, if you want."

"I'm fine. Um, shall we swap drivers now?"

"No. I'll keep on."

Was he determined to arrive at Puddles and Blivit's at the wheel of the car, at the helm, no matter if he wrecked his new knees? A flash of fury crackled through her head. Goddamnit, so be it.

BACK ON ROUTE 1, Tom drove on to Rockland, where Edna St. Vincent Millay had been born, then to Camden, where she'd lived in her girlhood. Route 1 was Camden's Main Street, and Snowy saw ghosts of herself, Bev, and Puddles walking along here, stopping at the taller-than-life-size statue of Edna St. Vincent Millay, who stood looking intently over her shoulder, wearing a long dress, a book clasped behind her back. A sonnet sailed into Snowy's mind, Edna's sonnet that began "Hearing your words, and not a word among them," with an image of the Maine island of Matinicus, wives of fishermen standing peering north, their skirts slapping in the wind.

Usually Snowy pointed out to Tom the Whitehall Inn where she and Bev and Puddles had stayed, even though he knew exactly where it was, but this afternoon she didn't and she didn't repeat the story of how Edna had recited "Renascence"

137

there. When they went past the road up which Bev had driven her and Puddles to the top of Mount Battie to see the ocean view that had inspired the poem, she stayed silent.

As promised by the forecast, the sun came out.

Tom drove on and on, until at last a road sign said: Long Harbor. He turned right, onto a quiet road meandering down Perkins Peninsula through the blueberry barrens, stretches of faded red bushes, splotches of snow. The first time she and Tom had seen the barrens, Tom had commented, "It reminds me of peat-cut areas," and had laughed and said, "Peat! You can read descriptions for years and still not believe it until you see it. Cutting and burning the earth in your fireplace! Instead of a chain saw and a woodlot, they get their shovel and go dig their fuel." And she'd said, "Remember visiting that Black House Museum, so authentic with a peat fire burning and we tourists started choking?"

Then came peninsula homes. Lobster boats and stacks of wire lobster traps in dooryards identified some as belonging to lobstermen, who must be figuring that it was time to start thinking about setting out their traps.

Long Harbor, the town at the tip of the peninsula, possessed what Puddles called the ugliest high-school building in the world. As they reached it, Tom behaved the way he always had, braking and staring in disbelief. The school stood at the top of a hill; you could not ignore the awful structure, built in the 1960s and designed by the head of the shop department. Tom, who had been the star of his high-school shop classes and briefly a shop major at Rumford Teachers' College before switching to an English major, now said what he always said, "One of these days the goddamn thing is going to fall down."

Its exterior of khaki-colored brick with chartreuse panels had apparently been an attempt to match the school colors of green and gold. The sign on the front lawn announced: Spring Sports Begin!

With the trees still leafless, you could see the school's view out across the town's rooftops. The contrasting emotions that the view usually ignited within her were excitement and a hint of serenity. Today the new sun glinted on the sea and she felt nerved up, exhausted. Farther away, the low silhouette of Quarry Island lifted to Hutchinson Mountain—which she and Tom had climbed a couple of times, though it really couldn't be called a mountain by Tom's standards. Maybe, she thought, maybe someday during these two weeks she and Tom could climb its easy trail very slowly.

The school's hilltop was so different from Oakhill's that the plunge down past houses didn't bother her. On the waterfront Main Street she said, "Let's hear and smell it," and pressed her window button down. Mewing of seagulls, salty tang of the sea. At the town wharf, the mail boat was moored, spanking white as if it had been repainted for spring. It was patriotically named the *Uncle Sam*. She and Tom would be taking it tomorrow, accompanied by Puddles and Blivit. Now that she would actually be getting into it, the boat looked too small for a voyage to an island on a horizon. Eek! No, it was actually much larger than a lobster boat. In Blivit's boat and the castle's boat, the trip took a half hour to forty-five minutes, depending. She had come prepared; her shoulder bag contained a plastic bag of peeled gingerroot, which didn't make you sleepy the way Dramamine did.

Tom snapped, "Too damn cold."

She closed the window.

Leander's Lobster Pound and the Seaview Café near the wharf were open year-round. Today Leander's sign bragged: Our Seafood Comes From the Best Schools! The Seaview Café's sign used the guilt ploy: Stop In or We'll Both Starve! But mostly the restaurants and gift shops and art galleries on Main Street were still closed for the winter, and their boarded-up fronts for some reason made her think of frontier ghost towns in Westerns. ("Head 'em up, move 'em on.") She glanced down Grove Street at the white clapboard house that was the Long Harbor Family Health Center where Puddles worked with a PA, a nurse, and a doctor who came three times a week from the hospital in the nearest city.

Snowy checked the dashboard clock. Four o'clock. Puddles didn't work here on Saturdays. Sometimes Blivit did work weekends at the ice-cream plant; he had handed over his CEO job to a cousin and returned to his beloved Research and Development experimentation. So Puddles and maybe Blivit would be awaiting them right now.

At a small roadside sign decorated with the Quarry Island Ice Cream logo of blue waves, green island, and white lighthouse, Tom turned onto Creamery Point. The Quarry Island Ice Cream Park surrounded the white building where the ice cream was made. In that building Puddles and Blivit had met. Earlier, Puddles had learned that she was remotely related to Quarry Island Ice Cream's Hutchinson family, so with her father and a cousin she had come to see the park. They had joined a group for a tour of the ice-cream plant, during which a pregnant woman had gone into labor. Puddles had leapt into action and delivered a baby girl on the sofa in the office of the stunned Quarry Island Ice Cream heir, Blivit.

Although the park's grounds and ice-cream parlor remained open throughout the winter, the gift shop, arts-and-crafts gallery, and farm museum were closed, and the bandstand sat silent. In the park's pasture, brown-and-white Guernseys grazed. Tom drove past the park to an unmarked gravel road, narrow between dark spruces. Partway along it a discreet gray-shingled gatehouse protected the farm, which lay out of sight down the road. But the gate bar was raised. The gatehouse was only manned by the gatekeeper from May to November when curious tourists might be tempted to explore. Or burglars. Evidently Blivit thought he could handle the situation during the winter.

Tom drove forward through the spruces. Then sunlight led to another pasture. Snowy wondered if Blivit's own small herd of Guernseys would be out of the barn and grazing—

Tom slammed on the brake. "Jesus fucking Christ!"

Nope, it hadn't happened at Cowshit Corner, it was happening here! And the cows weren't being escorted across the road, they'd trampled down a section of the wooden fence, they were loose, on their own! Spring fever! They frisked and bucked, jumping for joy, closer and closer to the car—

Tom blared the horn and began struggling out from behind the wheel, but Snowy was out of the car first, shouting at them, waving her arms. Down the driveway from the barn dashed Corey, Blivit's young farmer, his ponytail flying. His voice caught the cows' attention. They subsided.

"Sorry," he said to Snowy and Tom. "Sorry."

Snowy said, "It's spring."

"So it is," said Corey and began shooing the cows up the driveway to the gray-shingled barn.

Snowy and Tom collapsed into the car.

Then Snowy started laughing. "Remember the time you'd stopped to see me at Hurricane Farm and the Thornes' cows appeared in the yard with Cleora chasing them? Remember how you and I ran after them through the woods until they took a notion to head home?"

He said flatly, "I knew you were going to remember that."

Meaning what? Meaning she remembered too much?

He said, "We couldn't have chased them now."

"Well, let's be glad we could then."

"Lucky me, I've got Pollyanna for a passenger."

Tears stung. She blinked furiously. She would *not* arrive at Puddles's house crying.

Corey closed the barnyard gate on the cows and beckoned Tom to proceed. Tom did, up the driveway past the barn, and parked in front of the white salt-water farmhouse. Puddles came hurrying around from the backyard, her normally pale skin flushed, her expression pissed off. She was wearing jeans and a green sweat-shirt lettered in gold: Long Harbor High School Seafarers. She yelled, "What's all the racket, are the cows loose again?"

Snowy clambered out of the car. "They've got spring fever!"

Blivit followed Puddles, in his typical L.L.Bean attire, tattersall shirt, chinos. He'd lost weight since Puddles began overseeing his meals, and although he was still a big man, he appeared to be a healthy one. His gray hair hadn't receded any farther over the winter. Behind rimless glasses, his hazel eyes were anxious as he said, "You're okay? Corey has had to keep fixing the fence."

"He rounded them up," Snowy said. "Everything's okay."

Tom was getting out from behind the wheel. He had arrived at the helm.

Despite Snowy's warning, Puddles looked shocked by his thinness. However, uncharacteristically she didn't comment on this, at least not at once. She hugged Snowy hard, then hugged Tom. "How was your trip? No trouble in Wiscasset? This time of year, the traffic there isn't slower than cold molasses." She opened the back of the car. "Blivit, grab the suitcase."

Snowy said hastily, "We just need the overnight bag," and gave it to him, but then she took the hostess-gift tote bag and handed it to Tom, and off the backseat she hoisted the vanity case, which Puddles seized. So in addition to her shoulder bag she had only her laptop and briefcase to carry, not that she would probably need them tonight but what if an ocean gale blew the car away or another cow stampede squashed it? Then she wondered if she should bring the Cryo/Cuffs indoors. No. That would ruin Tom's triumph of driving all the way here.

Puddles led them at a measured pace into the backyard, glancing over her shoulder at Tom limping along.

Snowy paused, inhaling the breeze, and Blivit behind her stopped too. He said, "Maine welcomes your return."

Seagulls cruised across the view of the ocean, Quarry Island on the horizon. The flower beds on the sloping lawn were still heaped with salt-hay mulch. The guest cottage near the beach was shuttered for winter, and the dock was empty, the boats in storage. Waves jostled against the rocks of the shore.

Rewording the onesie she'd bought for Ruhamah's baby, Snowy said, "Hello, Maine."

PUDDLES WENT UP the back steps, ushering Snowy and Tom onto the screened porch, and here things were partly ready for spring, four wicker chairs set out. Puddles said, "We'd freeze our asses off sitting here today, and anyway, Tom, Snowy says you're feeling the cold a lot. Blivit's got a fire going in the living room."

Tom mumbled something. His thanks? Snowy wanted to tell him a lesson she had been taught in her childhood by a book titled *Summer at Buckhorn*, that a guest's first responsibility was to have a good time.

Snowy said, "A fire will be very—peaceful."

In the back hallway, they deposited the luggage on a sea chest already occupied by tote bags, and Blivit helped her and Tom off with their parkas, which he added to the row of parkas, jackets, and slickers on hooks. Below, a varied assortment of boots stood toes to the baseboard.

Lifting up the laptop and briefcase again, Snowy said, "At home, I learned that country living means boots. As islands mean tote bags."

Blivit said, "I think we're all ready to go barefoot, after this winter."

They followed Puddles into the kitchen, where Puffin the cat, the feline clown of the sea, uncurled from the rocking chair and stalked over to inspect the guests. Snowy put her laptop and briefcase on the pine kitchen table and crouched to pat Puffin's black-and-white fur, scratching the teardrop of reddish-brown fur behind his right ear, remembering Kit, her cat. Puffin purred. Then she took the tote bag from Tom and with a flourish pulled out the jug of maple syrup. "Coals to Newcastle, made in Woodcombe."

Puddles brandished the vanity case. "Hey, great. But come on and unload in your room."

However, Blivit set down the overnight bag and gallantly accepted the jug, studying the maple tree label. "I think we'll be having French toast for breakfast tomorrow. Thank you."

Then he and Snowy picked up their loads again and everybody went along the hall to the downstairs guest room.

Snowy was always assigned this pretty bedroom with its own bathroom, whether she was here with Tom or with Bev, who got an upstairs guest room. It had been where Puddles recuperated after the hip replacement, so a safety rail had been installed in the shower; Puddles seemed to think Snowy's scoliosis needed such security. Snowy saw that Puddles had provided more bedding than the blue flannel sheets and the duvet with a starfish-patterned cover. Atop the duvet were folded a blanket, a patchwork quilt, and a knitted afghan. Snowy babbled, "This is so thoughtful of you, so nice—"

Puddles gave her another hug. "We'll meet you two in the living room."

As Puddles and Blivit left and Tom went into the bathroom, Snowy looked through the white-curtained window. From here, did Quarry Island seem slightly closer? Bali Ha'i, attainable?

When Tom came out, she carried her vanity case into the bathroom. Blivit's mother had stenciled cute blue whales on the walls. The mirror over the sink had a frame made of glued seashells, as did some mirrors in the castle, also her handiwork. Both his parents had died before he and Puddles met, so Puddles had never known these in-laws.

Freshened up, Snowy stepped back into the bedroom. Tom was sitting in one of the two armchairs, but he wasn't looking out the window at Bali Ha'i. A little bookcase held a selection of books by Louise Dickinson Rich, Kenneth Roberts, John Gould, and other Maine writers, and also issues of *Down East* magazine, one of which he was leafing through.

She said chattily, "Here's hoping Puddles will have some substantial hors d'oeuvres. The crabmeat roll isn't sticking to my ribs. Maybe Blivit will make his mini-lobster-roll appetizers. If not, I'm hoping supper will be his lobster pot pie—"

Tom asked, "Is Blivit paying for the cottage?"

One good thing about his not acknowledging the trip had been his apparent lack of interest in details such as this.

"No," she said. "He and Puddles wanted to, but I wouldn't hear of it."

"How much is it costing us?"

She hesitated. "Off-season rates."

"How much?"

"Five hundred a week."

There was a knock on the door and Puddles called, "Have you two fallen asleep or got up to something else?"

Snowy didn't say: Not the latter. She laughed for Puddles's benefit and opened the door.

Puddles said to Tom, "Come warm up."

They followed her back along the hall, through the dining room with its Windsor chairs around the drop-leaf pine table set for four, into the long living room, which had paneled walls, Oriental rugs, and lots of Hutchinson family accumulation, including dark paintings of storm-tossed ships at sea and cabinets of little treasures

145

such as scrimshaw. Snowy knew that a housekeeper, Tammy, kept all this dusted. What must it be like not to have to think about cleaning a house? Puddles settled Tom into a wing chair beside the fireplace, fussing over him, offering an afghan that he refused—politely, to Snowy's relief. Snowy herself sat down in a nearby chair and looked out the small-paned windows at the ocean.

While Puddles bustled off to the kitchen, Blivit prodded the fire with a poker and asked them, "The usual?"

"Thank you," Snowy said.

Blivit went over to the liquor cabinet for glasses and a bottle of scotch. Out of the mini-fridge he took a bottle of chardonnay. He poured her a glass and brought it to her. This past week Tom had begun resuming a scotch in the evenings with TV, but it was not the single-malt Glenlivet that Blivit now poured him, stuff that cost a good part of a hundred bucks even in New Hampshire's state liquor stores renowned for low prices. Tom had bought a single malt to celebrate the millennium's New Year, and when else? Maybe he would this May to celebrate his seventieth birthday?

Giving Tom a glass, Blivit said, "You've mentioned you had a Jeep for ages."

Tom brightened. "I certainly did. It'll be like old times driving yours, though mine was a CJ2."

This was one detail that Snowy *had* mentioned to him. During Snowy's planning with Puddles over the phone, Blivit had insisted via Puddles that they use his island vehicle, an ancient Jeep Wagoneer, instead of renting the junker that the island's general store maintained for tourists.

So now Blivit and Tom talked Jeeps. Snowy sipped, turning her gaze to the open door of the room off the living room that had been the office of Blivit's first wife, Jill, a landscape designer who had died a year before he and Puddles met. After they married, he had asked Puddles what he should do about the office. Puddles had explained to Snowy, "I still have Guy's stuff in his den in the Hilton Head house, so I told Blivit to leave it as is. Not shrines. But." Thus it was still an office, with Jill's desk, Jill's gardening books on the shelves, and Jill's drafting table that reminded Snowy of the one Alan had had in his apartment when they met. Memories. Tom used to quote W. Somerset Maugham about how the infirmities of age were nothing compared with the burden of memories.

In came Puddles carrying a tray of cheese and crackers, carrot and celery sticks, which she set down on a coffee table. No mini-lobster-rolls. Then she accepted the glass of chardonnay Blivit handed her, raised it, and said, "Here's looking up your old address!"

They all burst out laughing. Even Tom! This was a toast from *M*A*S*H*, which Puddles had adopted last year after binge-watching DVDs of all the *M*A*S*H* episodes. Snowy suspected that when the series was on TV, Puddles had yearned to be the chief nurse, Major Margaret "Hot Lips" Houlihan.

Then Blivit left for the kitchen, and Puddles asked about Snowy's grandchild-to-be (Ruhamah would have the ultrasound this Thursday) and talked about her children and grandchildren. Blivit returned, and there soon wafted from the kitchen to Snowy the fragrance of lobster pot pie. She sighed contentedly, but then she had to answer his questions about the store's burglary. No, still no arrests.

At the dining-room table, Puddles presented a spinach salad and Blivit served the pot pie. When he had made it for Snowy and Tom the first time, Snowy had requested the recipe, and Blivit had said, "Lots of lobster meat picked out of steamed lobsters, some béchamel, some tomalley—you know, what Puddles calls the green stuff. For the crust, mix bread crumbs with butter and Old Bay Seasoning. Bake until hot and the crumbs are brown. Easy." But even though Snowy had jotted the recipe down, she had then begun to decide that lobster should always be eaten at the ocean, not inland, and thus she'd never made it. Now she was so glad that Blivit had that she couldn't resist complimenting it the Maine way; lifting a forkful, she said to Blivit, "Finest kind!"

He laughed.

He and Puddles talked about global warming's effect on fishing (bad) and the recession's effect on ice cream (people were still buying Quarry Island's). Puddles asked for Gunthwaite news; Bev had given Snowy permission to tell her about the summer theater, so Snowy related this. The flavor Blivit had chosen for the grand finale of dessert was lemon sherbet, and thus Snowy almost did get her lemon meringue pie. After the decaf, Tom excused himself, ready for bed, and after carrying dishes to the kitchen Blivit tactfully left Puddles and Snowy alone there.

Puddles immediately said, "Jesus, Snowy, you look like death warmed over."

Snowy opened the dishwasher.

"And Tom," Puddles said, "now that I've seen him with my own eyes—he's so thin, you must have to shake the sheets to find him." She rinsed a plate and passed it to Snowy. "I blame myself. Here I am, happy as a clam at high tide, too damn happy to take in over the phone how bad it's got."

Snowy slid a plate into the rack. Little did Puddles know. Snowy had not mentioned the rifle. To anybody.

Puddles fretted, "I'm a nurse, for God's sake, I should have—look, if out on the island Tom has a health problem you can't handle, call Aunt Izzy and she'll get hold of the island's emergency group, they just have first-aid training but it's better than nothing. Damn, I should have—"

Snowy patted Puddles's shoulder. "It's been—what's the word I want, 'cumulative'?"

"'Failure to thrive.' That's the term that hit me when I saw him, even though it's used for undernourished children."

Snowy repeated, "Failure to thrive."

"You told me he's only on Tylenol now? Are you absolutely positive?"

"Remember how you advised Bev and me to snoop in our kids' rooms for drugs? I've kept tabs on his meds. And other than the weight loss, he's doing fine physically. He is mending. That is, if he doesn't do long drives. He wouldn't let me spell him! Still, he's mourning Mount Pascataquac, not being able to work at the fire tower this year."

"So it's mental."

Snowy took a breath and said, "Like Alan."

THE WEATHER RETURNED to cloudy and dank the next morning, but the smell was delicious, heavy with brine. On Sundays, the mail boat made just one trip to the island, at the sedate hour of ten-thirty, heading back from the island at twelve-thirty. The French-toast breakfast had been leisurely and Puddles and Blivit casual about departure, while Tom grew antsy and Snowy had time to get nervous about seasickness. When Puddles and Blivit finally were ready, Tom drove them and Snowy to the wharf's parking area. After they all unloaded the car, he gave Blivit the car keys, for Blivit and Puddles's return this afternoon. Then they lugged everything down to the wharf to the mail boat. Nobody else was waiting here. Was nobody else crazy enough, wondered Snowy, to be arriving here on such an unappealing morning, parka hoods up against the wind? She realized that Puddles had seen her uneasy scrutiny of the harbor's choppy fringes, the open ocean's swells, and said, "Got my gingerroot with me."

149

Blivit was telling Tom, "The *Uncle Sam* can hold thirty passengers. The best place to sit is on the deckhouse, where they put lawn chairs. Not, however, in today's weather." A young man came out of the cabin, and Blivit added, "Hi there, Dylan."

"Hi, Blivit." Dylan, who must be the deckhand, stowed the luggage and tote bags on the deck.

Puddles remarked, "With boats, everything is in stages, load up, unload, unload, load up. That sounds like a sea chantey, doesn't it." She sang, "'What shall we do with a drunken sailor, early in the morning?'"

Dylan offered a hand to Snowy, who took it and timidly ventured from wharf to deck. Puddles next took his hand, but only to be polite, Snowy thought, because even with her titanium hip she stepped confidently. Next, he reached toward Tom. Oh God, what would Tom do, ignore Dylan, fall, and break his knees?

Tom said, "Thanks," and leaned on Dylan, maneuvering carefully.

As Blivit hopped aboard in the nimble way of some large men, a grizzle-bearded man came out of the cabin wearing a parka and jeans and what must be a captain's hat but one hardly recognizable as such, threadbare, its white cloth turned yellow with age, its black visor bent cockeyed. He boomed, "Well, now, Blivit, Puddles." His loud voice had the best Maine accent Snowy had ever heard. Puddles beamed at him, entranced.

Blivit said, "Good morning, Erroll. Looks like we're your only customers?"

"So it does."

"These are our friends from New Hampshire, Henrietta Sutherland and Tom Forbes. They're staying at Cotter Cottage for a couple of weeks."

Erroll nodded to Snowy and shook hands with Tom. "I guess you're avoiding the crowds. That's wise." He turned to Blivit. "Chilly enough for the cabin?"

Snowy looked. In the cabin were two wooden-slat benches down the middle and wooden-slat benches around three sides. Also, a propane heater.

Blivit glanced from Snowy to Tom to Puddles, who in turn glanced at Snowy before saying, "Fresh air is better for seasickness, isn't it. Let's start out sitting outside. If it gets too cold, we'll move."

Erroll said to Dylan, "Time to cast off."

Puddles and Tom and Snowy sat down on the bench on the right side of the boat. The right side, Snowy thought, meant starboard, didn't it? The deck lifted, buoyant, and the mail boat started out of the harbor.

Blivit smiled. "Every boat has its own sound." He went into the cabin. Snowy glimpsed money being handed from him to Erroll. During phone planning, Puddles had told Snowy that Blivit would take care of the tickets and that Snowy should not squawk about this. She didn't, and to her relief Tom didn't notice; he was looking at the shore, at Long Harbor.

Puddles whispered to her, "Erroll is one of those men who call their wives 'Mother.'" She delightedly gave it the full Maine pronunciation: Motha.

Blivit joined them on the bench. Gradually the view of the tiered town behind them diminished to a blur.

Puddles asked Snowy, "Had enough fresh air?"

"Not yet," replied Snowy bravely.

As the mail boat chugged onward and Quarry Island became more distinct, Snowy suddenly imagined approaching it by air. Seen from an airplane, would an island look not like a paradise or a fortress but vulnerable, disconnected, lonesome, a blob of green plopped down on vast blue? She dismissed the image. Anyway, Quarry Island had no runway, much less an airport.

Blivit and Puddles didn't repeat their tour-guide spiels they'd first done in the castle's boat when Snowy and Tom were amongst

151

the guests going from Long Harbor to the castle for Thanksgiving in 2001. Snowy knew what to look for, as did Tom, though today neither of them pointed at landmarks and exclaimed. The island was seven miles from north to south, three miles east to west, with a lighthouse at the northern end, Hutchinson Mountain at the southern. And now in the forest above South Cliff you could begin to discern the castle's red tile roofs, then gray stone towers and turrets. But Snowy was distracted from this usually fascinating sight by the wish that from here you could see around the northern tip to the eastern side of the island. That's where Puddles and Blivit said Cotter Cottage was.

The mail boat began angling toward the northwest harbor. A few lobster boats were moored there, and usually some regular boats as well as the castle's boat, but like Blivit's they must still be in winter storage. Beyond the big public dock the white houses of the village were strung along the rocky shoreline. A clapboard building, once a lobster cannery and long disused, was repaired and back in business, this time freezing lobsters, thanks to Aunt Izzy's efforts to restore industry to Quarry Island, population now thirty-five year-round, about a hundred in the summer. Last fall Aunt Izzy had given guests a tour of Quarry Island Seafood Products, during which Snowy and Tom watched the twelve employees processing whole cooked lobsters and packaging individual lobsters each in an elegant oblong white box where the lobster nestled like a great frozen ruby in a jewelry case. The main customers for this product were inland restaurants and supermarkets. Snowy had been dubious about frozen lobsters, but when the tour ended with a sample of steamed claw meat—well, if she hadn't known it was frozen, she might have been fooled, and Tom had commented, "Most people are used to them imprisoned in tanks anyway, not fresh from the sea, so maybe these taste like the real thing."

Snowy said to Puddles, "The island is still here. Sometimes I think I've dreamed it."

Tom startled her by speaking. "Woodcombe is an island. In its way."

Puddles said, "But you don't get a boat ride!"

Snowy braced herself as the mail boat edged up to what was called a float, a floating platform beside the public dock. Puddles and Blivit helped Dylan tie up and stepped onto the float. No wobbliness for Puddles, nor of course for Blivit, who took Snowy's hand and held her steady. When she was safe on the float, he hesitated about Tom, then held out his hand, which Tom gripped.

Then came the unloading of their baggage, for which Erroll appeared from the cabin. He told Snowy and Tom, "If this was a weekday, we'd have anything from propane tanks to lumber for cargo. And come summer, you wouldn't believe the tourists' bicycles. I hate bicycles."

Puddles giggled, giving Snowy the briefcase and laptop.

Blivit said to Erroll, "Puddles and I will drop in on Aunt Izzy, and then Tom will bring us back here by twelve-thirty."

"I won't wait," Erroll said. "If you're late, you'll be stranded."

Quiet amusement between him and Blivit.

Erroll said, "My best to your aunt."

Then came yet another of what Puddles had called stages, carrying everything over to the small parking lot, where, amid various vehicles seemingly half-dead, the Jeep Wagoneer awaited them, moldering contentedly. Puddles had explained that years ago on the mainland, when the Jeep was ready to be traded in Blivit instead had had it brought out on a barge to replace its predecessor junker, which had finally croaked. Snowy clutched tighter her briefcase containing a copy of the latest draft of the poem about island cars.

The Jeep wasn't locked, and they loaded it. Blivit produced keys from a pocket and handed them to Tom, saying, "I'll sit up front and give directions."

"Perishables," Puddles said, taking a folded tote bag out of her shoulder bag. "First we stop at the store for milk and whatever. Snowy and I will shop, you guys can sit in the Jeep and chew the fat."

So Tom drove past the dock to the little weathered-gray general store. A co-op operated by volunteers, it was open only three hours on Sundays, ten to one, timed around church-going and the mail boat. It had a look entirely different from any of Ruhamah's three stores: almost stark naked, no trees protecting it, no mountains hovering. And if it ran out of your favorite treat or ran out of food entirely, you couldn't jump in your car and drive to Gunthwaite's supermarkets. You could jump in your boat and head for Long Harbor—if you had a boat.

Puddles and Snowy went inside, where a half-dozen people made the place seem busy. Like the Woodcombe General Store, this store was a gathering place.

"Hi, Veronica," Puddles called to the woman at the checkout counter, whom Snowy had met before when stopping at the store's summer crafts shop to buy souvenir presents (a sea-lavender wreath for Lavender; a seashell bracelet for Bev; a bait bag for Ruhamah, who stored garlic in it). Veronica wore her gray hair as long and straight as she must have worn her hippie hair when she and her husband had come to the island in the back-to-the-land days of the 1970s. She also still wore tie-dyed T-shirts. Puddles explained, "Snowy and Tom are here on vacation, at Cotter Cottage. Tom's recuperating from knee replacements."

"Izzy was telling me," Veronica said. "*Both* knees at once, isn't it amazing what can be done." Leaning across the counter, she hugged Snowy. "You look like you could use an island vacation. How's Tom doing?"

Snowy almost burst into tears. "Fine, thank you." She hurried to the dairy section before she actually did start crying. Milk; whole here, the store didn't have skim. Eggs; it didn't have

Egg Beaters either, and anyway, wasn't the ban on eggs being lifted by the nutritional powers-that-be? Real butter, to melt for the lobsters they would buy tomorrow at the island lobstermen's co-op, which was closed on Sundays. The store of course stocked Quarry Island Ice Cream, in pints and quarts. The flavors were limited here but they had Tom's favorite, Chocolate Pure and Simple. She chose a quart and moved on to meat and vegetables, deciding on a package of sliced ham for lunch sandwiches, a package of ground beef and a cellophane-wrapped head of tired iceberg lettuce for tonight's supper.

Back in the Jeep, Tom and Blivit didn't look like they'd been chewing the fat. Tom looked as if he were flaked out after climbing Mount Washington, and Blivit looked at home, contemplating the harbor. Snowy and Puddles climbed into the backseat.

"Now," Puddles said, "Cotter Cottage."

Tom drove on past the teensy-weensy post office, the granite town hall with its granite watering trough, and the granite church whose steeple had a weather vane shaped like a fish. Snowy watched both Puddles and Blivit gaze at this church in which they'd been married. Then came the churchyard cemetery. Then the white clapboard one-room schoolhouse, then village houses, some fixed up by summer people, others lived in year-round, well-worn. On the outskirts were three small raw new homes, the result of Aunt Izzy's low-income-housing project.

Blivit said, "We're afraid one of these families won't be suited to island life after all. That'll bring the school population down to seven. Okay, now we take the dirt road after the lighthouse, before you come to the road to South Cliff."

The white lighthouse was automated but had once been kept by Aunt Izzy's uncle. Tom turned left onto the road, one they'd never been on before, a muddy bumpy track through woods, descending into the half shell of a little cove. Snowy's heart began to race.

155

Blivit said, "That's the driveway."

Tom turned left again, onto an even narrower gravel track, a driveway that led down to a bedraggled ranch house whose faded red paint was peeling. The snow squall in which Puddles had snapped the photo of the house had actually been merciful. Two rusty propane tanks hunkered beside the front door. Lichens covered the curling roof shingles like scabs. A woodshed tacked onto one end of the house was so ravaged by weather that it hardly sheltered the few sticks of firewood within. At the other end, a gray clothesline sagged across sparse brown grass to a skinny tree.

Puddles and Blivit had said the place needed some upkeep. It needed a wrecking ball.

This was her own damn fault. She'd rented a pig in a poke.

Feeling sick to her stomach, she climbed out of the Jeep. The wind was brisk and salty. From here she could see that the backyard dipped to a rickety dock, where waves were swirling green and frothy against rocks shaggy with seaweed.

Okay, she told herself, calm down. The cottage is awful but the ocean is—the ocean, right here.

The ocean.

What the hell had she been thinking? The ocean. Alan had had to go to the lake. Tom would have the ocean right at the door.

6

BLIVIT SAID, "THE KEY is here," and lifted a stone beside the doorstep. With the key he unlocked the door, then he stood aside, waiting for Snowy to enter first.

She did and found herself looking at the ocean again, this time across a living room through big picture windows. The windows seemed foggy. She ventured closer and inspected. They were made of thermal glass, and ocean gales must have stretched the glass and broken the seal and thus moisture had got in, blurring the view. This would drive her crazy. A maple dining table was placed in front of the windows, so you'd often be sitting here trying to see through the damn things. On the left, the plain glass of the back door's storm door was decorated with aluminum scrolls that interrupted a clear view of the cove.

His parka unzipped, Blivit showed Tom the propane heater set against the outside wall, saying, "You know how these work, see, the place will warm up quickly, and the fireplace will supplement—oh hell, I forgot to remind Ben to bring over some dry firewood and kindling. Well, I'll ask him to do it this afternoon."

Ben must work Sundays; he was the castle's gatekeeper and handyman and lived in the gatekeeper's cottage. Snowy turned to the rest of the room, to its knotty-pine walls, its fieldstone fireplace in front of which two threadbare slipcovered armchairs faced a rump-sprung sofa. And what was in the middle of this sitting area? A knotty-pine coffee table. On one side of the fireplace squatted a TV even older than the one she and Tom had. Everything looked neglected far longer than the amount of time Mildred Cotter had been away in the hospital and rehab place. Snowy thought of the first house she and Alan owned, across Pevensay Point Road from

159

the ocean, a falling-down shingled shack that had been a lobster-man's shed, called a fish house. They had fixed it up; they had made it a real year-round home. Frugality was one thing, but Cotter Cottage hadn't received tender-loving-care.

Yet the room was clean. Probably Aunt Izzy had asked Mary Frances, who did housekeeping at the castle, to tidy up. The braided rugs were becoming unbraided, but they had been vacuumed. Then Snowy noticed that on the far inside wall were two prints of paintings. In frames that maybe had come from Woolworth's ages ago, the prints were bleached pale by sunshine, but the styles were still obvious, and thanks to four years of rooming with art-major Harriet she recognized one as a Gauguin in Tahiti and the other as Seurat's most famous painting, whose title she couldn't remember. Beside them a doorway showed a little knotty-pine hallway with two doors ajar. Through the gap on the left she glimpsed a yellowed plastic shower curtain tucked inside a 1950s-pink bathtub; the gap straight ahead revealed a knotty-pine wall, the foot of a bed covered with a white bedspread, and, set beneath a window, a slant-top desk and its straight-backed chair, both painted a blue now badly chipped.

Blivit and Tom had progressed to inspecting the thermal glass, Blivit saying, "I can't convince Mildred to hire a glass company to send a person out to replace it."

Snowy crossed the living room into the narrow knotty-pine kitchen, where Puddles was emptying her tote bag onto the Formica countertop. Mr. Coffee already stood there alongside a row of old mottled chrome canisters. The kitchen was too small to hold a table. Then Snowy stepped to the sink, to the promised window, and the room opened up to the cove.

Puddles put the ice cream in the old refrigerator's little freezer. "I warned you about the condition this place is in. You can change your mind and accept Aunt Izzy's invitation to stay with her."

"No, no. It's so cozy."

"Okay, I'll tell her you're settling in." Puddles arranged the rest of the perishables on the fridge shelves. "Blivit! Time for the quickie with Aunt Izzy!"

Laughing, Blivit leaned into the kitchen, making it small again. "Shouldn't you rephrase that? Anyway, first we unload the Jeep."

Snowy and Tom went back outdoors with them, but Blivit and Puddles did most of the transfer, setting luggage and backpacks and tote bags down inside the front door. Then off they jounced in the Jeep. Tom went into the bathroom.

There were some hooks on the wall beside the front door. Snowy unzipped her parka, hung it up, and carried into the kitchen the tote bags of the groceries she'd brought from Woodcombe. She examined the old Revere Ware teakettle on the gas range. When had it last been used? Mary Frances had dusted it, as well as everything else. At the sink Snowy filled it, then put it on the stove, figured out which knob went to which burner, and in a tote bag located a box of Twinings Earl Grey tea bags. In a cupboard she found a surprising collection of souvenir mugs: Ernest Hemingway at his Key West house; the Grand Canyon; the Hollywood sign; the Eiffel Tower; Winston Churchill at Blenheim Palace. She chose the Key West mug for Tom, because it meant hot weather, and Blenheim for herself, for the memory of visiting it with Alan. She opened the rest of the cupboard doors to shelves of Blue Willow plates, glass plates shaped like fish, sturdy Libbey tumblers and wineglasses, Revere Ware saucepans, a CorningWare casserole dish, a set of striped mixing bowls, a big iron skillet, a small iron skillet, and a lobster steamer pot.

She heard Tom emerge from the bathroom. She said, "My turn," and went in. Pink washbasin and toilet to match the tub. A washing machine, fairly recent, probably brought here on the mail boat, a necessary replacement of an older one that had conked out. But no dryer.

Back in the kitchen, as she made tea she kept looking out the window. She could no longer see Quarry Island on the horizon; she was *on* Quarry Island.

She took the mugs into the living room where Tom, still bundled up in his parka, was huddled in the armchair nearest the fireplace, scowling at the cold hearth. She set the mugs on the coffee table, sat down on the sofa and sank deep. Should she try to make conversation?

She said, "I'm getting curious about Mildred Cotter."

He reached for his mug and did a double take at Hemingway, then at Churchill.

"Unless these mugs are gifts," she said, "she didn't spend all her summer vacations on the island and—or—she did a lot of traveling after she retired. And those prints over there—" She heard her cell phone ring. Where was it? She hurried to her shoulder bag amongst the luggage on the living-room floor.

Ruhamah asked, "Are you on the island?"

"Yes." Snowy checked her wristwatch. Almost quarter past twelve. Puddles and Blivit were cutting it close again. "You're at the Woodcombe store? How was the Sunday brunch crowd?"

"The usual, it was busy. How is Tom doing?"

The Jeep's horn honked. "He's fine," Snowy said, "and we're now taking Puddles and Blivit back to the mail boat, sorry, big rush, I'll phone you tonight. Bye."

Tom was off the sofa, limping toward the door. "You don't have to come."

"I'd like to." She grabbed her parka.

They clambered into the backseat and Blivit swung the Jeep around in the driveway as Puddles said, "Aunt Izzy says, 'Welcome!' and she'll let you get rested up before she pesters you to come to dinner later this week."

Blivit said, "Ben will be along with the firewood."

162

Tom asked, "But shouldn't this Mildred Cotter be supplying it as part of the rental?"

"Extended family," Blivit said somewhat obscurely and stepped on the gas.

At the dock's parking lot they all got out of the Jeep. Snowy and Tom followed Puddles and Blivit hastening down to the mail boat, where two teenagers were saying good-bye to parents before they returned to Long Harbor after a weekend at home.

Erroll boomed, "Well, well, I was about to leave without you," and Puddles hugged Snowy, whispering, "Remember, if you need anything, don't be shy, for God's sake. Call Aunt Izzy. And call *me*."

Then everybody was aboard, waving as the mail boat chugged away.

Snowy looked at Tom. He looked at her. The wind tugged at them, reminding her of the constant presence of the wind on the Isle of Lewis. Vacation, she thought. The sudden shock of vacation. She and Tom had never had a vacation quite like this trip to Quarry Island. They had traveled in Scotland. They had done backpacks in New Hampshire's mountains. They had spent Christmas with his mother in Florida. They had visited Puddles and Blivit in Long Harbor and at the castle. But two weeks together in a cottage? With no schedule, no routine?

"Lunch," she said. "I'll make lunch."

They walked back to the Jeep. Tom drove through the village, past the lighthouse, and turned onto the little muddy road to Dark Cove. As he parked in front of the cottage, she heard another vehicle.

Ben's black pickup rattled after them down the driveway loaded with wood. Ben parked beside the Jeep and hopped out, a lean man in his fifties, his thick hair white but his face young (maybe, Snowy had speculated, because of his carefree bachelor life in the gatehouse). Aunt Izzy once told Tom and Snowy that island-

163

ers had to be MacGyvers and referred to Ben's resourcefulness. To think that Aunt Izzy had watched the *MacGyver* TV show!

Ben regarded the woodshed. "That thing wouldn't protect a splinter. I'll stack some indoors. Brought a tarp for the rest."

Tom said, "I'll give you a hand."

Ben shot Snowy a glance, so he must know about the new knees, but he said only, "Thanks."

Indoors, taking off her parka, Snowy thought about Ruhamah's phone call. Usually Ruhamah would wait for a call from her mother. Why had Ruhamah called first? Just because of worry about Tom, or was something wrong? The baby. Should she call Ruhamah back now, not tonight? But Ruhamah was closing up the store and as always would be taking paperwork home. And wasn't that what Snowy herself should be doing, helping Ruhamah, working, not frittering away two weeks?

She carried the luggage and shoulder bag into the bedroom, now seeing the full room, the thin old white chenille bedspread on a basic bedstead; a double bed, not single. Had Mildred wanted the extra space for sprawling—or? A maple bureau. No photos on the bureau. She opened a drawer. Empty. On a captain's chair were piled extra blankets. Maybe Puddles's suggestion to Aunt Izzy, passed along to Mary Frances? Pushing open a closet curtain that had apparently been made from an old blue flannel sheet, she saw that the closet was empty too, only some wire hangers at the back, new white plastic ones in front. Aunt Izzy again, supplying coat hangers from the castle? Beside the bed stood a small two-shelf bookcase. Snowy fetched her glasses from her shoulder bag, leaned down, and started reading the authors. She stopped and stared. Mary Stewart. Were they all by Mary Stewart? Yes, yes, Mildred had all the novels except the Arthurian Saga ones. Mildred had arranged her collection in chronological order, from *Madam, Will You Talk?* to *Rose Cottage*, and, Snowy remembered, what a lot of armchair travel that included! Provence, the French

Pyrenees, Delphi, Crete, Corfu, Austria, Syria, Lebanon, various British locales—such as Skye in *Wildfire at Midnight*, which had kept her company at the hospital with Tom. But there was romance in Mary Stewart's novels as well as travel. Had Mildred had a love affair? More than one? Here on Quarry Island or in Portland or elsewhere? Had she lived her life alone because of a broken heart?

Listening to Tom and Ben stacking wood in the living room, Snowy unpacked clothes into the bureau's upper drawers and onto the new hangers, now and then pausing to touch the blue desk. Finally she opened its slanted lid. Empty. The ocean view from its window was clear, not fogged, but for a moment the waves seemed to be—well, waving, like the passengers on the mail boat.

She was getting punchy.

The noise of stacking indoors changed to outdoor noises. Returning to the living room, she saw out the front window that Tom and Ben were emptying the rest of the wood off the pickup onto the driveway. She carried her briefcase and laptop into the bedroom and put the briefcase on the floor beside the desk, the laptop within.

In the kitchen, she unpacked the grocery tote bags, setting out a bag of Wise potato chips, a loaf of Pepperidge Farm whole-wheat bread, a jar of Grey Poupon mustard, a jar of Vlasic dill pickles, a package of Vanity Fair napkins. She took two of the glass fish plates for sandwich plates. Was she playing house?

By the time she'd made the ham sandwiches and the teakettle was whistling, ready to make more tea, Tom had come indoors and begun meticulously placing kindling in the fireplace. He was an authority on kindling; he and David cut up some of their leftover pieces of lumber into kindling and sold bags of it at her store. She brought the plates and mugs to the coffee table, not the dining table.

"I'm starving," she said, and, instead of waiting for him, she bit into her sandwich.

After lunch, Tom fell asleep in the armchair that was now his. Asleep? She tiptoed near, watched and listened. He was breathing. If she tried to remove his glasses she would wake him up, so she let him nap wearing them. She herself should sit and read and relax. She didn't choose a book from her tote bags; she chose Mildred's *Madam, Will You Talk?*, sat down on the sofa, and read until she too nodded off. When she awoke, he wasn't in his armchair. At the fogged window, she saw him in the back-yard walking toward the shore. He was wearing his parka. You wouldn't put on a parka, would you, if you intended to—

Without her parka she tore out the back door, running disjointedly, uncoordinated in sheer panic, feeling as if she were flying apart.

He turned. She slowed and tried to look calm as she joined him.

"Napping," she said. "It's a well-known fact that the ocean air makes people hungry and sleepy."

He didn't reply. They walked together onto the dock and stood braced, the wind blowing against them, the surf churning saltiness.

THERE WAS A routine after all. A vacation routine.

The next day, Monday, dawn began along the horizon with smoky stripes of gray-blue and mauve, and then up swam a sunny orb, hooray! But Mildred's thermometer beside the back door registered an outside temperature of only thirty-four degrees. In his winter bathrobe, Tom fiddled with the propane heater and stirred up the embers in the fireplace. The chilly bathroom had an electric heater; Snowy hurried through a shower in the decaying pink tub and pulled on Levi's, a plain blue T-shirt and a blue Woodcombe

General Store sweatshirt, thinking over her phone call to Ruhamah last evening. Ruhamah had learned that D. J. would be coming home from Washington on Wednesday for the Thursday ultrasound. Ruhamah's voice when telling her this became light and giddy, and Snowy had tried to muffle the tears in her own voice. Happy tears, weren't they, but Ruhamah might not recognize that over the phone. Now she felt tearful again. Goddamn these tears! Think of that beautiful sunrise! And, inspired by the sunrise, she decided to make eggs sunny-side-up for breakfast.

Last evening she and Tom had eaten their hamburg patties and salad at the dining table, the fogged window just mildly annoying in the fading light. This morning she didn't care, she was too relieved that the day would be sunny, so when Tom emerged from his shower she served breakfast there. Then she did dishes, keeping tabs on the ocean out the window while Tom puttered with the living room's firewood. When she didn't hear him anymore, she stepped into the living room and saw that he was sitting sound asleep in his armchair, a Hamish Macbeth mystery fallen onto his lap.

Once again she tiptoed to him, watching his chest under his blue fleece vest, gray sweatshirt, white T-shirt. He was breathing. Okay, he could nap in the morning as well as the afternoon; he was on vacation. The house now felt very warm to her, but she went into the bedroom, picked up an extra blanket from the captain's chair, and softly draped it over him.

What to do with the morning? Go for a walk? No. She mustn't leave Tom. She returned to the bedroom. On the bureau, her cell phone and Tom's waited in their chargers. No. She mustn't phone Ruhamah again so soon. That captain's chair would be handy to sit in to put on shoes or slippers, but not with those extra blankets piled on it, so she should store them. In the bureau? When she'd unpacked, she hadn't used the bureau's bottom drawer. She opened it. At first she thought the paper in it was a drawer liner. Then she

167

leaned closer and realized it was a large folded map. Unfolding it on the bed, she saw islands. Her glasses were in the desk, which last night she'd decided to designate as their place; eyeglasses and keys had to have special places where they always were kept. She put her glasses on and read: Indonesia.

Indonesia? Mildred Cotter had certainly got around!

Then she noticed that there was a piece of paper still in the drawer. Blank. She turned it over and realized it was a print, this one botanical and geographic. Some kind of green plant with little white flowers entwined a blue-surrounded green island, which calligraphy at the top told her was St. Thomas. Puddles had honeymooned on St. Thomas with her first husband. More calligraphy at the bottom said: "The Love Vine. Considered an aphrodisiac, it is a parasite that kills the host plant. The love vine kills what it embraces."

My God. Chilled, she dropped the print back into the drawer and smothered it with the extra blankets. While cleaning, had Mary Frances mistaken the papers for a drawer liner or had she investigated and also recoiled, slamming the drawer shut, leaving Mildred's personal possessions seemingly undisturbed?

Snowy took the Indonesia map to the desk and sat down, trying to make sense of this and the print. Maybe Mildred had visited St. Thomas, had a love affair there. A shipboard romance? Or in Indonesia? A romance that had damaged her forever?

Let's not get carried away.

Last night, after watching some TV with Tom, she had been only semi-dozing in the unfamiliar bed, too tired for real sleep, when the sound of the ocean and wind brought a word into her mind: rote. A word from her Pevensay years, meaning the noise of the surf on the shore.

She opened the briefcase, took out the folder of poems and a legal pad, and picked up a pencil. A while later she glanced out the window and saw a cormorant perched on one of the dock's pilings, holding its wings out. Little Ruhamah at the Pevensay house had called cormorants "M's" because that's what they looked like.

Alan, we're going to be grandparents. You can come back now.

She heard Tom getting up, adding logs on the fire. When he went outdoors, she hurried to a living-room window and watched him tighten the sagging clothesline. When he started back, she retreated to the desk. Looking over her shoulder, she saw him in his armchair, reading the Hamish Macbeth. So she could concentrate again on pencil and legal pad. As noon neared, the wide sky's sun through the desk window grew so hot that she took her hiking cap off the closet shelf, and put it on—to shade her face indoors at the desk!

And thus the vacation days commenced. After breakfast Tom would fall asleep while reading; she would work at the desk. After lunch, they walked down the backyard to the rocks at the cove's edge, then into the woods along the shore until they came to a boarded-up gray-shingled cottage, an unknown next-door-neighbor's. The return route was the same but the views seemed different.

Then they would go for a drive, which reminded her of going for Sunday drives with her grandparents in her child-hood. Now she and Tom were the old folks. Their route took them around the island, and as Tom drove they kept an eye out for deer in the road. The island was overrun with deer, which Puddles said some people called rats with antlers. At Quarry Pond, Tom would unnerve her by slowing the Jeep down and staring into the pond, sheer and deep. Islanders swam here instead of the ocean. (Those who *could* swim; Blivit said that old-timers claimed—jokingly?—that there was no point in learning because the ocean was so cold it would kill you before you could swim a stroke.) Blocks of granite lay tumbled around the brim, remnants of the old quarrying industry.

Next came more history, the Hutchinson place under Hutchinson Mountain. The white farmhouse had been added onto in the traditional way, higgledy-piggledy, ells and sheds rambling to the gray barn. Aunt Izzy's granddaughter, Florence, now lived in the farmhouse with Mildred's grandnephew, Roddy, her lobster-man husband, and their children, Christopher age six, Priscilla age four. Snowy and Tom had accompanied Puddles and Blivit on visits here. Over the decades, the farmhouse had acquired all the conveniences that the ice-cream fortune could buy, but the genera-tions of Hutchinsons had deliberately not changed its essence, so the kitchen still hunched low, with plaster walls and crooked floors, and Snowy could imagine Flossie Hutchinson here in the 1890s making ice cream for her children, ice cream that soon was in such demand at the island's ice-cream socials and summer people's cottages that the busy kitchen hummed, children helping, the little business supporting the family now that Flossie's husband had been crippled in an accident. Eventually Flossie's oldest son built the ice-cream plant on the mainland.

In the pasture, the warm liquid gaze of the Guernseys didn't quell Snowy's apprehension about a spring-fever stampede.

Tuesday afternoon, as the road curved on to a cove where a lobster boat named *Florence* was moored, Snowy saw Florence and Roddy and the kids (the school day over) all busy at the farm's fish house festooned with nets and buoys, its open door showing an interior filled with a workbench, tools, cans of paint and gas and oil, yellow slickers. Roddy must be getting ready to set out his traps. The family waved. Snowy waved, and Tom raised an index finger off the steering wheel in the lazy style some guys affected at home and here. This was the first time she'd seen Tom do it. Lazy, on vacation?

They next passed the little Hutchinson cemetery she had walked around in with Puddles, reading the crumbling gravestones of ancestors and the most recent gravestones of Blivit's first wife and his parents. Puddles's favorite gravestone, old and blotched, belonged to a Lucy Hutchinson, wife of a sea captain whose gravestone was next to hers. Puddles said that according to Blivit, Lucy had always accompanied her husband on his voyages until their child was born. Lucy controlled her restlessness the following year, feeling that a ship was no place for a baby, but then the call of the sea overtook her; she left the baby with her parents and went with her husband on a voyage to the Caribbean. There she fell ill with a fever and died. "And," Puddles had related with relish, "her husband brought her home in a barrel of rum."

That terrible practicality never ceased to awe Snowy.

Now, somebody had set out several baskets of pansies throughout the cemetery. For color before Memorial Day's red geraniums? Usually the first sight of pansies each spring would make Snowy tell Tom that one of the old names for pansies was "Kiss-Her-in-the-Pantry." But she didn't this year.

Tom braked, and two deer leapt across the road, white pom-pom tails bouncing.

"Jesus!" he said.

Next came a little weathered sign marking the Hutchinson Mountain trailhead. Tom hadn't yet commented on it, so Snowy didn't. They continued past the castle's gate, open in off-season with Ben's granite cottage standing guard, and on around the island, looking at trees draped in silvery lichens, looking out to sea, braking for deer.

The first day she'd tucked their digital camera into her shoulder bag. But neither of them felt the need to take photos, on the drive or at the cottage.

They timed the drive so that they would reach the village just as the mail boat arrived from Long Harbor on its afternoon run. The island's lifeline! She and Tom would join the group on the dock watching the unloading of material for springtime construction and repairs. On each occasion Dylan and another

171

deckhand manhandled out a startling assortment of supplies, some of which Tom had to identify for her, such as reinforcing rods. There was also lumber, a big coil of wire, a boxed fiberglass shower, and Wednesday a crane on the dock lifted out, on pallets, sheets of drywall and sacks of concrete mix. Then there were the store's supplies, in which she took a professional interest, worrying over a case of milk set on the dock in the bright curdling sun, laughing as a village woman applauded paper products and exclaimed, "Thank heavens, toilet paper!"

When the passengers had boarded and the mail boat departed, Snowy would concoct an excuse to go to the store, to get an onion, an Almond Joy, while Tom waited in the Jeep. The store would be full of chat, with people leaning against the counter, a man sitting on the freezer chest, and behind the counter Veronica in her tie-dyes or an older woman, Anne, who sat on a stool knitting with string, making those net funnels that went inside lobster traps. Would the funnels actually be used or were they souvenirs for the summer crafts shop? (Monday, Snowy couldn't remember what they were called; Tuesday, she remembered they were trap heads.) Puddles had told her that Blivit differentiated between the manners of mainland locals and the manners of islanders, claiming that the mainlanders held back out of suspicion but the islanders did because of natural reserve. However, Snowy received friendly curiosity, everybody interested in how she and Tom were doing at Cotter Cottage. They asked her about Tom's knees and about the store on her sweatshirt. Explaining that her daughter was minding the store, she didn't mention that Ruhamah was also overseeing two other stores, but she did say that Ruhamah and her husband were expecting a baby. Which got smiles.

After the store on Monday, they stopped at the post office and Snowy went in to tell postmistress Cheryl that they were at Cotter Cottage for two weeks, on the off chance somebody sent a real letter instead of an e-mail. But Cheryl had already been alerted by Aunt Izzy. Snowy reported this to Tom, adding, "Remember how Aunt Izzy once held forth on the island's creed of 'Don't interfere'? She said it was a necessary creed, to maintain some privacy. But I think Aunt Izzy is a law unto herself."

Tom grunted. She decided to interpret it as agreement.

You can't eat lobsters for supper every night. Can you? On Monday and Wednesday she and Tom next stopped at the house in the village owned by the man in charge of the island lobstermen's co-op. Although it was early in the season, he had some to sell, and they bought two one-and-a-quarter pounders. But—moderation in all things!—Tuesday she served hamburg. Thursday she was distracted, worrying about the ultrasound. She made herself stick to the schedule of the afternoon drive, and after the mail boat left she dawdled in the store, buying a copy of the weekly *Long Harbor News* that the mail boat had brought, but all the time she was listening for the cell phone in her shoulder bag. When they got back to the cottage, she stepped into the kitchen, planning a non-lobster supper, spaghetti, and the phone rang.

She cried, "Hello, Ruhamah?"

"Hi, Mother. It's a boy! Alan Sutherland Washburn."

For once, the lurking tears didn't spill. Snowy leaned against the cupboards, looking out the sink window. "Oh, Ruhamah."

"Yes," Ruhamah said.

After a silence, Snowy asked, "Is everything—all right?"

"Yes. Now we'll phone Dudley and Charl. Bye!"

She went into the living room. Would Tom care? He already had two grandsons. Also, two sons, and every evening he'd been saying he should phone David to check on the workshop, but he hadn't.

She said, "That was Ruhamah—the ultrasound—the baby is a boy."

For the first time since the knees surgery, he went to her, put his arms around her, held her.

AT THE DESK that evening, Snowy phoned Bev. "It's a boy! Now I can do some serious shopping, except there are no shops here and anyway, I only really know about girls' baby clothes. Ruffles!"

Bev said, "Trust me, there are adorable baby-boy clothes. And you'll have plenty of time to shop when you get home. How is the vacation, how's Tom?"

Snowy glanced out into the living room, where Tom was partly reading the Long Harbor newspaper and partly watching a TV show, *30 Rock*. She said, "We're into a routine, but it's a different one from home. How are you?"

"Snowy, Roger has lost his mind! He's talking about going back to work! Either in Connecticut, and wouldn't Dick love that, having his aged father return to the firm, or else taking the New Hampshire bar exam and joining some firm here, as if anyone is hiring in these trying times!"

"Why?" But Snowy bet she knew why Roger was talking about work.

"Money. To get some money coming in. Our investments are—evaporating."

Snowy didn't know what to say.

Bev said, "Wasn't the weather lovely today, in the fifties here, it's supposed to be rainy tomorrow but clearing this weekend when we thespians are going to open up the barn and start getting it ready for the season. Are you eating lots of lobster?"

"Lots."

"Give Ruhamah my love."

"I will. Bev—"

"Bye."

Snowy sat at the desk, suddenly too exhausted to phone Puddles next with the news. She opened her laptop and sent Puddles an e-mail: "It's a boy!" Then she went into the living room and dropped into her armchair.

Tom suddenly laughed. Actually laughed. Not at the TV screen but at something in the newspaper. He looked up and said, "Here's a help-wanted ad from that lobster pound in Long Harbor."

"Leander's Lobster Pound?"

He read aloud, "'Must be able to lift at least one-hundred-pound crates and move barrels of bait.' Talk about local color."

She laughed. "I gather it's not an ad for a waitress?"

But he quickly went somber. "I could've done that years ago without thinking twice."

Work. Ruhamah juggling three stores. Was Ruhamah's plan still holding, the combination and consolidation of supplies? Bev had said, "These trying times." Snowy's mind sought Thomas Paine's words about revolution: "These are the times that try men's souls."

The next morning reminded her of a Mother Goose rhyme about a "misty moisty morning, when cloudy was the weather." But so far it wasn't raining. While Tom napped, at her desk Snowy opened her laptop to check for e-mail and found Puddles quoting another nursery rhyme. "'Snips and snails,'" wrote Puddles, "'and puppy-dog tails, that's what little boys are made of!' Have R. and D. J. decided on a name?"

Snowy realized that she hadn't told Puddles the boy-and-girl names they'd chosen. She wrote back simply, "Alan."

A reply came zooming back. "Holy shit. Are you okay with that?"

Out over the cove, seagulls were hanging on the wind. Snowy wrote, "I'm very happy."

She e-mailed Charl and Dudley, and then she closed the laptop, picked up a pencil, and on her legal pad started work on the new poem, about tote bags. Years ago at Hurricane Farm she had written about boots and country living.

Eventually she heard a car descending the driveway. Who could it be? She glanced at her wristwatch. Ten o'clock already! She hurried into the living room, where Tom was struggling up from his armchair, and together they looked out the front window as an old Volvo station wagon stopped beside the Jeep.

She said, "Aunt Izzy."

When they'd seen Blivit's aunt most recently, last autumn, she was still going strong, a small energetic woman darting around, white curls bouncing, and winter didn't seem to have slowed her down. Wearing a yellow slicker, she jumped out of the driver's seat and scooted for the front door, which Snowy hastily opened.

"A grandson!" Aunt Izzy said, entering full-speed-ahead, walking and talking. "Puddles phoned me with the news. And I thought, here Snowy is out on this island when she must yearn to be with her daughter discussing little boys, and since I'm going to be stopping at the school I thought you might like to join me and see some little boys. There are three; girls predominate. The youngest boy, age five, is in our kindergarten along with my great-granddaughter Priscilla. At age four, Priscilla might be deemed too young for kindergarten but in Maine this decision is up to the local school boards, and our school board knows our Priscilla. You come along too, Tom. After all, you were a little boy once, and probably you still are. Who was it who said that all men are six years old—was it Miss Marple?"

"Miss Marple?" echoed Snowy, her mind spinning, thinking of Bev as Mrs. Price Ridley in a Miss Marple play. She saw that under her open slicker Aunt Izzy was wearing old Levi's and a sweatshirt that said: Practice Random Acts of Kindness and Senseless Acts of Beauty.

Aunt Izzy surveyed the living room. "Are you keeping warm? Do you have everything you need? I know Puddles told you to let me know, but you make sure you do. Come along, the children will be at morning recess, and I've got the Friday surprise."

The surprise to Snowy was that Tom showed interest. He asked, "The Friday surprise?"

"Emily bakes a surprise snack for Fridays," Aunt Izzy said. "Whoopie pies today, mini-size—"

Emily Hewitt, an island native and granddaughter of Aunt Izzy's dearest island friend who'd died years ago, lived at the castle and looked after Aunt Izzy as much as anybody could.

"—with a seasonal touch, the filling is flavored with maple syrup. Put on those slickers I see on the hooks, but let's hope the rain holds off."

Tom asked, "Shall we follow in the Jeep?"

"No, no, don't bother."

Snowy grabbed her shoulder bag. They went outdoors to the Volvo in which she and Tom would ride with an octogenarian.

Aunt Izzy told him, "Sit up front with me," and added to Snowy, "I can't resist a handsome man!"

Tom obeyed. Snowy got into the backseat and sat beside a big Tupperware box. She puzzled over the seat belt, but Aunt Izzy didn't bother putting on hers and, unusual for him, neither did Tom, so she gave up.

Sedately, Aunt Izzy did her version of a three-point turn and ascended the driveway. On the little dirt road she said, "I expect that in your Woodcombe in the old days, there were several one-room schoolhouses in the various neighborhoods."

Tom said, "Yes. The historical society managed to rescue and restore a survivor, and it's open for events in the summer. The rest are gone, were moved to become a shed or something, or were abandoned. A schoolhouse in Little Harbor out on the main road to our hometown of Gunthwaite has survived as a café, the Schoolhouse Café."

Snowy wondered if this was the lengthiest speech he'd made these past months.

Aunt Izzy turned right onto the island's main road and said, "Little Harbor."

"Yup," Tom said with a grin, "we live in the Lakes Region, and we have fresh-water harbors. Also coves, dark and otherwise."

Murray Cove in Woodcombe Lake, where Alan had drowned.

But Tom wasn't thinking of that, thank God. Aunt Izzy, who didn't know, laughed. Then braked. On the lawn of the lighthouse, a deer watched the car approach. However, it stayed put as Aunt Izzy crept past and sped up, saying, "In the past, the island neighborhoods had their own schools, but when the population began dropping they closed, all except the village school, and parents brought their children there. We've also had several interesting versions of school buses. The most popular was Veronica's Volkswagen bus. Painted with flowers, you know. The village schoolhouse has of course been updated over the years, but it hasn't really changed. Probably Blivit has told you about the ever-present worry that the number of children will fall so low the school will have to close or that the teacher will want to move on. We've had young Amber since last September, coming here right out of the University of Massachusetts thinking that a Maine island is romantic despite our warnings. She learned the reality this winter. Although on the island it seems we keep even busier in the winter than in the summer—visiting and suppers and playing cards and sewing and knitting, volleyball in the town hall and skating on the pond, and it's the time to repair traps—where was I? Oh, despite keeping busy, winter can still begin to gnaw at you. I expect young Amber is now job-hunting on the Internet every spare moment."

Snowy thought of the past winter in Woodcombe. She remembered shoveling and shoveling, the blizzards, the noisy nights of wind and snow pelting the apartment windows; she remembered her fixation on suet pudding. How would it have been for a young woman on a Maine island, the claustrophobia of isolation, the unrelenting background roar of sea and gales?

Aunt Izzy said, "Here we are."

The village, Snowy supposed, would have been roused from its bleakness by the morning arrival of the mail boat at quarter of eight and departure at eight. Now it was lively again, with kids in the schoolyard, girls with jump ropes, boys on swings and the jungle gym. She found herself anxiously counting. Nine kids. However, hadn't Blivit said that one of the new families might be leaving?

Springing out of the car, Aunt Izzy called, "Owen!"

But all the kids turned at the sound of her voice, and they all came running. Aunt Izzy said to Tom, "Take charge of the Tupperware," and caught the smallest boy's hand. "Owen, I want you to meet my friend Snowy." She put his hand in Snowy's. "Say how-do-you-do." Then she was greeting her great-grandchildren and leading everyone toward the stark white schoolhouse.

Snowy said, "Hello, Owen."

"How-do-you-do." He shook her hand, let her hold on to his. A self-possessed five-year-old. His wind-ruffled hair was dark blond, his blue eyes alert. It was possible that he might resemble the combination of Ruhamah and D. J. But more important was his little-boyness. How had Aunt Izzy known? Well, Aunt Izzy had a son, a grandson, and a great-grandson.

Still holding Owen's hand, Snowy walked with him into the schoolhouse's hallway, where the kids hadn't paused to hang up their jackets in their rush to gather around the Tupperware box that Tom had set on the teacher's desk at the front of the

179

room near a propane heater. Young Amber, childlike herself, her dark hair in a cheerleader-perky ponytail, stood there with a stack of paper napkins and doled out the whoopie pies, her enthusiasm seeming strained. It had indeed been a long winter.

Snowy let go of Owen and said, "Great to meet you, Owen."

"Same here," he said suavely and made a beeline to the desk.

Beyond were the children's nine desks, a chalkboard on one wall, a map of the world and some crayon drawings of spring flowers (presumably) on another, a crammed bookcase, ocean views out windows.

Aunt Izzy said to Snowy, "Next, the library."

"The library?"

"I have a favor to ask. Tom, come along. We're making a stop at the town hall before I return you."

He looked questioningly at Snowy. Mystified, she shrugged, and they followed Aunt Izzy out to the Volvo. But as Aunt Izzy drove off, Snowy remembered that Blivit had once mentioned that the town hall contained the town library. Aunt Izzy drove past the granite church to this granite municipal building. It wasn't all that large, so the library within must be tiny.

"Oh, look," Aunt Izzy said, "the rain has begun." She parked, shooed them inside, and led them across a dark lobby to a closed door inscribed Quarry Island Public Library. Underneath this lettering were the days and hours: Monday, Thursday, Saturday, 1–6 p.m. Pulling keys out of a pocket of her slicker, she explained, "I'm on the board of trustees," and unlocked the door, switched on the overhead lights.

The library was a long narrow room squished narrower by its book-lined walls. There was a computer on the oak checkout desk, but also there were two dear old card-catalog drawers. Snowy had a tendency to go into a trance in libraries. She took her glasses out of her shoulder bag, patted the card catalog affectionately, and moved to the shelves, starting with Fiction. Louisa May Alcott.

Hans Christian Andersen. Jane Austen. She realized that adult fiction and young adult and children's must be organized together. Why not? Discoveries and rediscoveries for everyone. She stepped sideways to the B's and heard herself say, "You've got the Mapp and Lucia Series!" There it was, E. F. Benson's entire series, from *Queen Lucia* through *Trouble for Lucia*.

Aunt Izzy said, "Donated by one of our generous summer people."

Mildred Cotter's Mary Stewart novels. Perhaps someday Mildred would donate them?

"Now, Snowy," Aunt Izzy continued, "I want to show you this, over here in the Poetry section."

There was only a single shelf, mainly consisting of *The Oxford Book of English Verse*, *The Oxford Book of American Verse*, and the collected poems of Robert Frost, so Snowy could see plainly the bindings of all her own books. She said, "What on earth?"

Aunt Izzy smiled. "Donated by one of your generous friends."

"Puddles!"

"Yes."

Snowy snatched two off the shelf and looked at the title pages. They weren't inscribed. Puddles hadn't donated the copies that Snowy had given her over the years; she had bought a new set for the library. Had she done the same for the Long Harbor Public Library? Probably. What about her South Carolina libraries, had she bought extra copies as Snowy's books were published? "Oh, no," Snowy said, "I'm going to cry."

Aunt Izzy produced a packet of Kleenex from a slicker pocket and gave it to Snowy. "I've been thinking how much more these books would mean to the readers if they were signed by you. A real poet! Might I ask you to take time out of your vacation to stop by some day when the library is open and sign them? I did tell Puddles about this idea to make sure she likes it, and she said she hopes you don't get writer's cramp."

Drying her eyes, Snowy laughed. "Of course."

"Good. Now, I'll drop you off at your home. I hope you've settled in enough so that you can come to dinner tomorrow night. Florence and Roddy and the children will be there too. I expect you've mostly had lobster since you arrived. Tomorrow night it'll be Emily's Crock-Pot pot roast, guaranteed delicious."

Home. Aunt Izzy had called Cotter Cottage their home. Snowy looked at Tom. He wouldn't feel up to coping with a dinner party, would he? Did he remember how he'd hated the pot roast at the hospital?

He nodded.

So she said, "Thank you, we'd love to."

THE RAIN ENDED by noon on Saturday, and the sun was still out when Snowy and Tom arrived in the Jeep at the castle's open gate. In the two big granite urns atop the granite gateposts were more pansies, crowds of pansies, purple, blue, yellow, white, tiny faces frowning. The front door of the granite cottage opened and Ben leaned out, waving, his other arm around a hefty laughing woman; Ben also had company to dinner. Snowy waved merrily, but what she was feeling was trepidation. She and Tom had never been to the castle without the protection of Blivit and Puddles. Did she really mean "protection"?

Tom drove on up between high hedges that ended to reveal, on the left, South Cliff's sheer drop to the ocean far below. On the right above a wide lawn, still brown, where little Priscilla and Christopher were chasing each other, loomed a medieval fortress, a granite castle rising from its massive bulk into turrets and crenellated battlements and such. These examples of castle architecture had caught the eye of Blivit's ice-cream-empire grandfather during a European tour, and he had stirred them all together into this island extravaganza. Blivit acted embarrassed and amused by the place, saying it was a wonder his grandfather hadn't gone whole hog with a moat, but from Puddles she had learned how fond he was of it. Nearby were granite stables and the granite carriage house.

And in the driveway, pulled up past the castle's porte cochere, was Florence's middle-aged Subaru Forester. Florence and Roddy were tall, strong, capable, and were beckoning the Jeep to advance under the porte cochere. Although Florence had grown up in a Boston suburb, she had spent as much time as possible with her grandmother on the island. Here she had met Roddy, had worked as his sternman during summer vacations, and upon graduation from Radcliffe she'd married him and moved here for good.

Tom parked. He and Snowy got out, and when Florence hugged them Snowy felt the trepidation melt away.

Aunt Izzy called from the doorway, "Welcome!"

In the dining room there was the advertised Emily's pot roast at the lengthy oak table. Plus carrots and mashed potatoes. Also a cabernet sauvignon, which Aunt Izzy asked Tom to pour. Florence and Roddy (and the kids) abstained. Emily, a lighthearted young woman, sat down beside Snowy after serving and said, "If you're having trouble getting laundry to dry in this weather, bring it over here and I'll pop it in the dryer."

"Thank you," Snowy said, "but I found a wooden rack in the broom closet and I've been drying things in front of the fire."

Roddy sighed. "Great-Aunt Mildred and money. She'd steal the pennies off a dead man's eyes."

Florence reprimanded, "Roddy!"

Priscilla and Christopher giggled. Priscilla mimicked, "Roddy!"

Snowy said tentatively, "There aren't any photos in the cottage. I'm curious about what she looks like."

Aunt Izzy said, "She's taken personal things to the rehabilitation center. In case, I think, she can't return here. What does she look like? There's an old-fashioned term: chocolate-box pretty. Mildred Cotter was that. She still is, in my old eyes. You know she's a year older than I am? Oh, she was a belle at the island dances! But she didn't want to marry and settle down here."

Snowy asked, "Did she travel a lot? Her collection of coffee mugs, her books."

"In her imagination," Florence said. "She has nieces and nephews who travel. They send her souvenir mugs because of our Maine term for a snack, a mug-up."

Roddy said, "But nobody has sent her a mug from Indonesia. That's where she's always wanted to go."

Aha, Snowy thought.

Florence said, "She wanted to see far-flung islands, she wanted to see what islands were like far away from Maine. All kinds of islands, large and small."

"Gauguin," Snowy said. "The print in the cottage of one of his Tahiti paintings. I looked up the Seurat print on the Internet and learned it's on an island in the Seine, 'A Sunday Afternoon on the Island of La Grande Jatte.' And then in a bureau drawer I found a print of a drawing of St. Thomas, you know, the Virgin Islands."

Florence said, "I never saw any St. Thomas print, but she bought the Seurat and Gauguin in an art shop in Portland. Alas, Great-Aunt Mildred only got as far away as Portland. The failure soured her." She turned her attention to the kids, who were now bored by the conversation and poking each other with forks.

"Well," Roddy said, sounding defensive, "she's proud of her work at the law office. She brags about typing those contracts, those wills, a gazillion carbon copies, before computers."

Aunt Izzy said soothingly, "She must have been a splendid secretary. All that legalese she learned. She once told me that for some reason she always found the term 'common disaster' funny.

She'd type a clause about dying in a 'common disaster' and try not to laugh out loud."

Everybody except the kids pondered that as they finished the main course. Snowy and Florence helped Emily clear the table, carrying dishes into the old kitchen of soapstone sinks, glass-fronted cupboards, with a butler's pantry and a servants' dining room beyond. During Blivit's grandfather's time, the castle had employed thirty servants! Emily scooped Vanilla Bean ice cream into dishes, and back into the dining room they went, Emily carrying a tray of the dishes and thin cups and saucers, Florence carrying a pot of decaf, Snowy bringing up the rear with sugar bowl and creamer. The kids weren't blasé about Quarry Island Ice Cream; they cheered at the sight.

Aunt Izzy presided over the coffeepot, and as she handed Tom his coffee she said, "Now that you've seen the school, you'll understand when I tell you that volunteers are vital to it. The islanders volunteer their expertise, and we corral talented visitors. Such as you."

"Me?" Tom asked.

"You, Tom Forbes," said Aunt Izzy.

"Me?" he repeated. "Hell, I build"—he glanced at the kids—"um, coffins."

"An essential item," Aunt Izzy said. "We have people here who have done the same when necessary, not with your steady experience. And we do have islanders who volunteer to teach some shop. No, Puddles mentioned that earlier you taught high-school English. I was wondering if you might like to help out that way this coming week. With the school's three junior-high students."

Thrawn, Snowy thought, watching Tom's stunned face, waiting for his expression to go stubborn. He would rebel against Aunt Izzy's manipulations.

Aunt Izzy continued, "It would be just in the afternoons, discussing with them the books they're reading. Chloe and Lily are the eighth-graders, and they're now reading Willa Cather's *My Ántonia*. Trevor is the seventh-grader, and he's in the midst of *Treasure Island*. I'll lend you my copies so you can refresh your memory."

Snowy began to babble, to cover for Tom. "I didn't read *My Ántonia* until my junior year, how wonderful that it's on an eighth-grade reading list! *Treasure Island*—Robert Louis Stevenson's family built lighthouses, and we saw the one his father and uncle built on the Isle of Lewis in an impossible place, well, lighthouses are apt to be in impossible places, aren't they, this one is red brick and has turned almost pink—"

"Okay," Tom said.

The next morning he borrowed a pencil and a legal pad from Snowy and settled into his armchair with the books. Snowy sat at the desk looking out at the gray cloudy morning, wondering if he would fall asleep as usual and thinking of how it had been a whole week since she and Tom had arrived here. They only had this one week left.

Then she e-mailed Puddles, "I *will* get writer's cramp! That row of books, my entire—oeuvre, so to speak! Thank you, dear Puddles, for spreading the word. And you told Aunt Izzy about how Tom used to teach English? Has she been in touch to tell you she talked him into volunteering at the school?"

Puddles e-mailed back, "Just seeking more cures than lobster for Tom's 'failure to thrive.' With your books, think of me as Johnny Appleseed."

Next, Snowy e-mailed Bev, but she couldn't dredge up anything to say except, "I hope you haven't encountered any bats while cleaning out the theater." She e-mailed Ruhamah, and then she closed the laptop and picked up her pencil.

When she left her desk to make lunch, she found Tom still awake, reading Aunt Izzy's hardback copy of *My Ántonia*, taking notes. They didn't go for a walk, and they didn't do the afternoon drive.

The next morning was sunny, the wind whisking tree branches into a frenzy. As she started spooning ground coffee into Mr. Coffee, she heard an engine rumbling and looked out the sink window. Monday, and Roddy had started the season's work; the *Florence* was arriving in the cove. Tom came into the kitchen, showered and dressed in the best his vacation wardrobe could offer, a fairly new blue sweater and clean jeans. Together they watched the wire lobster traps being set out by Roddy and a sternman who wasn't Florence, motherhood having ended that job at least for a time. Both men were wearing the brown insulated type of coveralls. As a trap was shoved over the side, the warp—rope—whipped past and Snowy remembered that according to Blivit this was how the husband of Flossie Hutchinson had been crippled, getting his foot caught in a warp. He was lucky not to have been dragged into the sea and drowned.

Jobs. Work. Snowy went to her desk, Tom to his armchair and Aunt Izzy's leather-bound edition of *Treasure Island*. She knew he was becoming nerved-up. She hadn't known him when he was teaching, but from what he'd said about those years she'd gathered he'd been casually realistic. For lunch she made sandwiches from the leftover pot roast that Emily had sent home with them, but he ate only half of his. Damn Aunt Izzy! The renewed interest in food that the past week had brought him was wrecked by this volunteer work!

He said, "I suppose I could tell the kid—Trevor—about the Stevenson lighthouses. But the girls and Willa Cather, for an island connection?"

A brainstorm. Snowy exclaimed. "Grand Manan, the Canadian island where Puddles and Blivit went on their honeymoon! Puddles mentioned that Willa Cather summered there, owned a cottage. So Willa went from the Nebraskan prairie to an island in the Atlantic. Like Quarry Island. Well, bigger. They could look up details on the Internet."

"Grand Manan. Thank you. I guess I'd better be getting along."

As he drove off, she waved from the doorway, but he didn't glance back.

Now she had the cottage to herself. What to do? Dishes. While she washed the two glass fish plates and the Grand Canyon and Eiffel Tower mugs, she heard herself saying, "Patria. One's native country." Hadn't Willa written in *My Ántonia* about the narrator Jim Burden's Latin lesson in which "patria" in a poem by Virgil was translated as "country" and Jim's teacher, who was from New England, explained that "country" didn't mean a nation but the small neighborhood where Virgil was born? The emotion in the teacher's voice made Jim wonder if the rocky New England coast that the teacher often described was the teacher's "patria."

Bundled up in her parka, she went for a walk along the piece of coast that she was borrowing for one more week. The wind blew her hair straight back, and she touched her silver ear studs, secure. The sea was the blue-green of antique bottle-glass. Beautiful, breakable. What if Mildred didn't recover enough to return to the cottage? Would Mildred put it up for sale? Or would she save it for a niece or nephew?

Tom and I could buy it, Snowy thought. We could retire here. Cotter Cottage, which a week ago she had thought only worth a wrecking ball. Retire to a claustrophobic island? But the ocean . . . She'd already had her life on the ocean, with Alan. Her grandson would be living in Woodcombe. She and Tom had no money, they couldn't buy a cottage, they couldn't retire. And yet, and yet. Her mind was mayhem.

In the cottage, she worked at the desk until she heard the Jeep descending the driveway. She hurried to open the front door.

Tom got out of the Jeep, laughing. "I'd forgotten I learned to do an imitation of Robert Newton when I saw the *Treasure Island* movie a million years ago." In Long John Silver's voice he rasped, "Shiver my timbers!" and faking a peg leg he hopped into the living room. He hopped!

Snowy started laughing. "Things went okay?"

"I'd be keel-hauled if they didn't!"

She longed to hug him. She didn't dare; it might ruin his mood. She remembered her little schedule for this afternoon. "I should go to the library and sign those books; it won't be open again until Thursday. Would you like to come along?"

"I want to collapse. Only three kids. How did I manage teaching a whole goddamn day of classes?"

But he was still looking happy. She felt safe leaving him here alone. Didn't she? She hesitated, then on tiptoe she kissed his cheek above his beard. "Keys in the Jeep? I'm off."

He held her and kissed her properly before he went into the kitchen.

She knew she must be beaming and blushing as she climbed into the driver's seat. Then she realized she didn't have her shoulder bag with her, her wallet, her driver's license. Island freedom? Eek, she didn't have her glasses! Well, she was able to sign her name without them. Damn, she didn't even have a pen. To book signings she always brought her own pens and even a blotter. But the library would have those, or at least a ballpoint. She drove carefully into the village, on the lookout for deer.

In the town hall, the library was empty of customers. Anne, the woman Snowy had chatted with while she was knitting trap heads and tending the store, sat knitting at the librarian's desk and said before Snowy could explain her errand, "I don't think

189

we've been formally introduced. I'm Anne Davies, the librarian. We wear many hats on the island. Sit here, and I'll fetch your books."

So Aunt Izzy had told Anne that Snowy would be in sometime this week. Snowy took Anne's place at the desk and picked up a library pen. When she had finished signing, Anne said, "I don't suppose you'll be coming back in the summer, when the island is full? It would be such a coup to have you do a reading here."

"I'm awfully sorry, but no. Summer is our busy time too, at our general store."

"That's what I feared. Well, it's very nice of you to sign your books. We aren't exactly Barnes & Noble."

Snowy told her about a book signing she'd done at a Barnes & Noble during a thunderstorm that zapped the electricity; all the cash registers shut down and everyone was thrown back into the Dark Ages, helpless. She and Anne parted laughing.

As she drove home Snowy played make-believe, imagining Tom taking over from Young Amber, imagining herself volunteering at the store and library. The cottage would be theirs and they would fix it up.

Impossible. But when she walked in the door, Tom got up from the armchair and enfolded her close, and that afternoon Mildred's old bed became theirs.

And at suppertime, his other appetite had also returned.

Off he went to school Tuesday afternoon, Wednesday afternoon. Then he said, "I'll have done enough tomorrow. Only two days after that, and Saturday will probably be wasted getting organized to leave. Friday, let's climb Hutchinson Mountain and have a picnic."

Friday was sunny and suddenly warm. And it was Bev's birthday. After breakfast, Snowy phoned her and said, upbeat, "Happy birthday! Beautiful weather here, so I assume it is there."

Bev didn't sound like a birthday girl. She sounded wan. "Daffodils and everything."

Snowy persisted, "Oh, to be an April baby instead of March! Are you doing anything special today?"

"We're researching bed-and-breakfasts on the Internet. Roger's latest great idea. Instead of returning to the practice of law, he now wants to transform Waterlight into a B and B. He wants to call it the 'Inn at East Bay.'"

"Bev."

"He says it's the perfect setting and he'll be in charge of maintenance, which he thinks he already is but it's actually Leon. I'll be in charge of the guests. He says I'm decorative. Decorative! He expects I'll coo over them and coddle them— and coddle eggs. Does he think I'll be changing the bedsheets too? Well, enough of that! The weather people are calling this an 'orderly snow melt.' I've got daffodils poking up. You'll be home Sunday? I hope a vacation did help Tom."

"Yes," Snowy said.

"Thank you for phoning." Bev hung up.

Snowy went out to the backyard, where Tom was setting up two folding lawn chairs that had been stored in the broom closet. He looked serene. She decided not to tell him what Roger intended to do to the place Bev had described as "my dream house on the lake." She fetched Mary Stewart's *Thunder on the Right* (the French Pyrenees) and joined him reading until it was time to get ready for the hike.

She had saved some lobster from last night's supper, so the picnic she put into Tom's backpack was lobster-salad sandwiches, potato chips, cookies. Water bottles. Into her backpack went jackets, her cell phone. They drove down the island past the Hutchinson farmhouse, and Tom pulled off the road beside the trailhead sign. With their trekking poles they started slowly along the trail, which was more like a slanting ramp. It rose easily up the little mountain through woods to the open gray ledges of the summit. A low summit but—

"Jesus H. Christ," Tom said. "I forgot that you can see the world from here!"

He spread out the Space Blanket he used as a tarp, and they sat down to eat lunch and contemplate the world.

Eventually he said, "The kids were telling me how everyone says that the looks of summer people change from when they get off the mail boat to when they leave. They arrive looking strung out, they leave looking rested. Well, I suppose that's the point."

"Mmm," Snowy said through lobster.

"I was wondering. Would Mildred like to earn some more money and rent the cottage a couple more weeks? Could we arrange to stay on?"

She thought of all the reasons they couldn't. The baby, the store, the coffin factory. But would a return to Woodcombe mean a return of depression? Would they stave this off by staying longer?

"I know," he said. "We can't."

7

ALTHOUGH THEY REALIZED THAT Aunt Izzy would tell them not to if she knew what they were doing, they spent Saturday cleaning the cottage. Tom vacuumed; then he started on the bathroom. She dusted, caressing every single item she had discovered and had touched when these rooms were strange and unfamiliar. In the bedroom, she looked at the blue desk where she'd worn her hiking cap while working. Then she was confused by seeing an image of her office, by feeling her old desk's surface under her fingers. Was home tugging her?

As she put the map of Indonesia back in the bottom bureau drawer on top of St. Thomas, she had an idea. Crossing the hallway into the bathroom, where Tom was scrubbing the pink bathtub, she said, "Maybe on the way home we could stop and visit Mildred? Out of curiosity, after two weeks in her cottage. And to thank her for renting it to us."

"Better check with Blivit."

So she phoned Puddles, who shouted the question to Blivit and then reported, "Sure. He'll phone her and ask what her favorite ice-cream flavors are, and when we meet you at the wharf tomorrow we'll give you a gift box for her."

"The ice cream won't melt?"

"Dry ice," said Puddles. "Are you absolutely positive you don't want to spend tomorrow night with us and drive home Monday morning?"

"Back to work on Monday," Snowy said. Even if Mondays were her days off, this Monday she should be in the store making up for lost time, helping Ruhamah.

Puddles said, "Back to real life. Bye."

195

Snowy told Tom, "Blivit will arrange it and send a gift box of ice cream—eek! Gifts! We've got to find a gift shop in Long Harbor that's open and buy souvenir presents!"

Tom wasn't much of a one for gift shops, but he said gamely, "Okay." Then he added, "I guess I should finally phone David, let him know we're due tomorrow as planned."

The next morning they packed and took a last stroll to the cove. She remembered how she'd seen Tom alone in the backyard that first afternoon and had raced after him in terror of his intentions.

Allowing a lot more leeway than Puddles and Blivit would have, they drove to the village, left the Jeep in the parking lot, then walked down to the dock and were helped aboard the mail boat by Dylan. They were wearing their parkas, but unlike two weeks ago the day was sunny, the wind frivolous. No other passengers joined them. There weren't any high-schoolers going to the mainland; spring vacation had begun. As Dylan loaded their luggage and tote bags, Erroll boomed, "You two look like the ocean agreed with you!"

Snowy laughed, self-conscious. The change in Tom was obvious, but had Erroll thought she'd looked as if she needed a hug?

Tom said, "An ocean-air cure."

The mail boat set forth, the sun striking sparks on the smooth sea. She and Tom stood watching the village diminish to a white line. She realized Tom was singing very softly a Scottish song of farewell and hope, the hope that Bonnie Prince Charlie would return after his defeat at Culloden.

> Will ye no' come back again?
> Will ye no' come back again?
> Better loved ye canna be.
> Will ye no' come back again?

When the mail boat docked at the Long Harbor wharf, they saw Puddles and Blivit screeching into the parking lot, Puddles driving their Subaru, Blivit in his mainland Jeep. By the time the luggage and tote bags were unloaded, Puddles and Blivit were on the wharf. Puddles gave Tom a once-over, hugged him, then hugged Snowy and whispered, "Can I stop worrying about him? He appears to have begun to thrive."

"Yes," Snowy said, mentally knocking on wood.

They all transferred the stuff from the wharf to the Subaru, and from the Jeep Blivit brought the gift box, saying, "Mildred's favorite flavors are Vanilla Bean, Fudge Cordial, and Red Rhubarb. She'll be expecting you this afternoon." He stowed the box and took a slip of paper out of a pocket. "Here are the directions to her rehab place."

"Thank you," Snowy said. "Thank you for everything."

Puddles said, "Give my regards to New Hampshire."

Snowy hugged her; Tom and Blivit shook hands. It was truly time to leave. Tom drove out of the parking lot, Snowy waving, vowing not to cry. She swallowed and said, "Now, the search for an open gift shop."

Tom drove slowly along Main Street. A gas station's sign told them that the price was $3.41.

Snowy shrieked, "There!" An OPEN flag flapped above the Starfish Gift Shoppe.

She helped him choose T-shirts for his granddaughters. She chose a night-light shaped like a little lighthouse for Ruhamah, who'd be up a *lot* when the baby arrived, and, for the baby, both a plush lobster toy *and* a little lobster bib that said "Butter Me Up." Then she saw two white mugs with red roosters. At the counter, the clerk wrapped the mugs in tissue paper; this made Snowy think of them as presents for her mother.

Back at the car, they took off their parkas and settled in for the long haul, retracing their trip here. Up the hill out of town. Up the peninsula, past the blueberry barrens to Route 1. In Camden she remarked on the Edna sites. It wasn't yet supper

197

time when they reached Waldoboro, but she asked about stopping at Moody's Diner just to swap drivers. He replied, "Let's wait until Mildred's." In Brunswick they got onto I-95. As they passed the Freeport exit, she waved to L.L.Bean. Soon, out of her shoulder bag she took Blivit's directions and read aloud as Tom drove into the Portland suburbs to a sign at the end of a residential street: The Pines Manor Rehabilitation and Retirement Center. He turned onto the driveway.

The first thing you saw was a vast grassy leach field out of which white plastic pipes poked up like giant snorkels. Then the driveway circled onward toward a long three-story white building, just the one building, not Ivythorpe's mock village. The parking lot was smaller than you'd think it should be until you remembered that many of the residents probably didn't have cars anymore.

Snowy said, "Maybe this wasn't such a good idea."

Tom parked. "She's expecting us."

He lifted the box out and they walked to the front door. It was like entering a big hotel, an impression reinforced by the lobby's maroon wall-to-wall carpeting and polished reception desk. A groomed young woman greeted them, pushed forward a guest book, and asked them to sign in, saying, "Mildred is in Room 41, down the hall to your right."

The Pines Manor didn't smell of decrepitude. Vague air-freshener; dinner being cooked. They passed a room where a few white-haired people were sitting at tables working on jigsaw puzzles or playing cards. Past the elevators there were doors, some closed, the open ones revealing a combination of dorm room and hospital room.

Tom said, "Remind me not to get old."

She said, "Don't get old."

The door of Room 41 was closed. Snowy took a deep breath and tapped on it.

"Come in." The harsh voice seemed liver-spotted with age.

But when Snowy opened the door, the woman sitting in a recliner between a hospital bed and a walker did not look eighty-eight years old. As Aunt Izzy had mentioned, Mildred had retained her chocolate-box prettiness. Her gray hair was short and fluffy. She was demurely rounded in a pink sweater. Her denim trousers showed no indication of a cast still on the broken tibia that had landed her here.

"Hello." Snowy stepped into the room. "We're Snowy and Tom."

Mildred zeroed in on Tom's cargo. Her incongruous voice demanded, "Is that the ice cream?"

"Packed in dry ice," he replied. "Should I take it to the main kitchen's refrigerator or—?"

"No, no," she snapped. "Almost supper time. Just put it on the floor."

Tom did.

A pause. There was a straight-backed chair beside a window that overlooked the leach field, but no other place to sit except the bed. And Mildred wasn't inviting them to sit down. On the bureau Snowy could see a horde of framed black-and-white photographs and recognized what must be Mildred's high-school graduation picture. A grayish shingled Cape with a row of four children standing rigid out front might be Mildred's Quarry Island family home. Other photographs were indistinct from here. Could any be of a lover?

The pause had lengthened.

Snowy said hastily, "We wanted to thank you for our two weeks in your cottage. We had a wonderful vacation."

"I'll be back on the island as soon as I'm able."

"It's beautiful," Snowy said. "The island and the cottage."

Mildred's brown eyes suddenly were rimmed with pink, matching her sweater. She exclaimed, "I am so sick of living in one room!"

199

Snowy recognized a struggle with tears and started toward her, but Mildred radiated total reserve, so she stopped. Then she said before she knew she was going to, "I saw the St. Thomas print, in a bureau drawer. The love vine."

Mildred said, "It kills what it embraces."

"I've never been to St. Thomas. Have you?"

"You don't have to go to St. Thomas to encounter the love vine. You can have your heart broken anywhere. Your spirit broken. Killed. Even in Portland, Maine."

Snowy said, "I'm so sorry. So sorry." Inadequate.

Looking extremely ill at ease, Tom said, "We'd better be getting along."

"Drive carefully," Mildred said. "You don't want to die in a common disaster." And she laughed raucously.

At the doorway Snowy turned back, trying to think of something better to say, and she saw tears overflowing. But Mildred's barrier of reserve remained. Snowy followed Tom out the door.

ALWAYS BEFORE ON their way home from a trip to Maine, when they crossed the state line into New Hampshire Tom would peer ahead and joke, "What the hell's that cluttering up the horizon? Oh, it's mountains." And he did this afternoon.

She said to New Hampshire, "Puddles sends her regards," and continued driving west toward the setting sun, the mountains far away on the brink but getting closer, bigger. After two weeks in a place of blue limitless expanses of sea and sky, the change felt to her like a swoon into the land's contours. Spring had definitely arrived here. Although trees were still bare of leaves, grass was faintly green.

Tom's cell phone rang, a startling sound. He reared up in his seat belt and yanked it out of a jeans pocket. "David," he told her. To David he said, "Yes, almost there. You don't have to—okay, thanks." Putting the phone away, he explained, "He'll be at the barn to help us unload. I told him yesterday that wouldn't be necessary."

"He's a thoughtful son."

She turned off onto the road to Woodcombe, realizing that her nerves had tightened so much she was nothing but pure concentration on the moment. Down, down into the mountain valley. Down onto Main Street. The village looked more quaint than she remembered. Miss Marple's St. Mary Mead. If only Miss Marple were here to solve the store's burglary! Even though the store was closed, it still had a welcoming air, and there were lights on upstairs in Kelsea and Cody's apartment. But she braked, possessed by an urgent need to make sure the store was safe. No. She must get Tom reestablished. So she drove on to North Country Coffins. David's pickup was parked here, the barn's small door ajar.

They creaked out of the car and stretched thoroughly. Putting off entering? From the backseat she lifted out her shoulder bag, laptop, and briefcase. Tom went around to the back of the car and got the overnight bag and suitcase.

David emerged from the barn and said, "Welcome home!" He gave Tom an assessing look and a hug, then hugged Snowy and took the laptop and briefcase from her. "How was the return trip?"

Tom said curtly, "Uneventful."

Now she was possessed by the need to see and hug Ruhamah. No; that too could wait until tomorrow. Tend to Tom. She reached into the car, grabbed a couple of tote bags, and followed David and Tom into the workshop, thinking father and son might stop to discuss what had been accomplished in Tom's absence, but they continued toward the stairs to the apartment. She paused. The mental burden of the chores ahead grew heavier: unpack, see if

201

Ruhamah had watered the houseplants properly, do laundry, clean the apartment, and first of all make some sort of supper.

She set the tote bags on the workshop floor. "I'm going to go check the store," she said and ran outdoors, down the sidewalk, past the post office, to the store. From her shoulder bag she took her keys and unlocked the front door into its usual smell of the old wooden walls, pickle brine, coffee—and Sunday-brunch bacon. She switched on the lights, walked around. Everything was okay. The bulletin board's handwritten messages had new springtime announcements: "Bring in your bird feeders, the bears are out! I saw one crossing Pascataquac Road!" and "Parsnips for Sale" and "Wanted: Used Kayak" and "Piglets for Sale—Ironed, Wormed, Castrated."

So she left, locked up, went back along the sidewalk. Her commute. The routine. At the barn, David's pickup was gone and the car had been completely unloaded. She went upstairs, feet dragging.

Looking lost, Tom was standing in the kitchen amid tote bags on the floor. He yelled, "Where the hell did you put the presents for Elizabeth and Lilac? I was going to give them to David!"

She would not cry. She had added the presents to a tote bag containing soft stuff, his tam, her fleece cap, gloves. She found the right tote bag and lifted out the Starfish Gift Shoppe bag of T-shirts for the girls and handed it to him. She placed the bag holding Ruhamah's and the baby's presents on the kitchen table. Then she unwrapped the two rooster mugs, thinking of her mother's white-and-red kitchen. Had her father ever yelled at her mother? Not in front of their daughter, at least.

Tom said, "Shit. I'm sorry."

"It's precarious, the return." She carried her laptop and briefcase into her office and trudged back to the kitchen. Out of a cupboard she wearily took a box of macaroni and cheese.

While making supper she phoned Ruhamah and said, "We're home. I'll open up tomorrow morning, so why don't you sleep in?"

"No," Ruhamah said predictably. "It's your day off, spend it unpacking and catching up on everything."

"Ruhamah—"

"Okay, but take it easy, come to work late."

As Snowy entered the store the next morning holding the Starfish Gift Shoppe bag, she immediately saw Ruhamah at the cash register talking to her best friend, Kim, tall, black hair in a long ponytail, with perfect yoga-instructor posture that always reminded Snowy of dance majors at Bennington. Ruhamah and Kim both turned toward the door, and then Ruhamah was running out from behind the counter to her, arms wide. In her Woodcombe General Store T-shirt Ruhamah definitely looked halfway through her pregnancy.

Hugging hugging hugging, Snowy careful about Ruhamah's stomach, Ruhamah placing Snowy's free hand on it, saying, "He's begun doing somersaults. However, like any child he won't show off when asked to, will he."

But then Snowy felt her grandson move. Shakily she said, "Hello there, Al."

She hadn't realized until she said it that she'd given him this nickname. Alan had never been Al.

Ruhamah smiled. "D. J. and I have nicknamed him too." She sang the Paul Simon line, "'You can call me Al.'"

Carrying a pint of yogurt, Kim came over to them. "Welcome back, Snowy. Ruhamah, see you tomorrow."

As Kim left, Ruhamah told Snowy, "I've got Rita coming to help you tomorrow afternoon. Kim and I are going shoe-shopping. My feet are getting bigger, like the rest of me."

"How are you feeling?"

"Not so tired."

Ruhamah had never admitted to being tired. Snowy hugged her again and stroked her hair, which seemed an even thicker mane, and then gave her the bag. "Here are some souvenirs from the ocean—"

In front of the meat counter Janice Sewall made up her mind and called, "Steak tips! It'll be warm enough to use the grill for supper. It's spring! Last night we heard spring peepers tune up and get lively. I'll have Max grill us steak tips."

"Be right there," Ruhamah said.

"I'll do it." Snowy went to wait on Janice.

When she walked home to the barn after work, in the workshop Tom beckoned to her and led her onto the porch, from which she saw that the vegetable garden had been tilled and beside it was the love seat he had built this winter.

He said, "Don't worry. David did the tilling, not me."

"Oh, Tom."

Tuesday evening Bev phoned. "Would it be all right if I stopped at the store tomorrow morning? I know you're busy, but we haven't seen each other in ages."

"Of course." So Bev wasn't busy herself; Bev could spend a morning coming to the store to talk about—what? When Snowy had told Tom about Roger's bed-and-breakfast idea, Tom had asked, "It's her house, isn't it?" and Snowy had replied, "I don't think she changed anything about the ownership when he retired and moved in, but I don't know. Well, maybe it's just Roger's passing fancy."

On the morning news she learned that Hillary had won the Pennsylvania primary. Off to work she went, past daffodils and lilac buds, and her first customer was one-hundred-year-old Gladys Stanton, who said, "Hooray, don't give up hope!"

Later that morning in the store's din of coffee-break time, Snowy heard Bev's voice and looked up from serving coffee and sticky buns to a table of local women. Bev was greeting Ruhamah at the cash register, but even from a distance Snowy could tell that Bev's oohing and aahing over Ruhamah was forced. Then Bev came toward Snowy. Yes, Bev always looked beautiful no matter what (except during a crying jag) and so she did today but she looked slightly—unkempt. The cowl-neck of her purple pullover was askew, the Mimi-woven shoulder bag awry, and her hair, which never really needed fixing, should have been given a swipe with a brush after she pulled on that sweater. Bev hugged Snowy, sat down on a stool at the counter, and slumped. She didn't say anything about Hillary. She said, "I'm hiding from Waterlight."

Behind the counter, Snowy poured coffee into a Woodcombe General Store mug for her. "You're hiding from Roger?"

"He's spending his time walking through the house with a clipboard, making notes. I've abdicated."

"Bev—is the house still in your name?"

"Yes." Bev gulped coffee. "But we're married. For better or for worse. It's the worst now. And worst of a lot of worse over the years."

Snowy stared at her.

Bev said, "Maybe there's a possibility that Waterlight can bring in some money, so why not let him go ahead with his 'Inn at East Bay'? I haven't asked him how people can afford to splurge on an expensive lakeside vacation in this economy. Let him dream on and maybe it'll succeed."

Snowy couldn't think what to say except, "Would you like a sticky bun?"

"I would, but I shouldn't. How is Tom readjusting to being home?"

"Ordinarily he'd be up at the fire tower now. So his spring-time routine is out of kilter. He's working with David full-time."

"How are you readjusting?"

Snowy leaned against the counter to rest. "Well, I'm working here at the store and in my office. The routine resumed."

"Have the police found out anything yet about your burglars?"

"No. What's that pretty phrase, 'in the wind'? They're still in the wind. Or, as everyone says, in Massachusetts."

"Burglars! This is such a terrible year. And speaking of worse, from the sound of the news it's going to keep getting worse. I think I'll have a sticky bun after all."

Snowy brought the bun on a plate.

"Thank you." Bev took a bite, sat up straight, and at last smiled. "We thespians have almost finished cleaning the theater. Almost. The things we're accumulating for the yard sale will be underfoot until Memorial Day weekend. Have you and Ruhamah found anything to donate?"

Oops. Donations had completely slipped Snowy's mind; she'd forgotten to tell Ruhamah. "Not yet," she said.

"Phone me, and I'll come pick them up. During the cleaning, we decided to sell some old moth-eaten costumes from the theater's previous existence, but mostly the items have to be donations. When the sale is done, we'll concentrate on our schedule. I'll be painting scenery after all, as well as learning lines; it turns out we all play many roles. And I'm searching for an impressive hat for Mrs. Price Ridley. The Gunthwaite Summer Theater opens on the Fourth of July weekend with *Murder at the Vicarage.*"

"Matronly. I remember in the book she wore matronly hats."

"Remember the hat store near the movie theater? Imagine, a whole store just for women's hats and we took that for granted. What was its name?"

"Genevieve's Millinery."

Bev polished off the sticky bun. "Okay, wonderful to see you, now I'll go sit in my office and twiddle my thumbs. Ruhamah looks blooming, doesn't she?"

Knock on wood, Snowy thought, tapping the counter.

During the rest of the week she didn't have time to spare for a donations search, but on Sunday afternoon she scoured the store's cellar, coming up with several round wooden boxes that had contained wheels of cheese. At Ruhamah's farm she and Ruhamah went through the cellar and the barn; she asked Tom to see what his workshop had to offer. Phoning Bev, she described the cheese boxes and said, "From Ruhamah, how about old Ball canning jars, a couple of kerosene lamps, and a few milk pails? And Tom has some hinges and handles that don't look too funereal, plus some bags of kindling. We could keep them all at the store for you."

"Perfect," Bev said. "I'll pick them up Wednesday."

When Bev arrived at the store she said, "Happy May Day tomorrow," and after she and Snowy had loaded the donations into her car she took a poster from a stack on the passenger seat and presented it to Snowy. "Could you put this up? The publicity begins!"

The poster was decorated with comedy and tragedy masks and listed the plays and dates. Snowy said, "Remember when Puddles and I were on the Dramatics Club publicity committee for *Our Town*, putting up posters all over our very own town? Would you like to give me two more, for the other stores?"

"Yes! Here! Oh, this is great—it's really real, we're going to be performing plays in a barn! Of course it'd be more real if we were doing it for money and not just for love."

"Love?" Snowy repeated, thinking of Bev's falling in love with her leading man in the Ninfield Players.

"Love of the greasepaint, Snowy." Bev hopped into her car and off she drove.

207

MAY. WORK AND gardening usually saw her through May 9, when Alan had died. Twenty-one years ago, and this year there was Al.

Tom's May fifteenth birthday fell on a Thursday. For his seventieth milestone he did buy himself a bottle of single malt scotch. But he told her, "Let's keep to the routine, let it be an ordinary day." Although she agreed, at breakfast she astonished him by doing a Gunthwaite High School cheer that she'd updated:

> Tom Forbes,
> He's our man,
> He's turning seventy
> Like nobody can!

He had also told his sons not to make a big deal of it, but of course they ignored him. David and Lavender insisted on taking him and Snowy out to dinner that evening, so Tom and Snowy drove through the green dusk to meet them and Elizabeth and Lilac at the elegant Gilmore House. On Saturday, Brandon and Stephanie and their sons arrived to stay with David and Lavender and throw a party that included a banner saying: 1938–2008! Yes, Your Math Is Correct!

The price of gasoline at the store's pumps rose to $3.69 a gallon.

The Gunthwaite Summer Theater's yard sale was held on May 24, the Saturday of the Memorial Day weekend. Snowy had begun to get the feeling she should attend to see for herself Bev's new world, so she consulted Ruhamah and asked Rita to fill in for her that afternoon, then asked Tom if he'd like to accompany her. He said, "Maybe I can find that barbecue-grill pizza stone I've always wanted."

The day was cool, the sun coy. The price of gas was up to $3.88 a gallon. They drove to the Gunthwaite boardwalk, crowded with people strolling, tourists optimistic in shorts and flip-flops. Although some of the businesses were still closed (the pinball arcade, the bowling alley, the bumper cars, the beachwear shop), some had opened for this long weekend. A sign at the miniature golf course recognized the holiday: Home of the Free, Because of the Brave. The lake breezes wafted the fry-o-lator smell from the Boardwalk Buffet, which locals called Boucher's lunch stand.

Snowy said, "Maybe we should stop for a little something on the way home."

"Onion rings," Tom said, but he was scowling at the video-game arcade that had replaced the dance hall of their youth.

"Natch," she said. At this time of year the oil would be new and fried food at its best. Connoisseurs!

He drove away from the boardwalk to a side road to the summer-theater barn. Snowy hadn't seen the place since she and Bev and Puddles had driven past on their practice tour of Gunthwaite three years ago. Then, the barn had been boarded up and the field surrounding it overgrown. Now the barn was open, looking revived. Had Bev helped squeegee its old windows glitteringly clean? The field had been mowed and a parking lot roped off. Tom parked, and they walked toward the tables set up in the barnyard. The yard sale wasn't so busy as the boardwalk, but a reassuring number of people were browsing. She and Tom joined them. Dog-eared paperbacks, a standing lamp, an exercise bicycle, a pasta maker, a Havahart trap—

Roger! Behind a table displaying odds and ends of china (and plastic) stood Bev and, to Snowy's surprise, Roger. She had assumed Bev had kept him separate from this world and certainly wouldn't dragoon him into working at the sale; she had assumed he would only pay attention to the summer theater if it interfered with his life. But he and Bev were here together, wearing matching dark-red sweatshirts that looked brand-new, on the shoulders little gold versions of those comedy and tragedy

209

masks and across the front gold lettering that said Gunthwaite Summer Theater, the colors reminding Snowy of Gunthwaite's old movie theater's dark-red curtain and gold scrollwork.

"You came!" Bev exclaimed. "Your donations sold like hotcakes this morning. Thank you so much!"

Roger leaned across to shake hands with Tom. "Have you heard about our B-and-B plans? The place is a natural, the lake, the boats—"

Bev made her oh-horrors face at Snowy.

But Snowy saw her and Roger standing here, for better, for worse.

Bev said, "Hmm, which of my wares can I sell you? A teapot?"

"What?" Snowy said, blinking. "I already have a teapot."

"So you do. How about a cake stand?"

Snowy's eyes alighted upon four aqua Melmac dinner plates. "These, I'd like these, they're the right size to put under biggish houseplants."

Bev said, "Four dollars, please."

Tom paid and picked up the plates. Snowy noticed that another couple had decided on the purchase of a chipped soup tureen and were ready to pay for it, so she said quickly to Bev, "Bye," and she and Tom moved away from the table.

She asked him, "Will you marry me?"

He didn't drop the Melmac. But he looked thunderstruck. Then he said, "You bet."

There they were, in the middle of a yard sale, staring at each other. They both began laughing. He put his arm around her and hustled her across to the parking lot, into the car, and kissed her.

She laughed some more. "This is like going parking! We mustn't disgrace Bev and Roger!"

"Onion rings?"

"Okay."

He started the car.

Silence descended as he drove back to the boardwalk. She wondered if they'd gone into shock. He found a parking space between two cars, one from Connecticut, one from New Jersey. She tried to think of what to say next. And couldn't.

They got out of the car. He took her hand and they walked along the boardwalk looking at the view they'd grown up with, blue lake, green mountains.

Boucher's lunch stand, once owned by the father of one of Tom's fellow football players, had been handed down through the son to the son's daughter, Jeanine, a hospitable woman who greeted them, "Snowy and Tom! Holding hands, a sure sign of spring! What'll it be?"

Tom turned to Snowy. He stammered into speech. "This— this means a wedding?"

She said to Jeanine, "A small order of onion rings, please." A small order at Boucher's was more than enough for two senior citizens, even if one was Henrietta Snow, once renowned for her appetite. "And two Diet Pepsis." How silly, a diet drink and deep-fat-fried food!

Jeanine asked, "Did I hear 'wedding'?"

Snowy replied, hoping that Jeanine, like most everybody else, had assumed she and Tom had got married sometime in the past, "Friends of ours."

"Ah," Jeanine said, but watched with amusement Tom fumbling his wallet out of a back pocket of his jeans.

A few minutes ago at the yard sale he had done this maneuver in his usual second-nature way. A wedding, Snowy thought.

He paid, and he and Snowy waited in silence as Jeanine went to work and a group of tourists gathered beside them, noisily reading aloud the menu posted above the counter. A wedding. Tom's in a church, Joanne wearing white satin. On June 24, 1961, she and Alan had been married in her parents' living room by a justice of the peace. The only guests were his parents, his sister and brother-in-law and their daughter and son, Bev and Roger, and Bev's mother and stepfather. She'd worn a pale blue piqué suit with a corsage of pink rosebuds, her hair in a chignon. Theoretically she had thought a wedding should be private, should consist of just the man and the woman and some official to marry them, without an audience, but she had compromised on this small wedding for the sake of her parents. Her mother had baked a ham.

But now she could do what she theoretically believed. She took a wad of paper napkins out of the holder.

Jeanine said, "Here you go," and handed her two cans of Diet Pepsi, two straws. To Tom she gave a brimming container of onion rings. "Congratulations."

He didn't say anything. Snowy smiled and said, "Thank you."

They walked back to their car, where they sat and ate and drank and looked at the lake.

Yes, she could do what she theoretically believed, but finally she heard herself say, "How about a wedding like Ruhamah and D. J.'s? In the store with friends and family and invite the whole town to the reception. You won't even have to wear a tie. D. J. wore a polo shirt and khakis, remember?" Tom hated neckties.

After a pause he said, "Remember nine years ago when I asked you if you'd like a ring on your left hand and you said, 'I don't think we need one, do you?'"

"It did seem too formal. Unnecessary."

"Why the change of mind? I've put you through hell this year."

She said lightly, "I'm going to be a grandmother. Grandmothers should be married. And you should be married, as a step-grandfather."

"Snowy. That isn't an answer."

She looked at him, the white-haired septuagenarian she'd fallen in love with when they were teenagers. "It's site fidelity. I mean, you are."

Tourists ambled past their car. Beyond, a speedboat peeled across the lake.

DRIVING HOME IN silence, Tom eventually said, "I suppose I'd better phone David and Brandon. And won't they find this hilarious!"

"Well, it's a good thing that we do too."

After another silence he said, "I'm going to wear a tie. *And* a jacket."

She laughed, suddenly light-headed, dizzy. "Let's set a date!" Out of her shoulder bag she pulled her glasses case and her little 2008 calendar. "It's got to be a Sunday afternoon, when the store is closed, and let's not dillydally!" She put on her glasses and consulted the calendar. "How about two weeks from tomorrow, June eighth—" She stopped. Libby had been killed on Mount Daybreak on June 10.

"Fine."

She put the calendar and her glasses away.

After a while, he asked, "Do we have a honeymoon?"

She and Alan had taken a cruise to Nova Scotia for their honeymoon, and she had got seasick. Tom and Joanne, college students, hadn't had a honeymoon. She said, "The busy season has begun. We'd better wait until after Columbus Day. Where would you like to go?" She knew the answer.

"Not to wish Mildred ill," he said, "but if she isn't up to returning to Cotter Cottage . . ."

"If she is, we could see if Blivit could find us another place to rent off-season. If he can't, we can get him to ask Aunt Izzy to invite us to the castle."

"One way or another, Quarry Island."

They reached Woodcombe. She said, "Ruhamah, I can't wait to tell Ruhamah, could you drop me off at the store?" But how would Ruhamah react? By not marrying Tom, had Snowy remained faithful to Ruhamah's father?

Tom pulled up across the street from the store. "Do you want me to come in with you?"

"You'd die of embarrassment."

He laughed and kissed her, and she crossed to the store. She didn't recognize several of the cars in the parking lot, which meant, hooray, tourists. But the young man and woman sitting on the porch's bench weren't admiring the scenery; their heads down, they were engrossed in something on their smartphones.

Rita was at the cash register, where another tourist was buying a Woodcombe General Store T-shirt and a package of fudge. Snowy spotted Ruhamah scooping ice cream for a young family and joined in, wondering how to begin.

Ruhamah asked, "What did you buy? An exercise bicycle?"

"There actually was a used exercise bicycle!"

"People are always passing them on."

They handed the cones to the family and rinsed the scoops.

Ruhamah asked, "So what did you buy to help out Bev's theater?"

"Bev said we helped out a lot, our donations sold fast. And then I bought some lovely Melmac plates."

"*Melmac* plates?"

Keep it funny, Snowy thought. "After that big purchase, I popped the question to Tom. And he said yes. That is, he said, 'You bet.'" Oh God, would the shock of this news affect the baby?

"What? What? You *what?* You asked—you asked Tom to marry you?" Ruhamah burst out laughing and wildly hugged her.

Snowy tried not to cry, thinking it was certainly a good thing that Tom hadn't accompanied her into the store. And that Rita was too busy at the cash register to notice this commotion.

Ruhamah asked, "*Why?*"

Snowy decided to see if Ruhamah would accept the explanation that Tom had not. She said, "I'm going to be a grandmother. Grandmothers should be married."

"You're doing this for Al?" Ruhamah hugged her some more.

Snowy said, "We'd like to have a wedding the same as yours and D. J.'s, here in the store. On a Sunday afternoon, June eighth."

More hugging. Then, recovering, becoming efficient, Ruhamah said, "Let's begin planning. The eighth? D. J. is already scheduled to be home that weekend, campaigning. Only two weeks from tomorrow? It'll be a wedding campaign! Who will perform the ceremony? Because Dudley is D. J.'s father, we didn't have him marry us—too much family!—and we had one of D. J.'s friends, remember, Bob the judge? But remember how Dudley did Bev and Roger's renewal of vows? He'd be tickled to preside over your wedding."

Damn damn damn! Snowy hadn't thought this far. Would asking Dudley to marry her to Tom be like rubbing salt in wounds?

At the meat counter, Ryan Hopkins looked over at them yearningly. He wasn't the sort of bachelor who ate cereal three meals a day. Saturday was beans and hot dogs for him, and he was anxious to buy two hot dogs. The front door opened, and an elderly tourist couple (even older than Tom and I are, thought Snowy) advanced in a determined fashion, their quest obviously ice cream.

Snowy said, "Time to get back to work."

"You go home to your fiancé and start making lists!"

"Well, you phone me if things get hectic here."

"Go!"

Hurrying to the barn in a tizzy, she found Tom sitting in the wicker armchair on the back porch watching the red tube of a hummingbird feeder. She said, "Ruhamah is overjoyed, and she suggested asking Dudley to marry us, the way he remarried Bev and Roger, would that be all right?"

He looked alarmed. "Jesus, would we have to make up vows like they did? Can't we keep things simple?"

"As simple as possible." With the official vows trimmed. They didn't need the "for better, for worse" part of the ceremony; it went without saying.

He said, "I just was thinking. Your name."

A hummingbird thrummed, hovering. She had taken Alan's last name. Almost every woman had changed her last name back then. But she had remained Henrietta Snow professionally. Ruhamah hadn't taken D. J.'s name.

Snowy asked Tom, "Are you offering yours?"

He stood up. "If you want it."

"I want it."

"I always like to hear you say that."

Amusement. He kissed her.

She said, "Shall I ask Dudley to do the honors?"

"Sure." He added, "I phoned David, then Brandon. They're probably still laughing."

"I'll phone Bev—and everybody!" Rushing upstairs, she realized that Bev would be at the yard sale, so instead of phoning her first, in her office she phoned Puddles and said, "I'm finally making an honest man out of Tom. I asked him to marry me."

"Holy shit," Puddles said, sounding at a complete loss. "Holy shit."

"You and Blivit are invited to the wedding, needless to say."

"Holy shit. A wedding?"

"June eighth. A Sunday. It'll be like Ruhamah and D. J.'s." Which Puddles hadn't attended, still living in South Carolina then.

"Holy shit. Blivit, guess what! Snowy and Tom are finally getting hitched! That means lobster! Just a sec, Snowy." Muffled exchange. "Okay, remember how I sent a slew of shrimp from South Carolina for Ruhamah's reception? For yours, Blivit and I will be bringing lots of lobster meat and he'll make those mini-lobster-roll appetizers of his. Who's doing the knot-tying?"

"I'll ask Dudley—"

"What are you going to wear?"

"I don't know—"

"You won't be bothering with maid of honor and brides-maids and all that, will you?"

"No, no, a very simple ceremony—"

"And what about a honeymoon? It's got to be Quarry Island!"

"Yes, if possible, we can't leave here until after Columbus Day—"

"It will be possible, Blivit will see to that. But why the hell are you getting married all of a sudden after all this time? You're not pregnant, ha-ha!"

"I'm going to be a grandmother. Grandmothers should be married. And now I'll call Dudley and ask if he's free on the eighth."

"Tell him and Charl I'll be seeing them soon!"

Snowy waited to calm down before she phoned Dudley. Calm? Impossible. She waited some more. She wished she could tell her mother and father. She wrote an e-mail to Harriet, using her now stock explanation and inviting her and Jared. Would Harriet be traveling or able to attend?

Then she took some deep breaths and made the call.

Charl answered, saying, "Snowy? Is everything all right with Ruhamah?"

"Fine," Snowy said, knocking quietly on her desk. "I'm call-ing because I decided a grandmother ought to be married. So Tom and I are going to tie the knot." Ye gods, these expressions! "We're going to get hitched, we're going to get spliced, and we hope Dudley will marry us."

217

Charl screamed, "Dudley!" She clunked down the phone, and Snowy could hear her gasping the news.

Dudley picked up the phone. "I'd be delighted to officiate at your nuptials, pal of my youth." He did sound pleased.

Were they truly back to being sandbox playmates? She said, "Oh, Dudley, thank you. It won't be a big performance, just the basics."

"Short and sweet," he said. And as if he couldn't help himself he added, "Like you."

She laughed, pretending he'd made a joke. "I'll be inviting Darl and Bill. Oh, and Puddles says she'll see you and Charl here at the wedding. Thank you again, Dudley." She hung up.

That evening she phoned Bev. After asking politely about the conclusion of the yard sale and learning that the grand total hadn't yet been tallied, she asked, "Have you found a Mrs. Price Ridley hat, would it be suitable for a wedding?"

"A wedding?"

"A no-frills wedding, but if it were a formal wedding you'd be matron of honor and—"

"You and Tom are *getting married*?"

"On June eighth, at the store, like Ruhamah and D. J."

"How did this happen? *Tell all!*"

"I'm going to be a grandmother," Snowy began. She didn't tell even Bev about the sight of Bev and Roger standing together.

When she'd finished, Bev asked, "What are you going to wear?"

Snowy envisioned the decisions and errands ahead, the lists, while working full-time no matter what Ruhamah decreed. There would not be time for a shopping spree with Bev. Carrying the phone receiver, she said, "I'm heading for my closet," and left the office.

In the living room, Tom was watching a rerun of *Good Neighbors* on PBS. She waved at him and went into the bedroom.

Bev was saying, "You're thinking of the dress you wore to the fiftieth reunion. Flattering and comfortable—and recycling!"

As she flipped through the closet hangers, Snowy tried not to remember moving the .22 out of this closet to her office, where it still remained. She came to the blue-and-white floral wrap dress. She and Bev had found their reunion outfits at the Steeplegate Mall in Concord. Yes, this would be her wedding dress. She asked Bev, "Can it be both my 'something old' and 'something new' because I've only worn it once before?"

"Why not. It'll be something blue, too."

"And I'll have additional blue, the blue-beads necklace Ruhamah brought me from her trip to Israel with Harriet. 'Something borrowed'?"

"You can borrow my white stole Mimi wove, the way you did for the reunion, though you probably won't need it on a June afternoon. I'll stop by the store with it."

"Thank you. Dress decision made!" Snowy walked back to her office, waving at Tom again.

Bev said, "What about cake? You'll get one from Fay's Indulgences, won't you? For our renewal-of-vows cake, Fay tried to talk me out of the little bride and groom on top, she said it was passé, but I insisted, remember? Will you have a bride and groom on your cake? You didn't with—" Bev stopped.

"No, I didn't with Alan. I was trying to be unconventional within confines. I expect Tom did with Joanne, don't you? So this one had better have flowers on top instead. White roses?"

"Oh, Snowy, I'm going to cry. Bye!"

Snowy checked her e-mail. Harriet had replied, "I'm gobsmacked. You could've knocked me over with a feather. And I'm so happy! Jared and I will be there!"

Ruhamah recruited Lavender, who joined them in the closed store Sunday afternoon to make lists. Snowy began to feel as if she were riding a runaway horse, one that she herself had spooked. On Monday morning Ruhamah posted a big sign above the store's bulletin board: Come One, Come All, Wedding Reception Right Here, Sunday, June 8, 4 p.m. Who's Getting Married? Come and Find Out!

But of course by day's end everybody knew who was getting married, which was a big surprise to those who had assumed Snowy and Tom already were.

The morning of Wednesday, June 4, Snowy turned on the TV and learned that the results of Tuesday's last primaries had given Barack Obama the Democratic nomination for president. On June 7, Hillary conceded. Snowy phoned Bev, who said forlornly, "So that milestone won't happen." Puddles phoned, repeating what she'd said when Snowy phoned her the day of the New Hampshire primary, "I couldn't help hoping we'd have a woman president before we die."

At the store, Gladys Stanton came in and said to Snowy, "Hope springs eternal. I'm going to defy the odds and live to see a woman the president of the United States."

Sunday's weather was the dreaded three h's: hazy, hot, humid. The forecasters warned that the temperature could hit ninety. At least in recent years the store was air-conditioned, and so was their apartment. Ruhamah had ordered Snowy to take the morning off. Snowy and Tom spent it trying to stay cool mentally and physically by avoiding the Sunday news shows and sitting quietly reading in the living room. Snowy couldn't keep her mind on the Mary Stewart she'd got from the library, *The Stormy Petrel* (set in the Hebrides). She kept looking up from her book at Tom. He kept looking up from the latest issue of *Down East* magazine at her. They would laugh and glance back at their pages.

That afternoon when they began changing their clothes, she begged him not to bother with formality in this weather, but—thrawn!—with his khakis he put on a white oxford-cloth shirt, the Forbes tartan tie he'd ordered online for his wedding finery, and his navy blazer.

She said, "Devastating!"

"So are you."

Bev had been right; she wouldn't need the white stole today. But as she and Tom left the apartment, she picked it up anyway and carried it along for good luck.

She asked him, "You've got the rings?" They'd bought them at the same Gunthwaite jewelry store where they'd bought their high-school class rings.

He patted a pocket of his blazer.

They walked down the sidewalk to the store and saw for the first time the banner that David and Lavender had come up with for this occasion. It was strung across the front porch, rippling gently in the heat. It said: FINALLY!

Inside the store, amid the irises and peonies and roses that Ruhamah and Lavender had arranged on the counters and tables, guests were standing around or sitting on the store's chairs and the extra chairs borrowed from the library's meeting room. Snowy went momentarily faint at the sight of everybody: Ruhamah and D. J. and Kaylie; David, Lavender, Elizabeth, and Lilac; Brandon, Stephanie, Branny, and Tommy; Puddles and Blivit; Harriet and Jared; Charl and Dudley and Darl and Bill; Roger and—Bev in a pale green pantsuit and a pale green straw hat that Queen Elizabeth would have envied, dignified but jaunty, its style a chopped-off top hat, its brim foaming with pale green tulle.

Dudley stepped forward. "Shall we begin?"

Puddles called, "Hurry up, before they chicken out!"

Laughter.

Snowy draped the stole over the back of a chair, and she and Tom moved to stand before Dudley.

Dudley asked, "Do you, Henrietta Snow Sutherland, take Thomas Brandon Forbes to be your wedded husband?"

"I do."

"Do you, Thomas Brandon Forbes, take Henrietta Snow Sutherland to be your wedded wife?"

"I do."

Tom produced the rings. She had insisted they practice this, and the rings slid on over aging knuckles.

Dudley said, "You may kiss the bride."

Applause, cheers, and the reception began. As towns-folk streamed into the store with congratulations, Snowy and Tom stood near the door, greeting, hugging, shaking hands. David and Brandon were pouring champagne; Ruhamah and Lavender and Blivit were lifting hors d'oeuvres out of refrigerators and circulating with trays. She felt that she too should be working, waiting on people. During a lull, Tom gave her spine a quick knead and asked, "How are you holding up?"

"How are you?"

He put his arm around her shoulders. "We'll manage."

She remembered that on their first date, at the movies, he had put his arm along the back of her seat, but she was sitting so fashionably low, with her knees against the seat in front of her, that his arm would only officially have been around her shoulders if she'd sat up straight. Then he had begun stroking her ponytail. It had been the most romantic moment of her life.

She laughed.

And Dudley raised his champagne flute. "To Snowy and Tom, who personify that old proverb 'Better late than never'!"

More applause and cheers.

But Dudley wasn't finished. "And to Ruhamah and D. J.'s son, Alan, who will make Snowy a grandmother and Tom a step-grandfather!"

Snowy mentally knocked on wood. Then she leaned close against Tom.

Epilogue

Ruhamah Sutherland and Dudley Washburn Jr.
are happy to announce
the arrival of
Alan Sutherland Washburn
August 16, 2008
7 pounds, 8 ounces, 20 inches